THE WOMAN IN ROOM THREE

LAURA DOWERS

Blue Laurel
Press

This is a work of fiction. Names, characters, businesses, places, events, locales and incidents are either the product of the author's imagination or used in a fictitious manner. Any resemblance to actual persons, living or dead, actual places or locales, or actual events is purely coincidental.

ISBN (paperback): 978-1-912968-27-5

ISBN (eBook): 978-1-912968-28-2

1

DEATH OF A COALMAN

I washed the blood from my hands, the icy cold water of the examination room's bowl making me wince. The blood, so dark to be almost black, was like treacle, coating my fingers and creeping beneath my nails, so that I had to scrub my skin raw to rid myself of it. Drying my hands on the threadbare towel hanging from the washstand rail, I turned back to the table and the body of the coalman.

The coalman had arrived at St Eustace's Free Hospital only ten minutes earlier, wheeled through the teeming London streets on a handcart pushed by his mate. I had been on the point of leaving for the evening when the cart had burst through the large double doors of the hospital's entrance hall and the driver had shouted desperately, 'Somebody help me.'

A plea impossible to ignore, I shoved my gloves back into my overcoat pockets and hurried over to him.

I stared down at the man sprawled upon the handcart, his limbs dangling over the sides. There was a deep indentation in his chest, exactly like a rut in the road, and I knew he had been run over. His chest was crushed, and he was groaning, a scratchy, wheezing sound, painful to hear.

London is such a busy city. Its roads are almost perpetually jammed with horses, carts and cabs, and that is without all its inhabitants milling hither and thither. Road accidents are a daily occurrence. I had been at St Eustace's for almost a year, and apart from endemic diseases, traffic accidents were the most common reason for people coming to the hospital. The accidents varied in severity, from bruises to lower limbs where people had been knocked aside by vehicles, to broken bones where they had fallen beneath hooves or wheels. I had treated a variety of these, but had never seen an injury as terrible as this now before me. I could only imagine the pain the coalman was suffering and it made my stomach churn. What made me feel even worse was knowing there was nothing I could do to help him.

'Nurse Brewer,' I called, seeing her uniformed figure enter the lobby. She made her quick, confident way to me.

'Yes, Dr Cowdrey?' she asked, looking down at the coalman with a disarming lack of emotion.

'The examination room at once for this man, please. His friend can take him through on the cart.'

I followed Nurse Brewer and the handcart down the corridor and into the examination room. I watched as she commanded two male attendants to lift the injured man onto the examination table. The man groaned as they lifted him, and I bid them take care.

Nurse Brewer steered the coalman's mate out of the room and closed the door. She moved to the trolley and took up a pair of large scissors. 'There's nothing to be done for this man, doctor.'

I hung my coat up on the hook behind the door. 'We must try, nevertheless, nurse.'

'Of course we must,' she said, a little testily, 'but you must prepare yourself for the inevitable.' She cut open the man's shirt, having to tug it away from the skin where the wheels had driven it in. She shook her head at the sight she revealed. 'He cannot survive such an injury.'

She was right, of course, though I rather resented her telling me to prepare myself. I knew I had a reputation for weakness among the medical staff, and her words were simply a reminder that opinions of me were low. Nurse Brewer had been at St Eustace's for six years and seen far more injuries than I. Though no doctor, she could tell which patients we had a chance of helping and which were lost causes. But I could not stand by and do nothing, even if I wasn't at all sure what I could do to ease my patient's suffering.

With the ribcage sunken in this manner, the man's lungs would undoubtedly be crushed, probably even punctured by splintered ribs. To find out, I would have to open up his chest, something which I had never done before and which, frankly, I hoped never to do. Such surgery would probably kill him just as surely as his injury, and even if he did somehow make it through such butchery, there was no procedure I knew of that would restore his ribcage to its correct shape, nor any way to repair lungs riddled with holes and therefore incapable of inflating. As I ran my fingers over the man's crumpled chest, I wished I had left the hospital five minutes earlier and so spared myself this ordeal.

With every press of my trembling fingers, more blood spurted out of the coalman's mouth. It was dark, confirming my suspicions regarding his lungs, that there was a lack of oxygen in his blood. I could feel the broken ribs beneath my fingers, saw too the tips of ribs poking out through his sides. I racked my brains to remember my training, trying to find a treatment I could apply to make this man better. Nothing came to me. I was at a loss.

The coalman gave a sudden jerk, lifting his upper body off the examination table and spewing blood and froth over his soot-blackened trousers, and all over my probing hands. His body shuddered, his eyes widened, and then he fell back on the table, dead.

Nurse Brewer sighed. 'God is merciful.'

'If He was merciful,' I said, bile rising in my throat as I stared at the blood on my hands, 'He would have let him die at once, not made him suffer in this way.'

I felt her scornful eyes upon me as I hurried to the washstand in the corner of the room and plunged my filthy hands into the water.

Nurse Brewer had left to find a porter to take the dead man to the mortuary and the coalman's mate took the opportunity of her absence to poke his head around the examination room door.

'How is he, doc—?' He broke off as his gaze settled on his friend.

I moved to him and put my hand on his shoulder. 'I'm very sorry.'

'He's dead?'

His eyes were stark against the blackness of his skin. I wondered if the coal dust washed off or whether it was so ingrained that his skin would never be white again.

'His injury was too severe. You did well to bring him here, but there was nothing we could do to save him.'

The man clamped a huge hand over his mouth as if trying to stifle a cry, then let his arm fall to his side in despair. 'What am I going to tell his missus?' he said in a cracked voice.

'He had a family?' I asked, knowing it would be better for me if I knew nothing about the dead man's personal life.

'Three little 'uns.'

'Please pass on my condolences,' I said, thinking of three children, as soot-blackened as their father, waiting by a fireside for a parent who would only now come home in a box. I delved into my pocket and brought out some coins. A couple of sovereigns nestled amongst the coppers. 'Give them these, will you?'

The man stared at my palm. 'I'll look after them,' he said, glowering at me. 'We don't need your charity.'

I stepped back, dropping the coins back into my pocket, ashamed of my tactlessness. This man had lost his friend and his colleague, his friend's family had lost their father and husband, and I offered him two sovereigns in recompense, as if that could make up for the loss. I deserved his contempt.

I took down my overcoat from the hook and pulled it on. I grabbed my hat, took one last look at the man as he patted his dead friend's shoulder, and hurried out of the room.

I'd reached the entrance hall when I heard someone call my name. I groaned. Was I ever going to be allowed to leave the hospital? I turned towards the speaker, my fellow doctor, Horace Axeby.

He came towards me. 'I thought you left ages ago, Felix.'

'I meant to,' I replied, 'but an emergency came in just as I neared the door.'

'Oh, rotten luck. What was it?'

'A traffic accident. Crushed chest, punctured lungs.'

Horace winced. 'Nasty. Can't do anything about that, though. Waste of time having him brought here, really.'

'What do you suggest?' I said, dragging on a glove. 'That he should have just been left to die in the street?'

Horace drew himself up, affronted by my words.

'No, I'm not suggesting that. But it may have been kinder for him to die at home surrounded by loved ones rather than here.'

I put my fingers to my forehead and rubbed at the ache that had started there. 'I'm sorry, Horace. I shouldn't have spoken so. The truth is, the man's death has upset me a little.'

He put his hand on my shoulder. 'You really mustn't let these things affect you so, Felix.'

'I know you say that – everybody says so – but I can't help it. To see so much pain and know there is nothing we can do. Does it not make you angry?'

He shrugged. 'No, it doesn't. We do what we can, Felix. We're doctors, not miracle workers.'

'But should we not try to be?'

Horace's bottom lip curled inwards, his small white teeth biting into the skin. 'I'm going to tell you something, Felix, that you won't want to hear, but I want you to heed me. You won't get far if you're going to get this upset over every dead patient. If you wanted to save people, you should have gone into the Church.'

I pulled on my other glove. 'Thank you for those words of wisdom, Horace. I shall endeavour to be more like you and not waste a second thought on any of our patients.'

'That's not what I'm saying, and you know it,' he said, growing annoyed. He shook his head, despairing, and I saw his eyes glance up over my shoulder. 'Aren't you going to be late?'

I turned to the large clock above the entrance doors.

Its minute hand was nearing half past five. I groaned. 'Yes, I am, very late. I must go, Horace. And I will try to be more like you, I promise.'

I hurried out of the hospital, hearing Horace call after me, 'And pigs might fly.'

2

A FAMILY DINNER

It was Wednesday, and Wednesday evenings were sacrosanct in my family. These were the evenings when the Cowdreys gathered for dinner, and it was never permissible to be late.

There were three families of Cowdreys living in London at this time, all within a few minutes' walk of one another. My parents occupied 7 Milton Square, my brother Theo and his wife Abigail had number eight next door, and I and my wife Clara were at number twenty-one across the square. The reason for this proximity was due to my grandfather buying several plots of land in what was to become Milton Square some fifty years earlier, and upon each he had built a house. Numbers one to fourteen were the largest of the houses he had built. Numbers fifteen to twenty-three were similar in appearance but smaller, because by this time, my grandfather had discovered just how costly building houses could be and had made economies. Most of the houses had been sold but a few had been kept by the family and leased out. My grandfather had kept number six for himself and my grandmother, and made a wedding present of number seven to my father. My father had continued with this tradition, gifting number eight to Theo when he and Abigail married and number twenty-one to me when I wed Clara. He apologised at the time for giving me the smallest of the houses, but I assured him I was more than happy with my lot. It was the truth. Number twenty-one may have been smaller, but it had a distinct advantage. It was across the square from my family with a small park in between, and so gave me and Clara a sense, however misplaced, of independence.

As for Wednesday evening dinners, I cannot remember a time when they were not a Cowdrey family event. They always took place at my parents' house and were always served at six o'clock. Not leaving the hospital until half past five had put me very behind and I knew my father would not be pleased.

It was typical of my luck that no empty cab passed me on my way home so that I had to walk, and it was almost twenty past six when I turned into Milton Square and crossed the park to my house. As I drew near, I saw that the lace curtains at the bay window were pulled to one side and an anxious face was pressed against the glass. Clara was looking out for me, and she was turning first one way up the street, then the other in consternation. I felt a knot of irritation growing within me. When I hadn't arrived home before six, she should have gone over to my parents and explained that I must have been held up. Better that than we both arrive late.

As I took the front steps two at a time, her face disappeared from the window. Millie, our maid, must have been watching for me too, for the front door opened before I retrieved my key. I entered to see Clara hurrying into the hall.

'Where have you been?' she cried. 'It's almost half past.'

'I know what the time is,' I snapped. 'I got held up at the hospital.'

'But tonight of all nights. Oh, Felix.' Her hands slapped forlornly against her skirts.

'It wasn't something I planned. There was an emergency.'

'There's always an emergency,' she said sulkily. 'I had to send Millie to your parents with a note to explain we were going to be late.'

I shrugged off my coat. 'You should have gone over there yourself, not waited for me.'

'I'm not going there on my own.'

'For heaven's sake, Clara, they don't bite.' I had taken a few steps towards the stairs but stopped when I caught sight of the grandfather clock in the hall, and saw that it was indeed approaching six thirty. 'I shan't bother to dress,' I decided.

'Not dress for dinner?' Clara asked, horrified.

'They'll understand,' I said, heading for the door and taking my overcoat back from Millie who had been hanging it up. 'Come on, Clara.'

Millie hurriedly placed Clara's cloak around her shoulders. Clara's expression told me clearly that she didn't think it a good idea to go to dinner without dressing, but she didn't remonstrate with me. She took my hand, and I dragged her out into the chilly night air and across the square to my parents.

———

The lion-head door knocker glared down at us as we reached the step of number seven. I sighed as my fingers touched the cold metal and banged it hard against its base. Clara heard my sigh and squeezed my hand encouragingly.

The door opened and my parents' butler, Jempson, took the place of the lion-head knocker. His glare was just as forbidding.

'Good evening, Master Felix, Mrs Cowdrey,' he said, inclining his head ever so slightly and stepping aside for us to enter. We handed over our coat and cloak to the maid waiting to receive them, then followed Jempson to the drawing room. He opened the doors and announced us. As we entered, I heard someone, Theo, I think, say, 'At last.'

Theo and Abigail were seated on one of the rose damask settees, my mother on the one opposite. My father was by the fire, his fob watch in one hand, the fingers of the other moving the minute hand of the mantel clock.

'I'm sorry we're so late. It's all my fault.' I leaned

over the back of the settee and planted a kiss on my mother's cheek. Her familiar scent of rose water filled my nostrils and her skin was warm against my lips.

'You received my note, didn't you?' Clara asked.

'Oh yes, dear,' Mother said, smiling up at her.

'A lot of good a note does when dinner is spoiling,' Abigail said in a low murmur to Theo but loud enough for Clara and me to hear.

Mother heard it too and her expression became pained. 'Cook said the dinner will be fine,' she assured Clara. 'You gave her plenty of notice.'

I turned to my father and bid him good evening.

He looked at me, unsmiling. 'Good evening, Felix. Why so late?'

I opened my mouth to reply, but Theo stood up. 'Oh, don't ask him why, Dad. He'll go on and on and we'll never get to eat.'

My father ignored him. He was still looking at me. 'You haven't dressed for dinner, Felix.'

I smoothed my hands over my rumpled jacket. 'I thought it best not to, considering how late we already were. I'm sorry for it, but I didn't think you'd mind just this once.'

His expression told me he did mind, he minded a great deal, but Mother rose and said, 'Of course we don't mind. We know how busy you are at that hospital of yours. Come, let us go through to the dining room.'

That was Mother, always trying to pacify. My father moved to take my mother's hand and walked her towards the drawing-room doors where Clara and I still stood. We stepped aside and were about to follow when Abigail pointedly coughed at Clara, and she shuffled backwards, bumping into me, to allow Abigail and Theo to pass. Theo was grinning, keeping his face down so as not to be seen, but I saw him. I could have kicked him.

I gave what I hoped was an understanding yet encouraging smile to Clara and took hold of her hand. 'Into the valley of death,' I murmured in her ear. I was pleased I could make her giggle.

As much as I sometimes wished we could be excused these family dinners, I could not deny the dinners were always more than worth the eating. And I was very hungry. A snatched breakfast of eggs and bacon and a cup of tea and a bun at midday was all I had had, and my stomach growled as my nostrils caught the delicious odour coming from the tureen on the sideboard.

I saw Clara to her accustomed seat on the left-hand side of my mother, then took mine on Mother's right. Theo always sat on our father's right, Abigail on Father's left. In this way, our family's battle lines were drawn.

Mother told Jempson, who was waiting by the side-board, that he could begin serving, and I waited impatiently while he ladled the soup into everyone else's bowls. I was always served last. When my bowl had been filled, I picked up my spoon and tasted the soup.

Just a little pepper would make it perfect, and I reached for the cruet.

'Felix,' Abigail cried, 'what is that on your wrist?'

There had been some chatter at the table, but all that ceased with Abigail's shrill question. My arm still outstretched, I looked to see what Abigail was staring at in horror. My sleeve had risen up and exposed my wrist. On my pale skin was a splash of the deepest red. I snatched my arm away, taking my hand beneath the table and tugging my sleeve down.

'It's nothing,' I said, taking up my spoon again when I was sure my wrist was covered.

'It's blood,' Abigail said.

'If you know what it is, why ask?'

'Have you cut yourself, Felix?' Clara asked, concerned.

I shook my head. 'It's not my blood. I must have missed that spot when I washed at the hospital.'

Abigail made a sound of disgust. 'To think that we must sit here with you wearing the clothes you work in and the evidence of your vile trade all about you.'

My sister-in-law loves the sound of her own voice, and she delivered this sentence with all the melodrama of a stage actress.

'No one's making you sit here,' I said, biting into my bread roll, wiping away the butter that dribbled down my chin with my napkin.

'Should I be the one to leave?' she said, her hand going delicately to her bosom. 'I'm not the one disgracing the family.'

I spooned the soup into my mouth, unable to take pleasure in the taste now I had been so rebuked.

Abigail and I have never liked one another. We share a mutual antipathy. I believe that if we were both dogs, whenever we met, our hackles would rise, our ears would flatten, and we would snap and snarl at one another until one dared to take a bite. How much easier that would be. Regrettably, we are not dogs but civilised human beings, and so our antipathy must manifest in insults couched in polite and fulsome language. Such verbal sparring takes longer than a dog fight to conclude, and there is an awful lot of repetition involved, but the result is much the same: blood is drawn. In my defence, it is usually Abigail who begins these fights. I recently read one of Shakespeare's plays and found a very apt quote to describe my sister-in-law: *She speaks poniards, and every word stabs.* It had made me smile at the time.

When I had scraped my soup bowl clean, I pushed it away and reached for my wine. I drank all of it in one gulp, and setting it back down, tapped the rim for Jempson to refill it. I downed the second glass too. I have never been a heavy drinker, and I knew even as I asked for a third that it would do me no good to drink so much, that I would pay for it in more ways than one. But I had had a wretched day and Abigail's comments had stung. I'd reached a point where I no longer cared.

Jempson served the fish, and I foolishly began to hope nothing more would be said against me. But I had underestimated Abigail. She was still snarling.

'I suppose we shouldn't expect Felix to be any better than he is,' she said as she dissected her fish. 'We must blame the company he keeps. It is a free hospital he works at, after all. It must be degrading to mix with such people, day after day. Their rudeness rubs off. It isn't his fault.'

I banged my hand on the table, making the cutlery jump from the tablecloth. 'Such people! Is that what you call the poor unfortunate wretches I tend?'

Abigail was unmoved by my indignation. Her eyebrow arched at me. 'What else should I call them? I can hardly call them ladies and gentlemen, can I? To think you choose to associate with such people. I really cannot imagine what goes on in that peculiar mind of yours, Felix.'

My thoughts turned to the coalman who I had failed to save not two hours earlier. That common wretch had been going about his business, supplying the coal that fuelled our country's industry, that fuelled the very range our meal had been cooked upon, and who had left a wife and three children to fend for themselves in our unforgiving city. Had they been told of his death? Was his wife even now sobbing into her tattered skirts, torn between grieving for her husband and wondering how she was going to feed her children, while Abigail and I disputed the value of treating people of their class?

I held up my empty wine glass to Jempson. He looked to my father, asking for permission to do as I wanted and refill it. His impertinence maddened me.

'Just pour the wine, damn you,' I yelled at him.

'Felix!' my mother cried.

Abigail sniggered into her napkin.

'Serve the wine, Jempson,' my father said quietly, and turned to talk with Theo as the butler filled my glass and took my dirty plate away.

My father shouldn't have let me have that fourth glass. I might have been able to keep my mouth shut if I had stopped at three. And if Abigail had left me alone. She gave me a respite of a few minutes only.

'Why did you decide not to set up in private practice, Felix?' she said, spooning potatoes onto her plate. 'What made you choose to work at a free hospital instead? You've never told us.'

I sensed my mother's and Clara's agitation at her words. They both knew how close I was to losing my temper and were anxious that I should not. They knew too I was being provoked, but neither of them was an unkind woman, and they would not dream of telling Abigail to hold her tongue. Nor would Theo; on the contrary, he enjoyed watching his wife take bites at me.

'I didn't want a private practice,' I said, keeping my voice low, pretending to myself I had control of my temper. 'I didn't want to tend to women like you. Women with imaginary complaints, and old men with nothing more serious than gout. I wanted to help people who desperately need my help. But I don't expect you to understand that, Abigail.'

She laughed.

'What's so funny?' I demanded.

'You,' she said, covering her mouth with her hand in affected delicacy, 'helping people.'

What on earth did she mean by that remark? I turned to Clara, hoping to find an explanation in her expression. Her face was pained, evincing sympathy for me, but I fancied there was something more in the creases in her forehead and the anguish in her eyes. I was sure there was agreement with Abigail.

I dropped my fork. It clattered onto my plate. 'I do help people,' I cried indignantly at her.

Mother reached out and patted my hand. 'Of course you do, dear, we know you do.'

I snatched my hand away and pointed a finger at Abigail. 'You just wait. One of these days I'll make a great medical discovery and then you'll see I was right. You'll shut your big mouth when I find a cure for some terrible disease or, or ... or something.'

I knew even as I spoke I had gone too far. A gentleman doesn't speak to a lady so, no matter how greatly he has been provoked. I glanced over at my father and saw the disapproval, and worse, the disappointment, on his face. But I couldn't bring myself to apologise to Abigail. I hunched over my plate, hoping someone would say something that wasn't about me.

After what seemed an age, conversation resumed. My father, whether able to read my mind or just because it was the sensible thing to do, asked Theo about a case he was working on, and Abigail became all attention to her husband. She found Theo's work interesting, not because she found legal work fascinating, but because it gave her the opportunity to learn some scandalous secret. Theo, while honouring the confidentiality of his clients, often spoke about their cases to us, trusting we would repeat his words to no third party.

I continued eating, only half listening to Theo. My mind was fixed on Abigail's words, on her derision, and the worry I felt that she might be right. Could I, in all honesty, say I helped the people who came to St Eustace's? I hadn't been able to help the coalman, and there were plenty of other patients who had been turfed back out into the streets to manage with their illnesses as best they could because I hadn't been able to cure them. Had I been right to go into medicine, or should I have done as Theo had done, as my father had expected me to do, and followed him into the law?

Law was the family business and had been for five generations. The firm of Cowdrey and Burkett, Solicitors, Simon Burkett being my father's partner, was highly successful. All the best society came to Cowdrey and Burkett to have their legal troubles sorted out.

I had gone to Cambridge, intending to graduate and join my father and brother at the offices in Tremlett Street. But I had had my head turned at Cambridge. An older student friend inspired me with his ambitions of becoming a doctor. He spoke of helping people so passionately that his desire became mine. Gone were the ideas of settling into the law, and in their place, notions that I too could become a great doctor, help those who had not the advantages I had had, and make a name for myself. I knew myself well enough to know that this desire to become a doctor might be a passing fancy, and I was also aware that my father would be disappointed at my decision, so I continued with the studies I would need for the law, while taking on subjects, namely Greek and Latin, that were necessary qualifications for a medical career.

When I left Cambridge, I married Clara, to whom I had been engaged for two years, and went dutifully into the family firm. But the desire to become a doctor stayed with me, and after seven months at Tremlett Street, I told my father I was leaving. I had already arranged a position at St Eustace's Free Hospital so my father was unable to accuse me of not thinking the matter through.

My father was stunned into silence when I told him and didn't speak to me for half an hour afterwards. When the rest of the family found out about my decision at the next Wednesday family dinner, Theo called me an idiot, Abigail, an ungrateful wretch, and my mother asked if I was sure I was doing the right thing. Clara, who had had the right to be told before anyone else, but from whom I had reprehensibly kept my decision, said nothing, and no one asked for her opinion.

I had been very happy those first few months at St Eustace's. I enjoyed the hustle and bustle of the hospital; there was never a dull day. It was almost like being back at school, watching and listening to the masters, and taking my notes. I had progressed swiftly in my studies and become a doctor. I felt vindicated in my choice of career and certain my family had been wrong to doubt me.

But that feeling was leaving me. The hopes I had had of becoming an eminent doctor who would find a cure for a terrible disease felt further away from me than ever. As a doctor, I was no better than my peers. Any one of them was as capable of enjoying renown as I might be, perhaps even more so. The only discovery I had made, and what my colleagues had discovered about me very quickly, was that I felt my patients' suffering too deeply, and to feel so much wasn't helpful to anyone, least of all me.

Somehow, we got through the rest of the evening. At around eleven o'clock, Clara and I said goodnight, and I expect everyone was glad to see me go. Mother saw us to the door, and I heard Clara whisper an apology to her.

I gave Clara my arm as we left, but I think she was holding me up rather than me supporting her. I don't remember reaching our house or going to bed. I woke up, face down on the pillow, a little after ten o'clock the next morning.

3

THE DAY AFTER THE NIGHT BEFORE

The cotton of the pillowcase was sticking to my lips.

My head felt heavy and my tongue thick and furred, a sensation I had not experienced since my days at university when I indulged too freely in alcohol. I tried lifting my head, but the effort required was too great, and I let it sink back into the pillow. I opened one gummy eye to inspect the window. Sunlight bled through the curtains and I knew it must be morning. I heard the doorknob turn, and a moment later, Clara asking if I was awake.

'Barely,' I croaked. 'What time is it?'

'Ten past ten. Shall I have Millie bring your breakfast up?'

I groaned, and with a great effort, threw back the bedclothes. 'Why didn't you wake me?' I dragged on my dressing gown over my goose-pimpled skin. 'Is there any hot water?'

Clara opened the door and called down to Millie to

bring some up. She must have been waiting to do so, for she appeared with a steaming jug only a minute later. She poured it into the bowl and left the room. Clara busied herself taking my clothes from the wardrobe and laying them on the bed as I washed. Within fifteen minutes, I was heading down the stairs.

Millie was waiting in the hall with a cup of coffee. I snatched it off its saucer and downed it in one go. The coffee was very hot and burnt my dry throat, but it was just what I needed. I hurried out of the front door and through Milton Square to the main road, where I hailed a cab as I was too late to walk to work as I usually did. I settled into the cracked leather seat and closed my eyes, hoping the coffee would work its magic on my dull senses. I didn't open them again until the cab drew up outside St Eustace's.

As I entered the lobby, I glanced up at the clock above the large double doors. I was more than an hour late. The wooden benches in the hall were already filled with people waiting to be seen. Two nurses were passing along the rows, asking questions, determining which patients had urgent complaints and which could wait. I should be in one of the examination rooms, busy at work. I turned towards the corridor where the examination rooms were and halted as Horace came out of the first room, ready to call for the next patient. He saw me and gave me a look of strong disapproval. I hurried over to him.

'I'm sorry,' I said, unwrapping my scarf. 'I overslept and my wife didn't wake me.'

'We're very behind, Felix,' he said. 'I say, you look a bit rough. Are you quite all right? Haven't caught anything, have you?'

I shook my head. 'I'm suffering only from an excess of alcohol, Horace. I really am very sorry.'

'You'll be sorrier yet. Your absence at this morning's briefing was noted. Dr Hobkirk was not impressed.'

I groaned. That was all I needed. 'I shall see him later and apologise.'

Horace made a face that suggested an apology would not propitiate Dr Hobkirk and stepped aside for me to pass. As I entered one of the vacant examination rooms to begin work, I heard him call out, 'Next.'

The coffee had woken me up a little, but as the day wore on, I felt excessively tired, and a dull, persistent ache settled inside my skull. I was longing for five o'clock when I could leave, but I had one more schedule of ward rounds to complete before then.

The last ward on my list was the children's ward, and it was both my favourite and least liked of all the wards in the hospital because while the children were usually less complaining than their adult counterparts, I found them to be the more pitiable. All the children who entered St Eustace's were malnourished and had lice, while many of them had physical injuries too, either caused by mistreatment or accidents suffered while at their work. Others had deformities that were incurable or that could have been cured but which had gone untreated.

Sidney was one of these children. He was nine years old and had been born with a club foot. To his credit, he had managed well enough, wearing a specially shaped boot crudely fashioned for him by his father, and he had borne the disability with no great discomfort. But he had recently suffered an accident that had fractured the affected ankle bone and was refusing to heal. I had assigned him to a ward when I grew worried an infection was setting in, but had yet to find any treatment for the injury. For all his woes, Sidney usually put a remarkably cheery face on his predicament. It made my inability to treat him all the more painful to me.

I greeted him with a 'Good afternoon, Sidney,' putting on a smile just for him. He tried to return it, but I could see something was bothering him. I sat down on the side of the bed. 'What's wrong?'

'Can I go 'ome yet, Dr Cowdrey?' he asked. 'You said I might be able to last week.'

I patted his knee beneath the coarse blanket. 'I know I did, Sidney, but you are no better. If you were to go home now, your foot would worsen.'

'But I ain't earning while I'm here. Me dad was 'ere this morning, and he was asking when I was coming out. He needs me at 'ome. He said so.'

I didn't doubt Sidney's family did need him. Sidney came from a family of eight children and he was the eldest. With him in St Eustace's, his family would be struggling without his wages, pitiful though they no doubt were. 'I'm sure your father understands why you need to stay in here,' I said. 'He would want you to be better, don't you think?'

'I don't like it here, Dr Cowdrey,' he said, his bottom lip protruding sulkily.

I rubbed the back of my head where the ache was becoming particularly pronounced. I rather sympathised with the boy for I didn't want to be at St Eustace's at that moment either. 'I tell you what. When I was your age, I used to have a company of tin soldiers that I played with for hours. I still have them in my attic. Would you like them, Sidney? I can bring them in for you.'

His face brightened. I suspected he didn't receive presents often, if ever. 'Yes, please, Dr Cowdrey. Thanks.'

I ruffled his hair, now free of head lice thanks to the disinfecting carried out by the nurses on his arrival at St Eustace's, and rose. I made for the nurse's desk in the centre of the room to update the necessary paperwork that I had completed my rounds. Nurse Wood was sitting at the desk.

'You really shouldn't do it, Dr Cowdrey,' she said as I bent to sign my name.

'Do what, nurse?'

She took the pencil from my hand. 'Promise toys for the children. If you do it for one, they will all expect it.'

'And if I could do it for all of them, I would. Why should I not try to make their time in here a little happier for them?' I'm afraid I rather snapped at her, but tiredness and my headache had made me irritable.

'I'm thinking of you, Dr Cowdrey,' she said, only the smallest of changes in her expression to show that she was a little piqued with me. 'It doesn't do to become too attached.'

I stared at her for a long moment, wondering how a woman could be so cold, and towards children, too. I decided then that I had had enough, that I was done for the day, no matter it was not yet quite five o'clock. Gathering my hat and coat from my office, I sneaked out the rear of the hospital, not wanting to be seen, or caught, by anyone.

I decided to walk home to try to clear my head, but there isn't much fresh air in London and my head just became cold. As I walked, my thoughts turned to the previous evening and how badly I had behaved. I wasn't sorry for how I had spoken to Abigail – she had deserved my harsh words – but it hadn't been the act of a gentleman, and for that I was ashamed. I should have bitten my tongue as I usually did and complained about her later to Clara. I decided I would write a note of apology to Abigail and put that through the letterbox of number eight. It was cowardly, but I really couldn't face her.

My parents deserved more than a note of apology, however. When I arrived in Milton Square, I went to number seven rather than my own house, deciding I had better not leave it any longer. Jempson opened the door, and as he closed it behind me, I remembered how beastly I had been to him, too.

'I was devilish rude to you last night, Jempson,' I said, staring down at my feet. 'I'm sorry for it.'

'Most kind, Master Felix,' he said. 'You were a little overwrought last night.'

That was a polite way of putting it. 'I was,' I agreed.

'Mr Cowdrey is in his study,' he continued. 'Shall I announce you?'

'No, that's all right, I'll just go in.'

He left me to make my way to my father's study. I knocked on the door and put my ear to the wood. I heard my father's, 'Come in,' and took a deep breath as I turned the knob and opened the door.

'Am I disturbing you, Dad?'

My father was sitting at his desk, spectacles perched on the end of his nose. He looked up over the rims and waved me in. I stood before his desk, feeling rather like a schoolboy summoned to the headmaster's office.

'I've come to apologise for last night—'

'You can stop there,' he said, taking off his spectacles and setting them down.

'But I was—,' I began again, needing him to know how sorry I was.

'You were upset.' He shrugged. 'Perhaps you had reason to be.'

He rose from the desk and, holding out his arm, guided me towards the leather armchairs sited either side of the hearth. I settled into the one I normally took and heard the clink of glass and knew he was pouring us a drink. After the day I had had, a great sense of relief came over me. To be sitting with my father in the study I had always loved, and which had been a source of great joy to me all my life, was more than pleasant. It was a great comfort.

My father pushed a tumbler of whisky into my hand and bid me drink. He settled into his armchair and took a sip. 'So, what was that all about last night? Why did you become so angry?'

'Abigail always has that effect on me, you know that.'

'I do know that,' he said, nodding, 'but there was more to it. Is it the hospital? Is it getting too much for you?'

I looked at him sharply. 'Why do you say that?'

He took a deep breath before answering, staring into his glass. 'One of your hospital doctors is a member of my club. We've talked a little about you, and he said it is generally thought you may not be entirely suited to a free hospital.'

I slammed the glass down on the table beside me. A sharp, needle-like pain pierced my right temple. I put two fingers to the spot and rubbed hard. 'How dare he tell you that! And what are you doing talking about me to strangers?'

My father reached out and put his hand on my wrist. 'He dared because he was concerned for you. And it's not as if we were speaking ill of you or making you the subject of general gossip. It was a private conversation between two men who practise discretion daily. I asked him to explain what he meant by you not being suited for the hospital.'

I snatched the glass up again, hardly mollified, and took a mouthful of the whisky. 'What did he mean, then?'

'He said you were a good doctor, that you had the knowledge and skills to carry out your duties, but that you were too sympathetic.'

'That again,' I cried. 'I've been hearing nothing but that for the past two days.'

'From whom?'

'Oh, Horace Axeby, Nurses Brewer and Wood. I tell you, Dad, I'm sick and tired of it. All I did today was promise one of my child patients that I would let him have my old tin soldiers tomorrow, and Nurse Wood said I shouldn't do it, that all the children will expect the doctors to bring in playthings for them.'

'You don't think perhaps she was right in saying you shouldn't make such promises?'

'They're only little pieces of tin, they're not worth much. If Sidney would like to play with them, why shouldn't he have them?'

'I don't think that's really the point this Nurse Wood was making, was it?' my father said. 'Felix, if these nurses and this Axeby fellow have said the same thing as my acquaintance at the club, and if it's what all the doctors at the hospital are saying, there's obviously something in it. And besides all that, your mother and I don't like what this free hospital is doing to you.'

'It's not doing anything to me.'

'Oh, come now, Felix. You're tired, you're irritable, you're working such long hours. You're wearing yourself out for people who don't appreciate what you do for them.'

'You're just like Abigail,' I declared, annoyed that my father of all people was expressing such sentiments. 'You see the people at the hospital as just this mass of unwashed humanity that deserves everything it gets—'

'That's not true.'

'But they are the people who truly need my help. They don't ask to be poor or dirty or vulgar, it's just… just…' I had run out of words, and out of energy. I rested my aching head on my hand.

'You don't have to continue, Felix. You feel passionately about the hospital, I can see that, but all the passion in the world won't cure every one of the people who pass through it. There's only so much that can be done for them.'

'This is about me having a private practice, isn't it?'

'Don't the wealthy need your medical skills too?'

I shook my head. 'Not as much as the poor do. Oh, why can't I make you understand?'

I heard him sigh. 'Let's leave this conversation there, shall we?' he said. 'Finish your drink, my boy, and then you better get yourself off home. Just think on what I've said, that's all I ask.'

I did as he told me, draining my glass. When I arrived home, I went up to the attic to find the tin soldiers I had promised Sidney.

4

A PROPITIOUS MEETING

My father's mention of his club had reminded me it had been a while since I had been to my own. So, the next day, I left St Eustace's in the late afternoon and made my way to Sadlers, planning to spend an hour or two there before heading home.

Sadlers is, I admit, a rather second-rate gentlemen's club. My father would never have considered joining it, not even in his youth, but I rather liked it, not least because few, if any, of my colleagues at St Eustace's were members. Sadlers had been established fifteen years earlier to cater to gentlemen of science, but for those gentlemen who had yet to make their mark in their chosen field. Gentlemen who have gained renown in their field apply to join the Athenaeum, perhaps London's most prestigious gentlemen's club for men of science. I hoped that one day I would be able to apply for membership of the Athenaeum, but in the meantime, Sadlers did for me.

I handed my hat and coat to the steward, then made my way through to the library, for me, the most comfortable room in the entire club. Sadlers had a decent library, and I scanned the shelves for a book that would hold my interest for an hour or so. I was debating over a novel or a book of poetry when my eye caught a volume entitled *A System of Phrenology*.

I was aware of the theory of phrenology, of course, and knew that it had been pooh-poohed when first broached. But I knew too that it was enjoying a resurgence of popularity, and I must confess to being intrigued by the idea that it was possible to determine a person's character from the bumps on their heads.

I teased the book out of the shelf and scanned the room, looking for a vacant armchair. There were a couple of soft leather chairs in the far corner of the library and I headed for them, nodding at a couple of acquaintances as I passed. A waiter asked if he could get me anything, and I ordered a brandy and soda. Then I settled into the chair, the leather pleasingly warm, and began to read.

The book was interesting, and though still a little sceptical of the theory, I soon became absorbed in its contents. So absorbed, I barely noticed anything going on around me until a hard blow from a booted foot landed on my ankle and almost jerked me out of my chair.

'I'm so dreadfully sorry,' a voice above my head said as I bent to put my fingers to my throbbing ankle. 'Gave you an awful whack, didn't I?'

I pressed my fingers against the bone and the pain receded a little. 'It's perfectly all right,' I said, giving my ankle one last thorough rub before settling back in my chair. I gave my attacker a covert once-over as he dropped into the other armchair.

He was a little taller than me, about five foot ten, I reasoned, with black hair turning grey. Bright blue eyes sparkled out of a rather pallid countenance. He had high, jutting cheekbones and a dimpled chin. I supposed Abigail, who always judged people by their appearance, would have said he was handsome.

I reopened my book and resumed reading. Glancing up a few moments later, I saw that my new companion was looking at my book and smiling to himself. Wondering what so amused him about my choice of reading material, I turned it around so that its cover was towards me. All that was visible was the title and author name on the front and spine, and as far as I was concerned, there was nothing amusing about either of them.

'Forgive me,' he said when I gave him a querying look, and it occurred to me I was having to forgive my new companion rather a great deal in our brief acquaintance. 'It's just your book.' He shrugged. 'It makes me smile.'

'You think it laughable?'

'I think it absurd. That thing shouldn't be allowed on the club's bookshelves. It is one of the club's books, not your own?'

I nodded and set it down on the table between us,

suddenly ashamed of my interest. 'I was just curious about the theory. I don't believe we've met.' I held out my hand. 'I'm Felix Cowdrey.'

He took my hand and shook it. 'Miles Wakefield. Pleased to meet you. You a doctor?'

'Yes, at St Eustace's. Do you know it?'

'The name rings a distant bell. A free hospital, isn't it?'

I nodded.

'Then you're rushed off your feet, I expect. A doctor never gets a moment to himself at those places. Am I right?'

I laughed. 'You're right. Have you worked at a free hospital yourself, then?' I asked, assuming that if he knew about free hospitals, he must be a doctor too.

He made a face. 'Yes, in my optimistic youth, before I realised the error of my ways. But I suppose we must view it as all good experience.'

'You've moved into the private sphere?' I asked as the waiter appeared at our side.

Dr Wakefield ordered a large whisky. I declined his offer of another brandy and soda for myself.

'Yes, thank God. Isn't that what all doctors aspire to when they start off? Though it's not all wine and roses when you get there, I can tell you.'

'Working for yourself?' I asked in a surprised tone.

He grimaced. 'When you're working for someone else, you just don't appreciate all the other things that must be done. The paperwork, the bills, the managing of people.' He sighed. 'That's the real headache, let me tell you. Looking after patients is easy in comparison.'

'But it must be rewarding. Why else do it?'

The waiter set down his fresh glass of whisky and Dr Wakefield took it up. His blue eyes twinkled at me over the rim as he answered. 'The money can be very good, Cowdrey.' He tipped the glass up and downed its contents. He called to the waiter who had walked away, assuming nothing else would be required, and ordered another.

'Are you on Harley Street?' I asked, thinking that if he liked money so much, he would have rooms on London's most prestigious street for doctors.

'Lord, no. I'm not in London. I have a private establishment in Essex. Flete House.'

I wondered at the use of the word 'establishment'. I thought it an odd way of speaking of his practice and frowned. He caught my frown and nodded knowingly.

'Sorry, Cowdrey. I realise I sound cagey but the fact is, when I tell people the kind of establishment I run, I usually get raised eyebrows.'

Intrigued, I bid him tell me of it.

'I have a private lunatic asylum,' he said, setting his empty glass down. 'There, there it is,' he said, laughing and pointing at my face. 'The raised eyebrows. I told you.'

'I didn't mean them,' I said, laughing too and pressing my fingers to my offending brows. So, Dr Wakefield was an alienist, a mad doctor. How interesting. 'It's just I've never heard of a private lunatic asylum. I know of the public county asylums. And Broadmoor, too, of course.'

'Oh, everyone's heard of Broadmoor. But that place is for the criminal insane. My patients aren't criminals, they're just… troubled.'

'And wealthy,' I said with a shy laugh.

'Yes,' he grinned, 'they have money. They pay for their residency with us, and we make it comfortable for them. I'm afraid that's the best that can be done for most of them.'

'Your patients' madness is incurable, then?'

'I'm not sure there is a cure for lunacy. We doctors can pry and probe, but it's extremely difficult to know what goes on in the mind of another person, isn't it, sane or insane? No, the sad fact about the patients I have is that their families can't cope with their madness, so they place them with us where they can be controlled and kept safe. It's best for everyone.'

'It sounds interesting.' I gestured at the phrenology book. 'Part of the reason I was reading that is because I find the workings of the mind fascinating.'

'The mind is fascinating, but no one can learn what is going on in another person's mind by feeling for lumps on their head. The mind doesn't work that way.'

He sounded so sure. 'Have you made studies of your patients' lunacy?' I asked, thinking Dr Wakefield must be excited by the prospects under his very nose.

'I would like to, of course, but as I say, there's more to running an establishment like mine than simply chatting with the patients. I'm too busy, you see, Cowdrey. I just don't have the time to make studies and write papers.'

'That's a great pity,' I said. 'Perhaps you could take on some help.'

Dr Wakefield eyed me curiously. 'Yes,' he said after a moment, 'perhaps I could. Are you dining here tonight?'

'No. I've promised to take my wife out. There's a fair near us and she wants to go.' He looked disappointed we could not dine together, and I was flattered he found my company as pleasant as I found his. I too was sorry I could not spend another hour or so with him, but I had made a promise to Clara and I would not break it. 'In fact,' I said, taking out my fob watch and noting the time, 'I must be going.' I rose and held out my hand.

He took it. 'Pleasure to have met you, Cowdrey. Shame you can't stay, but we mustn't disappoint our wives, must we? They only pay us back in other ways.'

I expressed the hope that we might meet again and left Sadlers, thinking Dr Wakefield had opened my eyes to a new possibility. I had always believed a doctor could either be in private practice or work in a hospital, but now, it seemed a doctor could do both by opening a private specialist establishment. I thought a great deal about this as I walked back to Milton Square.

Such thoughts were still on my mind as Clara and I approached the park where the fair had set up. Torches flamed invitingly at the entrance gate and Clara clutched my hand and smiled up at me excitedly, nigh on dragging me through the gate in her eagerness. She took a rather childish delight in such fairs, darting from one attraction to another as if worried she wouldn't be able to see everything.

For myself, I have never been overly fond of fairs, but even I felt my troubles of the week ebbing away as we moved from booth to stall to tent, watching conjurers and contortionists, shooting at tin targets with air rifles, trying to knock coconuts off poles, and looking on with a mixture of curiosity and revulsion at specimens of dead freaks of nature floating in large glass jars.

We had wandered quite far into the park when we heard the unmistakable sound of a Punch and Judy show. Many a time, when we were children, had Clara and I watched show after show when they had been put on. Clara still loved the grotesque figure of Punch and his long-suffering wife Judy, but for me the knockabout comedy had long ago lost its charm, and I left Clara watching the show while I went wandering. The red and white striped Punch and Judy booth was near the end of the attractions, and the torches that had been a feature of the fair were fewer in number here. I wandered a little deeper into the darkness.

As I walked, the strangest feeling came over me. I felt the hairs on the back of my neck stiffen. The noise of the fair seemed to become muffled, and I suddenly felt so very cold, as if a fog had settled over me. I wanted to hurry back to Clara and the bright lights and noise of the fair. I turned to do so but then caught sight of a caravan between two trees, a small lamp burning in the opening, the opening itself draped with a frilled fabric. On the wooden steps below sat a gypsy woman.

And she was staring straight at me.

I still wanted to go, to return to Clara, but that woman's eyes held me there, made me stare right back. I had to wrench my gaze away, and then I only managed to shift my eyes to read the painted sign propped against the wheel of the caravan. The sign proclaimed the woman to be a fortune teller. I have never believed in such things, but I found myself moving closer.

She watched me as I walked toward her, her mouth curving into a smile as if she knew I could not resist the silent invitation she had given me. She had long black hair that hung loose around her sallow face, and her heavily ringed fingers toyed with the hem of her skirt so that I could see the tops of her boots. There was certainly no mistaking this woman for a lady.

'You were staring at me,' I said, glad my voice was still working. I had had my doubts before I spoke.

'*You* were staring at *me*,' she retorted, the smile still playing upon her lips. 'Do I interest you?'

I wondered what sort of woman she was that she should ask me such a question. Was she the worst sort, plying her vulgar trade at the fair, the fortune teller sign just a front? Before I could answer, she spoke again.

'Perhaps you want your fortune told.'

'And if I do?' I countered.

'Then I can tell it for you.'

I looked back to the fair. I could just see Clara from where I was. 'You're out of the way of the general thoroughfare here. That can't be good for business.'

'You found me,' she said, letting go of her skirt so it covered her boots.

'I might easily have missed you. You should move closer.'

'I would move closer if all I cared about was money,' she said with a bored sigh. 'Like some we know.'

I thought she meant me. 'I don't only care about money.'

She looked up at me, her head tilted to one side. 'No, I know. You're the doctor who cares too much about his patients.'

I gasped. 'You know me? How?' Had she followed me from the hospital? Had she been in Milton Square, looking through the windows at Clara and me?

Her coal-black eyes narrowed. 'I know what I know,' she said, 'and I don't demand to know how I know it.'

This was nonsense talk, and I wasn't prepared to listen to any more. 'I cannot think you will get much business with this manner of yours,' I said, and turned to walk away.

'Don't you want to have your fortune told, doctor?'

I halted, trying to walk away, but something held me there.

'Doctor?'

Her voice was enticing, almost seductive. I turned back. She was looking up at me, the left side of that thin, wide mouth curving up, mocking me. I fished in my pocket for coins and held up two shillings.

'Enough? Then tell me my fortune.'

She reached up and took the shillings. They disappeared into the darkness of her shawl. I held out my hand, thinking she would read my palm, but she shook her head and waved it away.

'I don't need that. Your destiny is written all over your face. You should leave well enough alone, doctor. No good will come of you taking a different path.'

'What path?' I scoffed. 'I'm not taking any path.'

'You should stay on the one you've made for yourself. Stay and learn your lesson.'

'I paid two shillings for this?' I scoffed. 'I should demand my money back.'

'My words are worth more than money, doctor. You should heed me.' She drew herself up, wrapping her shawl tighter around her breasts. 'But you won't, will you? I can see it in your eyes.'

Despite my desire to leave her, I was about to ask her to explain what she meant when I heard Clara calling me, and a moment later, felt her hand slipping around my elbow.

'You left me, Felix. What are you doing over here?' She looked the gypsy woman up and down, no doubt wondering at my speaking with such a creature.

'Nothing,' I said, giving the gypsy what I hoped was a disdainful look. 'Just wasting my time on nonsense.'

I turned Clara about and headed her back the way we had come, along the lighted pathway and out of the park gates. Clara protested that she hadn't seen everything yet, but I had had enough even if she hadn't and told her I was tired. As always, she put my comfort and desires before her own and complained no more at her evening's curtailment.

I didn't tell her about the gypsy woman's words to me, though she asked what we had talked about. I didn't want to revisit what the gypsy had said, even though I had dismissed it as nonsense. The truth was the gypsy woman had greatly unsettled me, and I had no idea why.

5

ONE DOOR CLOSES

Another Monday, and another week at St Eustace's to look forward to.

In fact, I was glad to get back to work. I know it sounds silly, but my encounter with the gypsy woman had played greatly on my mind. I tried to tell myself it was all nonsense, a show she put on for the fairgoers, but I couldn't help feeling that if that was all it had been, then she would have told me something to please rather than worry me.

Monday passed as all Mondays at St Eustace's pass, and by early afternoon, I was doing my rounds in the children's ward. I left Sidney till last, wanting to spend a little time with him as I could see as I tended to the other children that he was playing with the tin soldiers I had given him. As I neared his bed, he turned one of the soldiers to face me and imitated the sound of a rifle firing.

I made a face and clamped a hand to my heart as if I had been shot and collapsed onto his bed. 'How are you today, Sidney?' I asked.

He bounced the tin soldier over the blanket towards himself. 'Me foot's been hurting a lot, doctor. Can't you make it better?'

'I am trying,' I said. 'I just can't seem to find the right treatment.'

I had been scouring textbooks to discover a way to treat the poor boy's foot. I had even asked the senior doctors at the hospital for advice, but they had brushed me aside, saying it was a waste of their time to even ask. Nothing I seemed to do had any effect, and I was running out of time. His family couldn't afford to leave Sidney in the hospital and would come to take him home soon, whether he was better or not.

I stayed with Sidney a few minutes longer, playing with the soldiers, but I was conscious of my other duties and left the ward, desperate for refreshment. As I entered the corridor, I saw one of the hospital tea ladies pushing her trolley. It wasn't the done thing for a doctor to take his refreshment from one of these women – the senior staff thought it undignified – but most of my fellow doctors did partake, it being the only way we got anything to eat or drink during the day.

'Hello, Mabel,' I said, recognising the woman. 'Couldn't cadge a cup of tea from you, could I?'

She took up one of the chipped earthenware mugs and poured tea from a huge metal teapot. It was the colour of mud and would taste stewed, but I didn't care.

‘’ere you go, Dr Cowdrey,’ she said, passing it over to me. ‘Want summink to eat too?’

‘What do you have?’

‘Buns, if you want one.’ She bent to the lower shelf and took out a plate with dry-looking specimens upon it.

I took one. ‘Thank you, Mabel. You’re a life saver.’ I bit into the bun, taking a large mouthful.

‘Watch out,’ Mabel nodded as she pushed her trolley forward, indicating something behind me.

I turned and saw with a sinking feeling Dr Hobkirk walking towards me. There was nowhere I could hide in the corridor, no room I could back into, no one I could pretend to be speaking with. I tried to conceal the bun and mug of tea behind my back, but it was too late. I had been seen.

Dr Hobkirk was the most feared of all the senior doctors. He ruled over his student doctors with an iron fist, setting very high standards and criticising any who failed to live up to them, which was most of us. Only Horace seemed to satisfy his idea of a good doctor. I was, frankly, terrified of him.

Dr Hobkirk glared at me. ‘We have rules about taking refreshment from the trolleys, Cowdrey.’

‘Yes, I know, Dr Hobkirk, I’m sorry. But I haven’t had a chance—’

‘Don’t make excuses, man,’ he cut me off. ‘How can we expect the patients to respect us if they see us acting like this?’

‘You’re quite right, sir,’ I agreed. ‘It won’t happen again.’

He grunted, then looked me up and down. 'Time on your hands, Cowdrey?'

It was ridiculous to suggest I had nothing to do. 'No, sir, that is—'

'Then come with me.'

And he strode off before I could say another word.

I looked around for somewhere to put my mug of tea. There was nowhere, so I put it on the floor against the wall. I hurried after him, stuffing my half-eaten bun into my pocket. As I followed, turning corner after corner, I suddenly realised with a lurch in my stomach where we were headed. Dr Hobkirk was taking me to the operating theatre.

I had done my best to avoid the operating theatre since joining St Eustace's. I had only been there twice before, both times as a spectator standing in the gallery. Even from that remove, the sight of a man or woman lying on the operating table, fully conscious or anaesthetised with chloroform, about to be cut open by the knives and other implements that looked like instruments of torture, had made my insides shrivel and my heart pound.

Dr Hobkirk was the chief surgeon at the hospital, and he had a reputation for removing limbs before any of his spectators could blink. So fast was he that he often kept his patients conscious on the operating table, saying it would be a waste of chloroform to put them out. And so, his patients suffered terribly, thrashing and screaming as he cut through flesh and bone. No matter how fast he operated, I thought it callous to put his patients through such agony. They deserved not to know what was happening to them.

The stands were full. Not all medical men are like me. Most actually enjoy the show of the operating theatre, and there was a great deal of chatter as Dr Hobkirk entered with me at his heels. They quietened as they caught sight of the great man. I looked around and saw Horace in the stands. He was no longer a student, of course, but he always took the opportunity to observe surgery. He found it fascinating.

Dr Hobkirk was never one for pleasantries and he launched straight in to the reason why we were all there. He addressed his audience as he placed the cord of an apron over his head and moved for a nurse to tie it behind his back. The front of the apron was stained brown with dried blood.

'The patient today is a male child of nine years, born with a club foot deformity. He managed perfectly well with the club foot until he had an accident and broke the ankle. So severe was the injury that it has not healed, and infection is setting in. The only remedy is to operate to remove the diseased foot.'

A nurse was handing me another apron as he spoke, and so preoccupied was I with putting it on that it was only belatedly that I registered Dr Hobkirk's words. A boy, a club foot, infection. He couldn't mean, surely not—

'No!' I cried.

Dr Hobkirk turned to me, his brow deeply furrowed, his black eyes hard. There were a few smothered chuckles from the stands. 'Dr Cowdrey?' he growled.

I opened my mouth to say something, but no words came. There was a shuffling behind me, and I turned to see porters carrying a stretcher and on it, yes, on it was my poor Sidney. He was so small he only took up three-quarters of the stretcher. They had strapped him down, and I saw his terrified eyes darting around the room until they landed on me.

'Dr Cowdrey,' he screamed.

'Silence that boy,' Dr Hobkirk ordered, and one of the porters whispered something in Sidney's ear. I can't imagine what it was but Sidney didn't speak again.

'This patient,' Dr Hobkirk said, turning back to the students, 'has been under the care of Dr Cowdrey. Dr Cowdrey is here to assist me in the removal of the diseased foot as he has failed to cure it.'

I didn't care that he had publicly humiliated me. I could bear that. What I could not bear was to see the betrayal in Sidney's eyes as Dr Hobkirk accused me of incompetence. I saw it so very clearly: Sidney had lost any faith he had had in me. I had promised to help him and instead, I had delivered him into the hands of a butcher. He had appealed to me for help, and I was just standing there. I had uttered one pitiful protest, and that was all. What kind of man, what kind of doctor, was I?

Sidney was crying as the porters untied the straps that held him on the stretcher and lifted him onto the operating table. Here, he was tied down again, the porters having a difficult time of it because he was struggling so much. Ropes were tied around Sidney's wrists and ankles, and another tied over his right thigh. When they had done, one of the porters placed a bucket at the end of the table, just below Sidney's injured foot. I tasted bile as I watched, knowing what the bucket was for.

I couldn't stop this. Hobkirk would not listen to me. I closed my eyes and prayed that he would allow Sidney to endure this operation while under the effect of chloroform. *Spare him the pain*, I silently begged. *Can you please do that?*

Hobkirk clicked his fingers at me as he moved into position by the table. 'You will pass me the instruments, Cowdrey.'

I licked my dry lips and willed words into my mouth. 'I can administer the anaesthetic, sir.'

'No bother with all that,' he said, and I felt my breath shudder from my lips. 'It will all be over in a moment.'

I forced my legs to move; they felt like lumps of iron as they shuffled through the sawdust on the floor, thrown there to soak up the blood. I stood by the white painted trolley with its collection of medical instruments. I could see streaks and spots of blood on them from previous operations.

Dr Hobkirk was talking to the students. 'I must first cut the skin and retract it to expose the bone. Time is of the essence. If the patient suffers too great a loss of blood, he will die. It is imperative that the operation be carried out at speed. Cowdrey, I will need the curved knife.'

My fingers fumbled over the cold metal of the instruments. I took hold of the knife he meant and held it out to Dr Hobkirk. I saw how I trembled.

He saw it too and snatched the knife from my hand. 'Get a grip on yourself, man,' he hissed at me and placed his hand on Sidney's shin, gripping it tightly. 'Observe.'

I watched as he drew the knife around Sidney's ankle. Blood spurted, bright red against the rusty brown already on Hobkirk's apron. He set the knife aside and put out his hand for the saw. I gave it to him in a daze, my eyes on Sidney's leg.

Hobkirk bent over and positioned the blade of the saw on the bone. I held my breath for that brief moment as he summoned up his strength to make the first stroke.

It was Sidney's scream that undid me. The room began to move, sound washed in and out of my ears, and darkness came upon me.

I opened my eyes warily, not at all sure what I would see. Confused at first, I realised I was in the corridor outside the operating theatre, and that I was horizontal. I took a few deep breaths, testing my lungs, and wished I hadn't, for I felt nauseous and thought I might vomit. I swallowed a few times, pushing the feeling down.

'Well, that could have gone better.'

I turned my head. Horace was leaning against the opposite wall, arms crossed over his chest. 'Is it over?' I croaked.

'Yes, all over. Doesn't take Hobkirk long, does it? Steady, old man, take it easy.'

This last because I was sitting up. I wasn't sure it was such a good idea either, but I did it all the same. I swung my legs to the side. My feet hit the ground with a skull-juddering thud. I looked down at my legs. My trousers were filthy with sawdust and the palms of my hands felt gritty. I rubbed them together to remove the dirt. 'I made a fool of myself.'

'It wasn't your most impressive performance,' Horace agreed.

'Sidney?' I asked, looking up at him hopefully.

Horace's expression told me everything. 'The boy lost a lot of blood.'

'He's dead?'

''Fraid so, old man. Sorry.'

I couldn't help it. I sobbed, there, in front of Horace, and embarrassed him.

'Don't take on so,' he said, and I heard him shuffling his feet. 'The foot was diseased. Nothing you had done had made it better. It had to come off.'

'He was only a boy—'

'You must stop this, Felix,' Horace said, suddenly

stern. 'I've told you before, we do what we can for the patients. It's inevitable that many of them will die. It is God's will.'

'And my incompetence.' I laughed bitterly. 'You heard Hobkirk, everyone heard Hobkirk say so. It's not a secret any longer that I'm a lousy doctor.' I waited, looking up at him. 'You know it. You can't even bring yourself to contradict me.'

Horace uncrossed his arms and tugged his jacket down. 'Hobkirk wants to see you in his office as soon as you are able.'

He didn't need to say any more. I was in trouble. I nodded understanding, and Horace left me. I stayed on the bench until I felt sure my legs could carry me to Hobkirk's office. They trembled a little as I walked, but I kept going.

Dr Hobkirk had the best office in the hospital, which wasn't saying much. I had been there only once before when I had first taken up my appointment at St Eustace's. There was a large window that let in a great deal of light. Hobkirk's desk was placed before it, and the great man was sitting at this desk when I entered. With his back to the window, his face was in shadow, but I didn't need daylight to tell me his expression was thunderous.

'What do you have to say for yourself?' he demanded without preamble.

'I apologise for my behaviour, Dr Hobkirk,' I began. 'It was unprofessional and insulting to you.'

'I'm glad you acknowledge both of those facts,' he

said, putting his pen down in the silver tray and folding his hands across his stomach. He looked me up and down. 'You're an intelligent young man, Cowdrey, and a hard worker, but I'm afraid to say I think we've come to the end, and not just because of this afternoon's debacle. It's something I've been considering for a while now. I don't believe you are suited to such an environment as St Eustace's.'

My heart thudded once, twice, then I took a deep breath and said, 'I agree with you, Dr Hobkirk.'

He frowned. 'You agree?'

'I do. I assume you are dismissing me from my post?'

'Yes, you are dismissed,' he said. I think I had rather taken the wind out of his sails. He had expected me to argue, perhaps even to beg. I was glad to disappoint him in that. 'You will clear your desk and pass on your case notes to your fellow doctors. Your salary to this day will be forwarded to you in due course.' He attempted kindness. 'It's for the best, Cowdrey. This is no place for you.'

'What place is for me?' I wondered.

'Be a General Practitioner,' he suggested in a tone that implied he thought he was being helpful. 'Private patients who will appreciate your bedside manner.'

I thanked Dr Hobkirk for his advice and for the opportunity he had given me. I expressed regret at my proving a disappointment. Then I bid him good afternoon and made my way to my office, emptying my desk drawers of my personal belongings. There were only a few. A couple of handkerchiefs, a pencil, a few coins. I pocketed them, gathered my files, placed them on Horace's already overladen desk, and put on my hat and coat. I took one last look around, then exited, closing the door behind me.

6

ENVY AND OPPORTUNITY

People talk about carrying the weight of the world on their shoulders and it always sounds like an exaggeration, but I can honestly say that as I walked out of the large double doors of St Eustace's that late afternoon, I felt the most immense relief I had ever felt in my life. I realised then, as I dodged pedestrians and had my trouser legs splashed with filth, just how pressured I had felt at the hospital. It became clear to me, as it never had before, that Dr Hobkirk and my father were right. A free hospital was not the place for me and I would never have been happy at St Eustace's or any other similar establishment.

I don't mean to imply that I wasn't worried. Of course, I had concerns about my immediate future. I was free from financial concerns, but I did not want to be known as a gentleman of leisure. There was shame in that. And there was also the ignominy of being dismissed from my position to be got over. I didn't doubt that I would have to suffer some embarrassment, even humiliation, at the hands of my family, especially Theo and Abigail. How pleased those two would be to hear of my dismissal! But what concerned me most was what I was going to do next. Was a private practice really my only option?

By the time I reached Milton Square, I had decided to get it all over with. I would collect Clara, take her over to my parents' house, invite Theo and Abigail to join us, and tell them my news. But this plan of mine was thwarted almost before I stepped inside my front door. Clara called to me from the sitting room.

'There you are,' she said, beaming up at me as I entered, and my first miserable thought since my dismissal came to me, that my news would make that lovely smile fade. 'Now, don't be cross, darling, but Abigail has invited us to a small gathering at your parents' house tonight. She and Theo have some news.'

'What news?' I asked with a sigh. I could think of nothing more tedious than an entire evening spent in their company.

'Abigail wouldn't tell me,' she said, putting her needlework away and getting to her feet. 'Said it was a surprise. I did wonder if she is…' she made a face, her eyebrows rising, and she gestured at her stomach, 'you know.'

'Who else is going to be there?' I asked, a little grumpily now my plan had gone to pot.

'Only the Burketts, Abigail said.'

I shook my head. 'They wouldn't invite the Burketts to announce a pregnancy. It can't be that.'

'Then I wonder what it is,' Clara said, her brow creasing.

We had our dinner, the gathering at number eight being an after-dinner affair. I said nothing to Clara, but I had my suspicions what the news would be. For some time now, Theo had been taking on the criminal cases at the firm and had been making a name for himself. He had probably concluded a big case, made a lot of money for the firm, and now wanted to show off.

During dinner, I pondered over whether to tell Clara about my dismissal from St Eustace's, but I decided against it as I didn't want to spoil her evening. My news could wait until the morning. At half-past eight, with Clara wearing her best silk gown and me properly attired – Clara had seen to that – we set out, arm in arm, across the square.

Abigail breezed into the hall as we entered my parents' house, her smile as wide as I had ever seen it. She held out her hands to each of us, and as she pulled us into the drawing room, Clara and I slid a bemused glance at each other, wondering what on earth had come over her.

The Burketts had already arrived. Mr Burkett was standing with Theo by the window, both of them looking extremely pleased with themselves, while Mother was chatting with Mrs Burkett. I say chatting, but really, Mother was only listening, as Mrs Burkett rarely paused for breath. My father was standing in front of the fireplace, watching Theo with pride evident upon his face.

'Here they are,' Abigail called, announcing us.

Mr Burkett hallooed us by raising his glass, and I moved towards him, hand extended. 'How nice to see you again, Mr Burkett,' I said.

He shook my hand vigorously. 'Well, well, young Felix, it's been a while, hasn't it?'

'It certainly has,' I agreed.

I bowed to Mrs Burkett, then checked to make sure Clara was being taken care of. Mother had patted the seat beside her, and Abigail was pressing a sherry glass into her hand. Abigail was still smiling. Whatever this celebration was, it had to be more than just the successful closure of a case.

'So,' I said, taking a glass from Theo and looking around at everyone, 'what are we celebrating?'

No one answered me. Abigail smiled at Theo expectantly, but Theo just grinned. I grew a little exasperated.

'Mother?' I asked.

She shrugged. 'I don't know, Felix. No one has told me anything.'

'We wanted everyone here for this,' Abigail said, sliding her hand around Theo's arm and smiling up at him. It was really very odd to see her so happy and, for once, not spitting venom. 'Go on, Theo. Tell them.'

Theo's cheeks actually coloured, something I had never seen before. He looked down at his feet, shuffling a little in his embarrassment. Abigail tugged on his arm, and I saw a little of her old self in the annoyed narrowing of her eyes.

'Well,' Theo said eventually, 'Dad and Mr Burkett already know this, of course, but for those who don't, I've been dealing with the firm's criminal cases over the last year, and… well… I've been rather good at it.' The red in his cheeks deepened, and he seemed unable to continue. He looked shyly at our father.

Dad nodded. 'I'll spare Theo his blushes. Theo's been doing quite a bit better than rather good. He's brought a lot of business to the firm, and we're being talked about as the only people to go to for those facing criminal prosecutions.' He held out a hand to Mother. 'I know you ladies think it's all rather seedy, delving into crime, but it is profitable, and I would like to point out that not everyone charged with a crime is guilty. Theo has worked extremely hard to make contacts with chambers in Lincoln's Inn, and I know how much of his success in wooing those contacts is owed to Abigail.'

Abigail didn't blush.

'But I'm dragging this out, aren't I?' Dad said, laughing as he looked around at his audience. 'So let me get straight to the point. We are all here to celebrate Theo becoming a full partner at Cowdrey and Burkett.'

My mother cried out in delight and jumped off the settee to drag Theo into an embrace. Mrs Burkett raised her glass and said, 'Congratulations.' Mr Burkett said, 'Here, here.' Clara caught Abigail's eye and smiled.

Then she looked over to me, her smile slowing shrinking.

'Felix?' Theo asked quietly.

I suddenly realised all eyes were on me. Had I really not said anything? 'Congratulations, Theo,' I said. 'I'm very pleased for you, and for you, Abi.' I must have sounded insincere, for one by one, everyone's expressions faltered, just a little. Evidently, more was expected from me. I cleared my throat. 'I knew you would be made partner one day, even if I didn't think it would be quite so soon.'

It was the wrong thing to say. I realised that as soon as the words were spoken. I was damning with faint praise. But after the day I had had, it was difficult to summon up genuine pleasure at my brother's promotion. My prospects were heading in the opposite direction, and yes, I'll admit it, I was jealous.

Clara came to my rescue. 'We think it's wonderful,' she said in a voice unusually loud for her, drawing the attention that had been fixed on me. 'Felix never knows what to say at times like these, you know. He always sounds so reticent when really he is bursting with admiration. And Abi, now I know why you were so happy when you called round this afternoon.'

Abigail's hard face softened only a little as she replied to my wife. 'Yes, now you know, Clara. Perhaps one day you will have as much reason to be proud of your husband as I have of mine.'

She moved to brush past me. 'Though I won't hold my breath,' she hissed at me as she passed.

The evening wore on. Fortunately, my lack of enthusiasm didn't dampen everyone else's joy, and the company became quite convivial without my intervention. I thought no one would notice if I escaped. I just needed to be by myself for a little while, have a respite from pretending to be pleased, and so quietly left the drawing room to hunker down in my father's study for half an hour.

There was a copy of *The Times* on the table by the fireside. I sat down in the armchair and turned the pages without taking in any of the news. I had not been there ten minutes by my reckoning when I heard the door creak open. I pretended not to have heard and kept my eyes bent upon the newspaper. But then I felt my father draw near and he sank down into the chair opposite. I folded the newspaper up, laid it on my lap, and waited for the rebuke I knew was coming.

He looked at me out of the corner of his eyes. 'What was all that about earlier? And don't pretend you don't know what I mean.'

'I am happy for Theo, Dad,' I insisted.

'Are you? You made a damned poor show of it.'

'I'm sorry.'

His eyes narrowed. 'Has something happened?'

I sighed. 'You could say that. I've been dismissed from the hospital.'

'Ah, now I understand. Can you tell me why?'

'I can, but I warn you, you'll be ashamed of me.'

'Just tell me.'

'Dr Hobkirk ordered me to assist him in an operation. I've never been very fond of what goes on in the operating theatre — it's more like torture than surgery — but he insisted and I couldn't get out of it. My stomach was already lurching, but then they brought in one of my patients. A young boy.'

'Not the one you gave the tin soldiers to?'

I nodded grimly. 'Dr Hobkirk was going to cut off his foot.' The memory of Sidney's eyes came back to me and I buried my face in my hands. 'The boy, he looked at me with such terror and blame. But there was nothing I could do. When Dr Hobkirk started to cut and the boy screamed, I... well, I fainted, Dad. There, I've said it. Now, what do you think of me? I don't give you anything to be proud of like Theo.'

I didn't dare look up. I kept my face in my hands and managed at least to hold back the tears threatening to squeeze out of my eyelids. I felt my father's hand grasp my wrist.

'I'm always proud of you, Felix,' he said.

I looked up at him in astonishment. His expression was sincere. He actually meant it. He kept his eyes on mine for a long moment, then released me and sank back in his chair.

'Did Hobkirk give you a character?' he asked.

I shook my head. 'I didn't think to ask. I suppose I could apply to him for one, but I doubt it would be particularly glowing.'

'I know Charles Hobkirk. Leave that to me.'

'No, Dad, I can't involve you—'

He waved his hand to quiet me. 'I'm your father, Felix. Why shouldn't I be involved? I don't doubt you did excellent work at the hospital, even though it hasn't been a great success for you. And you'll need a character to get another position, unless you mean to set up privately, of course.'

'I'm not ready for that, Dad,' I said hurriedly. 'I need more experience.'

'But you are planning to stay in medicine?'

'What else?'

'You could come back to the law. Had you stuck with us, you would have made an excellent solicitor. You would have shined just as much, if not more, than Theo, I promise you.'

I was grateful to him for saying this, but a return to the law wasn't what I wanted. 'I'd like to stick with medicine, Dad.'

He nodded. 'Is this news of yours a secret?'

'I was going to tell you all tonight,' I said. 'But Theo and Abigail got their news in first. I haven't even told Clara yet.'

'Well, we won't say anything tonight. Let's not spoil the evening. And I don't think we need to make a big announcement. I'm sure you don't need or want to do that, do you?'

He was right about that, but I didn't think I had any alternative. 'They will have to know. They'll realise I'm not going to work each day.'

'Of course they must be told, but it doesn't need to

come from you. I can tell them you've chosen to leave the hospital, if you would prefer.'

'That would be a lie.'

My father gave me a look that suggested I was being tiresome. 'Not every truth needs to be told, Felix. All Theo and Abi need to know is that you've left the hospital. They don't need to know why if you'd rather they didn't.'

'Would *you* prefer they didn't?' I asked.

His jaw tightened and I saw I had annoyed him. 'I am not ashamed of you, Felix. The hospital was not right for you, that's all.'

I was contrite. 'I was rather dreading telling you all,' I admitted. 'You may not be ashamed of me, but I'm ashamed of myself. If you can spare me having to tell the truth, I'd be grateful.'

'Then leave it to me. You must tell Clara, of course.'

I agreed and thanked him.

'Are you all right for money?' he asked.

'I have enough for a little while. Hopefully, it won't take me too long to get another position.'

'Well, you know you can always come to me.'

He was being too kind; I didn't deserve it. I rose. 'We should get back to the others, Dad.'

My father got to his feet. 'Yes, indeed, and try to put a smile on your face, Felix. Theo has earned his partnership, and I want you to be pleased for him.'

I promised him I would try.

Clara was wonderful. I told her of my dismissal as we lay in bed that night, keeping as many of the grisly details of the operating theatre from her as I could. She fussed over me when I told her I had fainted, suggesting I had caught something at the hospital that had weakened me. I blessed her for that, but told her it was not true. I had been womanish, weak, and there was no getting away from it. She tried to make light of my unemployment, declaring happily that she would see more of me for a little while until I had a new position. Clara always was an optimist.

I had to get a new position, that was a fact. How was I to go about it? Positions weren't advertised in the newspapers. The kind of position I would be interested in came via word of mouth, which meant that I would have to put myself about. Part of me revolted against going to my club to find out what I could. I had an idea my dismissal would be the club's common gossip and I would be laughed at as soon as I set foot inside Sadlers. Or worse. I might have been blackballed in my absence and not allowed through the door.

But after a week of lounging around the house, I decided I had to brave Sadlers. I made it through the front door, the doorman nodding to me as I passed, so I obviously hadn't been thrown out. I went to the reception desk and greeted Wilson. He returned my greeting and said he was glad to see me as a letter had arrived and he wasn't sure whether he should have forwarded it to my home address. I waited, wondering who would have written to me at my club, as he turned to the pigeonholes allocated to members behind the desk and plucked out a letter from mine.

Handing it to me, I studied the handwriting. I didn't recognise it. I thanked Wilson and retreated to the smoking room to read my letter. I ordered a coffee, biscuits and a cigar, and plumped down in an armchair.

I opened the envelope and took out the letter. The letterhead bore the legend, *Flete House, Essex.* My eyes sought the signature, thinking it could only be from one person, and yes, there was the signature of Dr Miles Wakefield. I read eagerly.

> Dear Dr Cowdrey,
>
> Forgive me for sending this to Sadlers, but I had no address other than St Eustace's Hospital for you, and I thought it best not to write to you there.
>
> When we met, I was in London to acquire the services of a competent doctor to work at my asylum. My former employee, Dr Dennison, rather left me in the lurch when he was compelled to depart quite suddenly for health reasons. Unfortunately, I failed in my endeavour and was despairing of finding any qualified doctor to fulfil the position. It is truly amazing how ill-fitted for lunatic patients most of our brethren are.
>
> Then I thought of you. I remembered how interested you were in my asylum, and though I daresay you are perfectly happy where you are, I would like to know whether I can persuade you to join me at Flete House, if only for a short while. I

know you are a London doctor and would probably not want to be closeted away in the country for long, but the position need only be for a few months, just long enough to give me a little breathing space to find a more long-term replacement for Dennison. Then you could return to London and take up your old post at St Eustace's (I know they would be pleased to have you back). I will be the first to admit that the proposition may not be an attractive one. I daresay I cannot match the salary you enjoy at St Eustace's, but I can promise you interesting work.

What do you say, old chap? Will you help me out of a hole?

If this interests you at all, please write to me as soon as you receive this letter and I will write back with any details you require.

Yours sincerely,

Miles Wakefield

I had to stop myself from laughing out loud with joy. This was the answer to all my problems. I jumped up and dashed over to the writing desk beneath the window. I pulled out a sheet of Sadler's writing paper and began scrawling my reply to Dr Wakefield.

Dear Dr Wakefield,

I am very interested in your proposition. Please write to me with full details of the post and its duties, as well as any accommodation that would be available to me.

I paused and nibbled the end of the pen. I didn't want to appear too eager. There was no need for Dr Wakefield to know I was out of a position at the moment. As far as he was concerned, I was gainfully employed at St Eustace's. I put my pen back to the paper.

If the details you provide are acceptable, I would be glad to take up a temporary position at Flete House, just to get you out of the hole you say you are in – ha ha.

I would, in the meantime, like to thank you for thinking of me, and for your belief in my ability to successfully work at your asylum when your opinion of our brethren is so low.

Yours sincerely,
Felix Cowdrey

I gave my home address, signed and sealed the letter, then hurried out to Wilson to have it posted without delay.

7

DECISION MADE

I received an answer from Dr Wakefield during breakfast two days later.

I had said nothing to Clara of his first letter, foolishly perhaps thinking that to speak of his offer would be to doom it in some way. I had an image in my head of receiving a letter from him that said he had actually found a doctor after all, and he now didn't need me. I don't think I could have borne such a disappointment coming on the heels of my dismissal, so I decided to keep his offer to myself, at least until I definitely had the job.

I opened his letter with shaking hands. That I had received an answer so soon gave me hope, and I was right to have that hope. The post had not been filled and Dr Wakefield provided particulars.

I would be an employee of Dr Wakefield and his wife. I would answer to him on all medical matters and to his wife on all administrative ones. I would have the charge of the female patients, the male patients being in the care of Dr Wakefield. Daily duties would include checks on the patients' welfare, the diagnosing and treating of any ailments or injuries they had, and ensuring they were kept occupied throughout the day. I was quite surprised. The duties seemed light compared to those I had had at St Eustace's.

As for accommodation, Dr Wakefield was sorry, but all he could offer was a single bedroom in the asylum that Dr Dennison, being a bachelor, had occupied. No provision was available for a married man such as myself. He supposed rooms might be available in the village a little way off, but he would prefer me to be resident on the premises, as indeed he and his wife were, occupying as they did the lodge within the asylum's grounds.

This gave me a pang. I was rather used to home comforts and having the run of a house. I did not fancy being reduced to a single room, and that room in the same building as lunatics, but there it was. I really had little choice in the matter. I considered taking rooms in the village of Flete as Dr Wakefield said, but I felt to pursue it might count against me in his estimation.

'Good news, darling?' Clara asked as she buttered her toast.

'Possibly,' I said, and put the letter back into its envelope. 'I think I'll pop in to the office today and ask Dad to lunch at Simpson's. You don't mind, do you, Clara?'

She shook her head. 'No. I promised your mother I

would go with her to the Home for Unmarried Mothers today. In fact,' she caught sight of the time from the clock on the mantel and hurriedly chewed her last mouthful of toast, 'I had better hurry.' She rose and bestowed a kiss on my temple, telling me to give her love to my father.

I wasn't accustomed to dropping in on my father unannounced and I hoped he wouldn't be annoyed by my appearance in the office, but I wanted his opinion on Dr Wakefield's offer. Although I had already decided to accept it, I wanted my father to confirm I was right to do so. I didn't want to make another mistake. I also needed to ask him about Clara.

It felt a little odd to enter the offices in which I had spent a dissatisfied seven months years earlier. Nothing seemed to have changed. The chief clerk, Mr Whitly, looked up at me as I entered, and did me the honour of recognising me. I asked if my father was free to see me and he hurried away to check, returning a minute later to inform me that my father was free and ushering me through to his office. It was the finest in the firm, with a very large desk bearing a silver double inkwell, a bust of Thomas Erskine, the famous barrister, and a great many papers which almost hid my father from view. He could have been less busy if he wanted, but my father enjoyed his work and delegated little of it.

'Felix, what are you doing here?' My father looked worried, as if he feared some new calamity had befallen me.

'I thought I might take you to lunch, Dad.'

He relaxed. 'I'm sorry, my boy, but I can't. I have an appointment with Lord Morley at one.' He took off his spectacles. 'I could put him off, I suppose, if—'

'No, no, no,' I said quickly. 'It was just a whim of mine. I should have known you would be busy. I just wanted to ask your opinion on something, that's all.'

He pointed me to one of the visitor's chairs. 'Ask me now.'

I sat. 'I've had the offer of a job.'

'Felix, that's wonderful,' he said, and I could see the relief as well as the surprise in his expression. 'And so soon.'

'Yes, quite a bit of luck.' I told him all about Dr Wakefield and his asylum. I noticed Dad's lip curling at my mention of lunatics, but he made no comment and let me continue.

'It sounds like an excellent offer,' he said when I had finished. 'And you seem to have already made up your mind to take it, so what do you want my opinion on?'

'It's a bit awkward. You see, there isn't any room for Clara. Dr Wakefield can only offer me a small bedroom at the asylum, and that's not good enough for Clara, is it? If I take the job, I'll have to leave her behind.'

He frowned. 'It's not ideal, I can see that, but if that's how it must be, then that is how it must be. And it will only be for a short while. This position is temporary, you say.'

'It is, and you're right, of course, I must take it.' Now that I had his approval to accept the position, I hurried on. 'But I don't like the idea of leaving her alone in the house. I wouldn't feel she was safe.'

'What you're really asking is if we will take her in.' He rolled his eyes at me taking so long to get to this point. 'Of course we will have Clara come live with us. Your mother will be delighted.'

'Thank you, Dad,' I said, relieved he had agreed. Everything was working out perfectly. There seemed to be nothing in the way of me going to Flete House. I scribbled a letter to Dr Wakefield then and there to accept the position, and told my father I would post it on the way home. As soon as I got home, I would tell Clara my good news. I knew she would be as pleased as I was.

'I won't do it!'

The cushion Clara hurled struck me full in the face. I picked it up from the floor and threw it back on the settee.

'You have to, Clara. I've taken the job and there is no room for you there.'

'You've accepted a position that doesn't allow you to live with your wife?' she shrieked. 'What were you thinking?'

'Of being employed, that's what I was thinking,' I shouted back, shutting the sitting-room door so our quarrel wouldn't be heard by Millie and Mrs Sugden, the cook, quite so easily. 'I must earn a living, Clara.'

'There are other positions here in London. Any

hospital would be glad to have you. Why accept a position in the country? And in a lunatic asylum, of all places?'

'It is of interest to me,' I said. 'The chance to study maladies of the mind rather than of the body will be excellent experience.'

'And what of me?' she cried, laying her hands on her breast. 'You haven't given a moment of consideration to me. Oh no, I'm to be packed off to live with your parents as if I'm nothing better than a dog.'

This wasn't what I had expected from Clara at all. That she would be so angry with my decision hadn't occurred to me. It was so unlike her. I had to make her understand. 'I've done what I believe is best for everyone.'

'You've done what's best for you, you mean.' She dropped onto the settee with a great sigh of resignation.

Seeing the fight had gone out of her, I knelt before her and took her hands in mine. She tried to pull them away, but I held them fast. 'It will be for no longer than six months,' I promised, 'perhaps even a little less. It is a temporary position only. And Dad is overjoyed at the prospect of having you to live with them. Mother will be so very pleased.'

'I'm very fond of your mother and it will be pleasant to be with her. But,' Clara looked around the sitting room, 'this is my home, Felix. Mine. I will feel I'm a girl again if I go to your parents, not a married woman.'

'It is for a few months only,' I repeated, not really understanding her objection. 'And it wouldn't be economical to keep the servants on when it is only you here.'

She sighed and wiped her eyes. 'I can say nothing to persuade you not to do this, can I?'

'No, my love,' I admitted, stroking her cheek. 'I have accepted, and everything else has been worked out.'

'Yes, you and your father have managed it all,' she said sourly. 'You didn't even ask me what I wanted.'

I was tempted to say that it didn't matter what she wanted, that as my wife she had vowed to obey me, but now was not the time. She needed consolation, and I gave it to her. I took her in my arms and told her she was the best of wives. Then a note arrived from Mother telling us to come over for dinner so we could discuss all the arrangements for Clara moving in.

Clara made no further complaint. She sat quietly while my parents and I discussed her removal to their house, the shutting up of our own, and the dismissal of Millie and Mrs Sugden. Clara may not have been happy at this turn of events, but for my part, I was glad everything had fallen into place so easily.

8

FLETE HOUSE

Within two days, I was ready to leave for Flete House.

I had given Millie and Mrs Sugden a month's salary in lieu of notice, Clara had moved into my old bedroom at my parents' house, and I had packed two bags with everything I thought I would need.

And yet, something within me was telling me I should not go. A misgiving, I suppose you could call it, brought on by the dream I had during my last night in London.

With Clara already across the square, I was sleeping alone — I was planning to leave early the next morning and didn't want to disturb her, so had spent my last night in my own bed — and the bed did indeed feel strange without her. I must get used to sleeping alone again, I told myself, and tucked the covers tight around my neck.

I was so anxious about leaving in the morning that it

wasn't until the early hours that I actually fell asleep. I almost wished I had stayed awake.

I dreamt I was back at the fair. This time I was alone, no Clara by my side. All the booths and shows I remembered were there, the performers, the flare of the torches, but there was no sound. Not a whisper, not an utterance. The people I passed, their mouths were moving, but I could hear nothing of what they said. I was walking down the middle of the fair – it was arranged neatly on either side of me, not as it had been in reality – and I had the pathway to myself.

I didn't stop at any of the amusements. I put one foot in front of the other without knowing where my feet were taking me. And yet, I did know, really. They were taking me to the one place at the fair where I didn't want to go. I was heading for the gypsy fortune-teller.

She was sitting there on the steps of her caravan as she had been when first I saw her. The fringed shawl was draped around her shoulders, her black hair hanging down about her face, and she fixed me with those same dark eyes as I approached.

'I've come back,' I said, though the words didn't seem to come from my mouth.

'I knew you would,' she said.

'I'm going away.'

'You should stay.'

'I can't.'

'Why can't you?'

'I need the work.'

'Ah,' she grinned, 'but does the work need you?'

The sound of the fair suddenly broke in on me. It was loud, far louder than it should have been. It hurt my ears, and I squeezed my eyes shut. After a time, I do not know how long, I opened my eyes. The gypsy was gone, though the caravan was still there. I looked around for her desperately, but I couldn't see her. The noise grew louder and louder, and I couldn't bear it, it was almost painful.

I awoke on a shout.

I was soaked in sweat, my legs tangled in the bedsheets. Daylight was bleeding in through the gap in the curtain. I checked the clock on my bedside table. It was approaching eight o'clock. Time I was up.

I ate a breakfast of cold ham and bread, washed down with a glass of milk, then made my way to Bishopsgate Street and the terminus of the Great Eastern Railway. I handed my bags to a porter, purchased a newspaper from the W. H. Smith's stall and took my seat in a first-class carriage.

I chose the seat by the window and had to keep moving my feet as more people entered until eventually the carriage was full. The whistle blew, and the train began to chug, steam billowing around the window until we had passed out of the station and picked up speed.

Once past Mile End, the view outside the window improved, and I set my newspaper aside and watched as we left London behind and travelled into the countryside. As the miles hurtled by, I wondered about Flete House and its inhabitants. The past few days had been so full that I had barely had time to consider what my new place of work would be like.

The further the train went into the country, the fewer people remained with me in the compartment until there was only one other man beside myself. He was an elderly man with abundant white hair and rosy cheeks. Like many elderly people, he seemed to feel the cold keenly, for his muffler was tied several times around his neck and he had kept his gloves on all this time. He must have seen me noticing the empty seats.

'It's always like this at this time of day,' he said. 'Are you staying in Colchester?'

Flete, being only a village, didn't have its own train station; I would have to disembark at Colchester.

'No, I'm going on to Flete,' I said.

'Are you really? So am I.'

'Do you live there?'

'Oh yes, all of my life. May I ask why you are going there?'

'I'm a doctor,' I said proudly. 'I'm going to Flete House to work.'

His white eyebrows rose a little. 'The asylum. Yes, of course.'

'Do you know Dr Wakefield?'

'Indeed I do. He and his patients are my parishioners.'

I was surprised. 'You preach to the patients?'

He smiled and folded his hands, one over the other, on his lap. 'They are God's children's too, Dr... forgive me? I don't know your name.'

I told him it and he introduced himself as Reverend Timothy Bute.

'And Mrs Wakefield is very devout,' he continued. 'She insists on the patients attending services. Those that behave themselves, of course.'

'And those that don't?'

'For those, I go to the asylum and perform a private service. But most do behave. Even so, some of my other parishioners feel less than comfortable having them in the church. Less than comfortable having the asylum so close, actually.'

'Flete House isn't popular in the village?'

Reverend Bute shrugged. 'When we first learnt the house had been bought, the villagers were pleased. The house had stood empty for some years, you see, and we were all very glad it was to be occupied again. But then it was discovered to what use the house was going to be put to and...' He shrugged again and made a face.

'Is the village still against the asylum?' I asked, a little perturbed at this information.

'Oh, they've settled down. Village folk, you know, they're always slow to embrace new ideas.' He smiled encouragingly, showing a full set of fine teeth. 'So, I assume you are Dr Dennison's replacement.'

'That's right.'

'I see.' He looked out of the window. 'It won't be long now before we arrive. Is anyone meeting you?'

'A Jim Danby? He should be meeting me with a dogcart.'

'Danby,' Reverend Bute said in a rather disapproving tone. 'Now there's a strange fellow.'

'He's not one of the patients, is he?'

The reverend laughed. 'Oh no, no, no. Although, I do wonder if perhaps he should be. No, Jim Danby is one of Mrs Wakefield's 'finds'. Took him out of the workhouse, I believe, and reformed him. He was a great drinker but now doesn't touch a drop.'

'That's very laudable of Mrs Wakefield.'

'Yes, very laudable. And now he's devoted to her, but only to her. He's surly to absolutely everyone else.'

'Not to you, surely?'

'Oh yes, even to me. One just has to accept his nature, I'm afraid. My advice is don't try to engage him in conversation when you meet him, if you are so inclined. It will be a waste of breath.'

'Thank you for the warning.'

He nodded happily. 'You must come and have tea at the vicarage once you're settled, Dr Cowdrey. My wife would enjoy meeting you.'

'I'd like that,' I said. It was cheering to have an acquaintance in Flete before I'd even arrived. I wanted to ask Reverend Bute what else he could tell me of Flete House, but we were coming into the station and he rose to take down his bag from the rack above our heads. I offered to help.

'I can manage, thank you,' he assured me, and opened the carriage door. We stepped down onto the platform.

'I have to wait for my luggage,' I said, feeling a little awkward.

'Of course. Well, it's been a pleasure to meet you, Dr Cowdrey,' he said, extending his gloved hand. 'I hope to see you again very soon. Remember, tea at the vicarage.'

'I'll hold you to it,' I promised, taking his hand and wringing it. 'Goodbye.'

He waved at me as he entered the ticket hall and then was gone. My luggage arrived a moment later. I passed through the ticket hall and looked around for a man in a dogcart. Sure enough, there was a very unpleasant-looking individual holding the reins of a pony sitting in a dogcart just outside.

'Mr Danby?' I asked.

'That's me.'

'I'm Dr Cowdrey.'

'Get in.'

He didn't offer to put my bags in the cart, and I realised Reverend Bute hadn't exaggerated Danby's character. I lifted my bags into the back and climbed up beside Danby. Before I was barely secure on the wooden plank, he had flicked the reins and we were off.

It was a dreary journey to Flete House. Danby was not at all inclined to speak with me, and following Reverend Bute's advice, I made no attempt to speak with him. Danby sat on what I suspected was a straw cushion and had a blanket across his lap, but he neither offered to share the blanket with me nor provide me with another. By the time we trotted into the village of Flete, I was chilled to the very bone and had lost all feeling in my backside.

Flete was a small village, little more than a hamlet. To my London eyes, it was very quaint, a relic almost of the previous century. There were a few shops: butcher, baker, general store, post office. The largest of all the commercial buildings was a public house, The Black Dog. Sitting in the middle of the dusty street was a stone hut where troublemakers could be locked up until the authorities carted them off.

The village was busy at this time of day and faces turned upwards to stare at me. These were the villagers who were opposed to Flete House, and I wondered if they guessed who I was and what I had come to do.

Danby took us straight through the village and out onto a narrow road with hedges rising high on either side. I saw a church tower above them. Before I knew it, Danby was turning left into a gated driveway and drawing rein. Flete House was only a stone's throw from the village, and I could understand why the proximity had made the villagers nervous. Danby jumped down from the cart and took a large black key out of his pocket and forced it into the lock. I heard the tumbler drop and he pushed the heavy gates open. It occurred to me as he clambered back up and snapped the reins across the pony's back that it was unusual for gates to be locked during the day. Was this the first evidence that

Flete House was not an ordinary country house but a prison for the insane? This seemed to be confirmed when we were just inside the gates, and Danby dropped down once again and locked the gates behind us.

I looked around while waiting for his return. On my left was the lodge, and I remembered Dr Wakefield saying this was where he and his wife lived. It was a pleasant little house, but there was evidence that it was as yet unfinished. The garden was nothing but turned earth and was crying out for some flowers or shrubs, though of course, little would have been in flower at this time of year. I supposed the Wakefields had been too busy ensuring the main house and the lodge were fit to be lived in to tend to their own garden.

We carried on up the short drive and Flete House was suddenly before me, a house of red brick in an Elizabethan style with white stone ornamentation around the bay window jambs and corners of the walls. It was three storeys high, with small windows at the top where the attics would be.

Danby drew rein once more outside the white stone porch and remained seated. Evidently, I was supposed to descend. I did so, very stiffly, my feet crunching the gravel of the drive, and reached back into the rear of the cart to retrieve my bags. I had barely caught hold of their handles before Danby drove off.

Cursing the man, I turned as I heard footsteps on the flagstones of the porch behind me. Out of the shadows of the porch stepped a woman. She was short, not more than five feet tall, and very compact. Her dark brown hair was pulled into a bun that sat beneath a white cloth cap. Her skin was of a sallow hue and appeared very dry, for there was flaking around her nose and lips. Her eyes were heavily lined, and I put her age to be around forty-five years. She jangled as she moved, and I saw a bunch of keys hanging from a thin belt around her waist. I took her to be the housekeeper.

'Welcome to Flete House, Dr Cowdrey,' she said. 'I am Leonora Wakefield.'

I did my best to hide my surprise. This was not the Mrs Wakefield I had imagined. What a blow to my imagination this creature was. Where was the sophisticated woman I had thought such a man as Miles Wakefield might have as a wife? What had he been thinking in tying himself to such a dowdy woman as this? And what a disappointment she must have been to her parents, who had bestowed upon her the beautiful name of Leonora.

I put down my bags, stepped towards her, and held out my hand. She gave me the topmost part of her fingers only briefly before withdrawing them. 'Mrs Wakefield,' I said. 'I'm very pleased to meet you.'

She looked me up and down in a way that was not altogether flattering. Then she pointed at me to pick up my bags and turned back into the house. She didn't wait for me. I gathered up my bags and hurried after her.

I entered a spacious hall. A round oak table occupied

the centre, atop which sat a large vase stuffed with flowers. Off to the left and right were two sets of double doors that I supposed led to the principal reception rooms. An uncomfortable-looking settle was placed against a panelled screen that divided the hall in two and sat opposite the front door. To the left and right of this screen were archways. I followed Mrs Wakefield through the left-hand archway and emerged into the back part of the hall. Here was a central staircase and doors on either side, indicating more rooms.

'I'll show you to your room, Dr Cowdrey,' Mrs Wakefield said as she mounted the stairs. 'You can settle yourself in, then join Miles and myself at the lodge for lunch.'

'Thank you,' I said, wishing she would slow down a little.

'I hope my husband made it clear to you that we can only offer you a bedroom. I'm afraid we simply don't have the space for the doctors to have a private sitting room as well.'

'Yes, he wrote to me of the room. It will be fine, I'm sure.'

We climbed the stairs to the second floor, and she led me to the very end, turning the corner into a short corridor. There was only one door here, and it was different to the ones we had passed. Those had each had a small blackboard hanging from a hook beside them. Upon each of these blackboards a name had been written in chalk, Mister this, Mister that. I realised those rooms must belong to the inmates.

‘I’m on the same floor as the male patients?’ I asked, and there must have been something in my tone that indicated unease because Mrs Wakefield gave me a queer look, amused, condescending.

‘Yes, Dr Cowdrey,’ she said. ‘It’s the best place for you to be. I would have thought that obvious.’ She turned the handle, and the door creaked open.

I followed her in, and my heart sank a little, I must confess. The room was rather small, perhaps no more than ten feet by eight, about a third of the size of my bedroom in Milton Square. A narrow bed was against one wall, a one-door wardrobe tucked into the corner near the window, and a chest of drawers with a jug and bowl on it against the other wall. Beneath the window was a small writing desk and chair. The rug beside the bed was thin and threadbare. Two paintings adorned the walls, a religious picture above the bed and a water-colour of a country house above the chest of drawers.

‘Will it do?’ Mrs Wakefield in a tone that dared me to answer in the negative.

‘Very well,’ I said as cheerily as I could. I heaved my bags onto the bed and it squealed beneath their weight.

‘When you’ve unpacked,’ she said, ‘kindly return to the entrance hall and wait for me there. I have to see to the midday meal for the patients but I will be along soon enough.’

With that, she left, closing the door behind her. I took a deep breath, relieved to be out of her presence. Moving to the window, I was a little cheered by the view for here I looked out onto the garden. A wide lawn rolled down to a pretty stream with trees hanging thickly on the farther side. To the left was a long brick wall which I supposed housed the kitchen garden, and by pressing my face to the cold glass, I could see a series of outbuildings beyond which were probably the stables and perhaps a dairy.

I turned to my bags and unpacked. In the chest of drawers I placed my undergarments and in the wardrobe I hung up my shirts on the few hangers supplied. By the jug and bowl, I placed my hairbrush and shaving equipment. I threw the now empty bag on top of the wardrobe, eyes widening apprehensively as the rickety construction creaked and wobbled. I wondered what to do with my doctor's bag. I didn't need it for lunch, and I had not yet been shown my office (I presumed I would be given one), so decided to put it in the bottom of the wardrobe until needed. Then I left the room, snatching up the key Mrs Wakefield had left on the chest of drawers, and locked the door after me.

I retraced my steps down the corridor, avoiding the temptation to take a peek into one or two of the rooms, and made my way back down to the entrance hall. There was no one there, and I wandered back and forth around the oak table, leaning in to sniff the flowers before realising they were wax, and studying the two paintings that hung on either side of the front door. They were feeble paintings, a mediocre moorland landscape and a still life of dead pheasants and hares.

I caught the unmistakable sounds of cutlery upon

crockery coming from behind the left-hand door beyond the wooden screen, and I remembered Mrs Wakefield's statement that she was seeing to the patients' midday meal. As I was wondering how long I had to wait for her to finish, I saw a door open and Mrs Wakefield walk briskly out.

'There you are,' she said to me, picking up a cloak that hung over the arm of the settle and whipping it around her shoulders. 'Come along, Dr Cowdrey. I expect you are hungry.'

I was hungry and followed her out of the front door. We went back the way I had come on the dogcart, down to the lodge, she talking about the weather and my train journey, nothing of any consequence. I quickly grew bored at the way she was dominating our conversation and decided to ask a question.

'I assume you have only recently moved into the lodge?'

She gave me a sharp sideways look. 'What makes you say that?'

'The lack of a garden,' I said, pointing at the bare earth beds. 'It's the wrong time of year for planting anything. You're waiting for the spring?'

'We are waiting until we have some time,' she said, and I got the feeling she thought I was criticising her and her husband for not having an immaculate garden. 'We've been very busy getting the house into a fit state. I'm afraid making the lodge look pretty has had to be a minor consideration. I think you'll find the interior to be all above board.'

'I'm sure you've made it very welcoming and homely,' I said as she pushed open the front door.

She didn't answer, but waved me inside.

'Nora, is that you?' a man called, and I recognised the voice of Miles Wakefield.

'Yes, it's me. I've got Dr Cowdrey.'

She made me sound like a parcel she had picked up from the post office.

'Bring him in,' Dr Wakefield called. 'Ah, there you are, Cowdrey,' he said, making his way around the sofa to take my hand. 'Can't say how glad we are you agreed to come. Aren't we, Nora?'

She nodded, tight-lipped, and banged a cushion to plump it up. A fire burned in the hearth, and I could feel the chill leaving my bones.

'Nora showed you your room?' Dr Wakefield asked.

I nodded. 'Yes, very comfortable, thank you.'

'Well, it's not all that comfortable, I daresay, but it's the best we can do, I'm afraid. Now, food. Hungry?'

'Very,' I said.

'Then let's go through to the dining room.'

'It's just cold meats and potatoes today,' Mrs Wakefield said. It almost sounded like an apology, but I felt sure it wasn't. In all honesty, I could have done with something a little more warming, but cold meat and potatoes would have to do.

A small, round mahogany table stood in the centre of the dining room and three places were laid. Dr Wakefield told me where to sit – opposite him, next to Mrs Wakefield – and I did so. A maid brought in a dish of steaming potatoes with butter sliding over them to join the cabbage already sitting by the platter of ham and beef in the centre of the table.

'Don't stand on ceremony, Cowdrey, help yourself,' Dr Wakefield instructed.

I needed no second telling and forked a slice of each meat onto my plate.

'You had better tell Dr Cowdrey his duties, Miles,' Mrs Wakefield said as she spooned a meagre portion of potatoes onto my plate.

'Yes, of course, my dear,' Dr Wakefield said. 'Well, the first rule, Cowdrey, absolutely not to be broken, is to keep your wits about you. The patients here may be mad but they're not stupid. Far from it, in fact. They can be very sly.'

'Indeed. We had some worrying escape attempts when we first set up,' Mrs Wakefield said.

'Attempts? So they weren't successful?' I asked.

She speared me with her eyes. 'Of course not. We're very careful.'

'But that won't stop them trying,' Dr Wakefield said. 'So, just be on your guard.'

'I will,' I promised.

'Second rule. Don't get personal with the patients. You may be tempted to tell them about yourself. Don't. They'll store it all up and then embarrass you by telling their relatives your deepest, darkest secrets when they come to visit.

'Rule number three. Don't imagine you can cure them of their madness.' Dr Wakefield held up his hands.

'I know you probably will want to. I remember our chat at Sadlers, and I'm not going to stop you trying, but ready yourself for disappointment in that regard.'

'I would like to study some of the more interesting cases,' I said. 'I was hoping to get a paper out of one or two of them.'

'Oh, study away. There's no harm to be done there.'

'There may be harm done in giving the patients false hope, my dear,' Mrs Wakefield said. 'Dr Cowdrey must take care to avoid that.'

Dr Wakefield looked chastened. 'Nora is quite right. As always.' He cleared his throat. 'Just understand, Cowdrey, that the patients are here, first and foremost, to be kept under control. That's what their relatives are paying us to do.'

'And if you do intend to write a paper, Dr Cowdrey,' Mrs Wakefield said, cutting her meat with surgical precision, 'you must maintain the confidentiality of our clients.'

'Oh, yes, of course,' I said. 'I would change names and all that.'

'Good. Well then, what else?' Dr Wakefield looked to his wife. 'Have I missed anything, my dear?'

'You must maintain a professional distance at all times, Dr Cowdrey,' she said, looking me straight in the eye. 'This is especially important, as you have the care of our female patients. Propriety is paramount.' She glanced out of the corner of her eye at her husband, perhaps expecting him to interject. But he allowed her to continue, finding the food on his plate of great interest. 'Our clients have placed their female relatives in our care knowing they will be looked after properly. Any behaviour that risks compromising them is unacceptable.'

'I understand completely, Mrs Wakefield,' I said, and felt compelled to add, 'I am a married man.'

She laughed humourlessly. 'Oh, wedlock is seldom a bar to indecent behaviour, Dr Cowdrey. Men will be men, when all is said and done.'

I assured her she had no fear of me. I would never betray Clara with another woman, and the idea that I would forget myself with a lunatic.... Well, that was absurd.

Dr Wakefield coughed. 'Your duties, Cowdrey, will be light, I imagine, after the rigours of St Eustace's. Your first job of the day will be to check with the attendants whether there have been any disturbances during the night, any incidents, illnesses, that sort of thing. The patients are not allowed to remain in their rooms during the day. They have to be in the communal areas where they can be watched. The only exceptions are if they are ill and need to be kept in bed. During the day, you'll talk to each inmate, ask them how they feel. You'll need to probe. These aren't your usual patients who are only too eager to tell you what's wrong. They like to keep things to themselves and may pretend that they are well when they have a chesty cough or a pain in the side, that sort of thing. Some of them can't articulate what they feel properly, so your diagnostic skills will certainly be needed. I suppose you could say you are going to have to be something of a detective. So, Cowdrey, how does all this sound? Not too terrifying, I hope?'

'Not at all, Dr Wakefield,' I assured him. 'It's all perfectly clear. I'm eager to get started.'

'Excellent. Then after lunch, I'll take you back up to the house and show you around.'

He stabbed a potato and popped it in his mouth whole, grinning at me.

9

SETTLING IN

We finished lunch and Dr Wakefield and I returned to Flete House, leaving Mrs Wakefield behind. I was glad to be rid of her, to tell the truth, for there was something about her that was entirely repressive. I fancied Dr Wakefield felt the same, for his mood seemed to lighten as we walked together.

I heard music as we entered the hall. Someone was playing the piano. I expressed surprise to Dr Wakefield.

'You have to get it out of your head that this is a prison, Cowdrey,' he said. 'This is, to all intents and purposes, a hospital, just like St Eustace's. The patients come here because they are sick in the head rather than the body, and they come here to stay because the mind is a lot more difficult to mend than a broken bone. I don't deny that back in the dark days of the last century and yes, until quite recently, asylums were prisons, and the inmates were punished for their lunacy, as if they could help themselves. But restraints and ill treatment, thankfully, are a thing of the past. Nothing like that happens at Flete House.'

'No restraints at all?'

'We only use a straitjacket when the patient is violent and in danger of harming themselves. It calms them down. I think we've had cause to use one only three times since we opened.'

He showed me around the ground floor. The reception room on the right was the men's dayroom, the one on the left, the women's. These, he said, were where most of the patients stayed during the day when the weather was cold, and indeed the rooms were both quite full. Some inmates looked round as we stood in the doorways, but others ignored us. We moved on to the music room and watched as a male inmate played the piano with great skill. Whatever his lunacy, it certainly didn't affect his ability at the piano. The piano was a grand and though it sounded well enough, it was a little battered. When he noticed us watching, the man slid his hands from the keys and kept them still in his lap, his eyes downward.

'Do carry on, Mr Darrow,' Dr Wakefield said, but it was only when we had passed through to the library that the music started up again.

No one was in the library, and I glanced at the books on the shelves. Many of the shelves were empty, and those that had books bore titles of very little interest or recency. I could tell at a glance that they had been bought by the yard and were not likely to inspire many of the inmates to take them out and peruse their pages.

Beyond the library was a small sitting room that Dr Wakefield said was mostly used when relatives visited, but that I was at liberty to use it whenever time and my duties allowed. It looked out onto a paved terrace and then onto the lawn I had seen from my bedroom window.

The last room on that side of the house was Dr Wakefield's office.

Crossing the hall by the stairs, we entered the dining room. It was rather large and housed two long refectory tables with benches on either side, one for the men, the other for the women. At the end of these, on a raised platform and set horizontally to them, was a smaller rectangular table and this, Dr Wakefield informed me, was where I could take my meals if I so wished. The fare for me would usually be the same as the inmates, so it would be easier for the staff if I did so. Dr Wakefield, however, appreciated I might want some time to myself and would want to eat in private. He opened a door in the corner of the dining room that led into a much smaller room.

'This,' Dr Wakefield declared, 'is your office.'

It was only a little larger than my office at St Eustace's, but at least I had this all to myself. It needed tidying. The desk had books piled precariously on its edges, pens were sticking out of the inkwells, and the blotter was covered in ink. Shelving on the far wall was bowing under the weight of books, and these were shoved in with no attempt to make them look attractive or ordered.

'Well, that's everything down here,' Dr Wakefield said. 'The first floor is dedicated to the women's bedrooms. The second floor, where you have your room, to the men, and the attendants have the attic rooms. The bedrooms are locked overnight and there's a night watch station on each landing.'

'Are the bedrooms all the same?'

'No, not quite. The four at the front of the house are the largest and they are the most expensive. The other rooms are smaller and therefore cheaper, but they're still quite comfortable. Yours is actually the smallest room, but then you're not paying for it, are you?' He laughed, and I smiled politely.

He continued. 'When it gets a little warmer, if you're still here, that is, and haven't deserted us, we want the patients out in the garden as much as possible. They need to be gainfully employed, you see. It helps them.'

I asked what he meant by gainfully employed.

'We have a kitchen garden here,' he said, 'and we encourage all of them to have a hand in it. It's very good for them, tilling the soil, watching life grow and all that. It's also helpful when it comes to having vegetables for the kitchens, not having to buy them in. Not all of them are suited to gardening, of course. Some would cause more harm than good, and those we just let wander about the garden, reading, painting, playing a game, this and that. They're supervised at all times, of course, if you're wondering.'

'But they can't leave the grounds?'

'Of course not.'

'I met Reverend Bute on the train here,' I said, and Dr Wakefield's face clouded a little. 'He said there had been some opposition from the village about you setting up a lunatic asylum here.'

Dr Wakefield thrust his hands into his jacket pockets. 'He's right, there was. I suppose they thought the patients would be wandering about the village, causing havoc. People don't like lunatics, you may have noticed, Cowdrey. They're scared of them. Too unpredictable, too dangerous. That's what they were worried about. Needlessly, as you can see. The gates are locked during the day as well as the night, and the stream acts as a barrier in that direction. And to be quite honest, none of the patients we have now feel particularly inclined to leave. They see Flete House as a sanctuary. The outside world scares them. They'd rather be safe in here. And I think the villagers have got used to us now.'

I said I was glad to hear it.

'Well, I'll let you settle in here,' he said, gesturing at the desk. 'Begin work first thing tomorrow, eh?'

———

Left alone, I began to explore my new office.

It soon became apparent that what I had taken to be a mess was actually quite in order; it was just that there was so much of it. Dr Dennison had been a copious note-taker and a methodical one. I found a small cabinet containing buff-coloured folders labelled with his patients' names, all quite thick with papers about their conditions, the interviews he had had with them, and the medicines or treatment he had considered or used.

I moved to the bookshelves and began taking the books out, turning them around, putting them back in neatly. There were the usual books to be found in any doctor's office, but also some that surprised me. An explorer's book on the poisons used by African tribes, a naval surgeon's memoirs, and a book on the benefits of tobacco. I picked another that had its spine turned to the wall, and this one made me smile. It was the same book on phrenology that Dr Wakefield had caught me reading in Sadlers and in which he had taken such amusement. Evidently, Dennison had had the same interest in the theory as I and perhaps, fearing Wakefield's derision, had done what he could to keep his interest hidden. I put the book back on the shelf with the spine facing outward, the title clearly visible to anyone who cared to look.

I returned to the desk and set about tidying, moving piles of papers and placing them on a table by the wall. I sorted through the drawers, finding pen cloths stained with ink that I set aside to be laundered. I checked the ink pot – it needed filling – and used a clean cloth I found at the back of the drawer to clean the pens I found in another.

I carried on in this way, making the office my own until a maid knocked on my door and asked if I would like tea and if she could light the lamps. I hadn't realised how dark it had become and told her she could, asking her name. It was Edith, she told me with a shy smile, and I reasoned she was about the same age as Millie.

I asked her about the servants in the house, how many there were and their names. In addition to Edith, there was the cook, the butler, a scullery maid, and a boot boy. I was surprised by how few there were. My parents had the same number in Milton Square. Surely, an establishment the size of Flete House needed at least double that number? But then, I remembered the attendants who supervised the patients. Dr Wakefield had told me there were six in total, three attendants for the men, three for the women. It was likely that these took on the domestic chores relating to the patients, emptying chamber pots, laundry, etc, and that Edith and her fellows were restricted to serving the Wakefields, and now me, alone. I was about to dismiss Edith when I remembered Jim Danby and asked what role he served within the household. Edith made a face and said he looked after the single horse the Wakefields possessed and did all the outdoor work. It was evident Danby was as unpopular with the servants as he was with Reverend Bute and me.

Edith returned shortly with my tea. A little before six o'clock, I heard noise coming from the dining hall and realised it was time for the evening meal. Deciding I would eat with the patients on this, my first evening, I left my office and stepped into the dining hall.

The patients were being led in by the attendants. They formed two snaking lines, like children being taken out for a walk by their schoolmaster. The men were taken to the refectory table on my left, the women to the one on the right. The patients seemed rather docile and sat down on the benches with apparent meekness. Few seemed to have an interest in their surroundings, preferring instead to keep their eyes down.

I took my seat at the smaller table at the end of the room. As I did so, I spied Mrs Wakefield wandering around the hall, watching the attendants and patients with an eagle eye. I wondered if she was intending to join me at my table, half hoping she would not. She came up to the table but made no attempt to sit down.

'You have settled into your office, Dr Cowdrey?' she asked.

'Yes, thank you, Mrs Wakefield,' I nodded, and out of politeness, indicated the spot beside me.

'Thank you, but I always dine with my husband,' she said, managing to sound and look as if I had insulted her by suggesting she sit with me. 'When the meal is over, I will lead the patients in prayer and then they will be taken to their rooms.'

She continued to walk around the dining room as the inmates ate. My supper was the same as theirs: bread and cheese, and a half pint of beer for the men, the women having water. One very thin female patient had an attendant encouraging her to eat, telling her to open her lips, which she did, but only reluctantly. I supposed she had some kind of eating malady, and left to her own devices, might very well starve herself to death. One of the men was similarly accompanied, but it seemed his problem was not a lack of appetite but an inability to control the shaking in his hands. The attendant fed him to ensure his food ended up in his mouth rather than down the front of his shirt.

It was common in hospitals for the main meal to be given to patients at midday, and for them to have only a light supper before bed, and it was no different here. I was used to more hearty fare of an evening and I ate my meagre supper contemplating what delicious dinner Clara and my parents would be sitting down to. They would be having meat and gravy, followed by sweet puddings and fruit. If bread and cheese suppers were the norm at Flete House, I would have to modify my idea of what made a decent dinner and relish the meals I would have when I returned to London.

I occupied myself during supper by observing the patients, making the women my main concern, as they would be the ones in my charge. There were more women inmates than men, ten women to seven men. I supposed that was to be expected, women being more inclined to hysteria. I was relieved to see that none appeared to be manic or violent, and that were it not for the attendants and the absence of conversation, these women could easily be considered not to be lunatic at all, especially as though the attendants wore a uniform made out of a dull grey cloth, the inmates were dressed in what appeared to be their own clothes. These, though not extravagant in any sense, would not have been out of place in any gentleman's home.

When the food had been eaten and the plates and

cups taken away, the inmates sat quite still and I realised they were waiting for Mrs Wakefield to begin her reading from the Bible. I wished I had realised this earlier, as I would have made a discreet exit, but once she had begun reading, I felt sure it would be looked on unfavourably if I left.

I endured a full half hour of Mrs Wakefield's dry, monotonous voice reading a passage from Corinthians, followed by near fifteen minutes of prayers, with the patients mumbling the required responses. Then Mrs Wakefield bid the inmates good night, and the attendants led them out of the dining hall. I heard them tramping up the stairs to their bedrooms.

I retired to my office and wrote a letter to Clara, informing her that I had arrived at Flete House and of my first impressions of the house and its occupants. I told her of my meeting Reverend Bute on the train and his invitation to tea (Clara would like to know that I had made a friend, and so soon), his warning about the surly Danby and how that was soon borne out. I told her of Mrs Wakefield and how disappointed I was in her appearance, something, I assured Clara, would never be said of my wife. I explained that I had not yet had a chance to talk at any length with Dr Wakefield, but that I hoped such an opportunity would arise once I had settled in.

When I had finished my letter, I went to the library and selected a book from the shelves, an old novel that appeared on first glance interesting but which proved to be something of a bore. I persevered for an hour or so, but the busyness of the day began to catch up with me and I found myself yawning over the pages.

Resolving to retire, I took my letter and popped it in the postbag on the entrance hall table, and climbed the stairs to the second floor, nodding at the night watch attendant as he sat at his desk on the landing.

My small bedroom was chilly as I undressed for bed and I did not linger over my prayers but hurried beneath the cold blankets. I felt something of a child again, sleeping in such a narrow bed and without my dear Clara by my side.

What I found particularly strange, and, to tell the truth, not a little alarming, was my sleeping in a house full of lunatics. With a sudden remembrance, I hurried out of bed and turned the key in my bedroom door's lock. I knew all the inmates were locked in their rooms overnight, but as I saw it, it did not hurt to be extra careful.

10

THE FIRST WEEK

I rather overslept that first morning. I had a restless night, waking several times, perhaps because of the strange bed or perhaps the night noises made by the nocturnal wildlife of the country, I cannot be sure.

I washed and dressed hurriedly, noting as I strode down the corridors that all the inmates' doors were wide open, the rooms vacant. No one was about as I clattered down the stairs, but I heard the slight hubbub from the dining room and knew everyone must be at breakfast.

Mrs Wakefield raised a disapproving eyebrow as I entered. 'Breakfast is served at eight o'clock, Dr Cowdrey.'

'I'm so sorry, Mrs Wakefield,' I blustered. 'I woke up late. New surroundings, strange bed, you understand.'

'I hope you get used to your surroundings quickly. The patients must not be neglected.'

'They won't be,' I assured her, and made my way to

the top table. The inmates' breakfast consisted of cocoa and bread. I expected to be given the same, but happily, a bowl of porridge awaited me.

I hurried through my breakfast and had only just finished when the attendants began leading the patients out of the dining hall. Two of the attendants, one male, one female, remained behind counting the cutlery, ensuring that none had been pocketed by the patients. As I made to follow, Mrs Wakefield approached me.

'I trust you are ready to begin your duties, Dr Cowdrey,' she said.

'Ready and eager,' I replied with a smile which entirely failed to thaw her.

'I would not recommend you be too eager. The patients will not appreciate it and it may lead you into error. Tread carefully. It is much the better way.'

Nothing I said seemed to meet with her favour. She walked away without another word. I collected my notebook from my office and made my way to the women's dayroom, where I expected most of my charges to be.

There was a definite stiffening of bodies as I entered the room. It was only natural, for I was a stranger in this place and the inmates were wary. Some turned their backs on me, glancing over their shoulders, while others openly stared. To the nearest of these braver souls, I moved first.

I need not weary the reader with details of those first interviews. They were a struggle, certainly in comparison to similar interviews I had had with patients at St Eustace's. As Dr Wakefield had predicted, most of them were disinclined to talk with me, and nothing they did say was of any great interest. I did, however, glean that none had suffered injury or complaint during the night and so my doctoring skills were not required. I thought it best therefore if I removed to my office and familiarised myself with my patients' case histories.

Pulling out the buff-coloured folders from the cabinet, I put them in a pile on the right-hand side of my desk and began working through them. I discovered a wide range of mental maladies.

Miss Golderson, in her early thirties, claimed to hear voices that no one else could hear and would do their bidding no matter how reckless their commands might seem. Miss Rushbridger was nineteen and had been mute for seven years, ever since an accident that had killed her younger brother, and would often refuse to eat or drink. I wondered if she was the lady being helped to eat at dinner the previous night. She had nearly died at home and had been committed to the asylum more for the constant care she would receive rather than for any demonstrable lunacy. Fifty-two-year-old Mrs Riggs had a history of inflicting wounds upon herself. Mrs Millsop, a woman in her sixties, had stolen babies, and several of the mothers had been persuaded from prosecuting her on the condition she would be committed to the asylum. Mrs Grigson, thirty-three, cherished the belief that she would likely be the victim of an assassination and would often peer around doors and corners to be assured no one was waiting with a knife or axe to plunge into her body. Mrs Fawcett, thirty-six, had made several attempts to kill herself and was of a perpetually melancholy disposition. Miss Trew, a woman in her late forties, had the habit of suddenly screaming and shouting at anyone and anything, which made for a frankly alarming proposition. Mrs Blake, a widow in her mid fifties, suffered extreme fright of the outdoors and would not venture out of Flete House. Miss Bonamy, a woman of twenty-eight, though never having been married, had been found to be unchaste, throwing herself at any man, of any station, who she happened to find attractive. So great had been her adventures in this regard that her family had not known what to do with her other than incarcerate her in Flete House, where she could be controlled. The last file belonged to a nineteen-year-old lady by name of Miss Hebron. Her lunacy was described simply as presenting a danger to others.

During the afternoon, I sat in a corner of the dayroom and simply watched the women, allowing them to become accustomed to my presence and putting faces to the files I had read. With a little perseverance, and some questions put to one of the attendants, I was able to identify all the women, with the exception of Miss Hebron. Upon querying this with the attendant, I was told Miss Hebron had left the asylum for an as yet unspecified period.

Over the course of my first week at Flete House, I insinuated myself into my patients' consciousness until they no longer viewed me with alarm but mostly with tolerance. I soon came to understand the routine of Flete

House, and it proved to be far less exhausting than the routine I had been used to at St Eustace's.

When Saturday came around, I received an invitation from Mrs Wakefield to dine with her and her husband at the lodge that evening.

I was surprised by how little of Dr Wakefield I saw during my first week. I caught sight of him dashing through the rooms and heard his voice through his office door, but not once had he stopped to talk with me. Of course, he had the male patients to deal with as I had the female, but he never seemed to have a moment to himself, and I supposed it must not only be a great emotional burden running a private lunatic asylum, but a physically draining one too.

I was glad to receive the invitation to dine at the lodge, for I had been feeling a little starved of intelligent conversation. I saw that all the patients were put to bed for the night before braving the cold night air and walking the short distance to the lodge. I knocked on the door and the Wakefield's maid, Judith, opened it and took me through to the sitting room.

Dr Wakefield was on the sofa, legs stretched out in front of him, his head resting on the back. His eyes were closed. He didn't seem to have heard me.

'Dr Wakefield?' I said hesitantly.

He jumped, confirming my suspicion that he hadn't been aware of my arrival. 'Cowdrey. Didn't see you there. Come in.' He waved me over to the opposite sofa.

He looked tired and I must have conveyed this in my expression because he gave me a thin smile and said, 'Long week.'

'Has it been?' I asked a little guiltily, knowing it had been far more restful for me than any week I had spent at St Eustace's.

He rolled his head back and stared at the ceiling. 'I never could have imagined there would be so much paperwork when I opened this place. Do yourself a favour, Cowdrey, and never open a private asylum.'

I laughed, not entirely sure he was joking. 'Why did you?' I asked, wondering why he had not set up a small private practice instead. He seemed to me the type of doctor who would thrive in such a practice.

'I'd had enough of working for others,' he said. 'It made me miserable. And it takes an age to build up a patient list as a private doctor. I didn't want to wait. Nora and I wanted independence before we were too old to enjoy it.'

'And we achieved it,' Mrs Wakefield said, entering the room. She stared at her husband. 'We have exactly what we wanted, don't we, Miles?'

'Of course we do, my dear,' he said, holding out his hand to her. 'I was just explaining to Cowdrey here that it takes a great deal of hard work.'

'As it should,' she said, ignoring his hand. 'God rewards those who work hard.'

Dr Wakefield let his hand drop back onto his leg,

and I felt he was avoiding my eyes. Mrs Wakefield had embarrassed him and by association, me, and I wondered if I would have done better to decline the dinner invitation, although I suspected a refusal would have been taken as an insult.

'Is dinner ready?' Dr Wakefield asked.

'Yes,' Mrs Wakefield nodded, 'come through.'

We both followed obediently to the dining room and took the same places we had occupied on my arrival. The dinner was served and I kept quiet, not knowing what to say. The business of serving occupied us all for a few minutes, but then the silence became oppressive, and I thought I simply had to speak. I was trying to think of something to say when Mrs Wakefield spoke.

'How have you found your first week at Flete House, Dr Cowdrey?'

She had caught me with a mouthful of food, and I had to force it down before I could answer. 'Very interesting,' I said, wiping my mouth with my napkin. 'And very different from what I've been used to. You were right about the patients' unwillingness to talk to me, Dr Wakefield.'

He nodded. 'It will take a while for them to get used to you. But you've kept an eye on them?'

I assured him I had. 'And I've read all the female patients' case notes. I think it quite incredible the different ways madness has manifested in these women. I wouldn't have thought such diversity could be found in so small a group of women. I wonder how many more manifestations will appear when you have a full house of lunatics.'

'We are only a little under-capacity,' he said stiffly. 'It takes time for word to get around, you know.'

I hadn't meant it as a criticism, and I was growing a little tired of my words being continually taken the wrong way. Both the Wakefields seemed so damnably touchy.

'Of course,' I said, trying to sound understanding. 'You have only been going, what, how long?'

'Not quite two years,' Mrs Wakefield supplied.

'Well,' I said, 'that's not long at all.'

'No,' she agreed with me, probably the first time she had done so. 'And it was very brave of my husband to leave his London work to open this asylum.'

'Nora,' Dr Wakefield murmured repressively, but she ignored him.

'And it has taken much hard work, many sacrifices and a great deal of dedication to get to where we are now.' She fixed me with a hard stare.

I wanted Dr Wakefield to distract her, to rescue me, but he began cutting his meat noisily, the knife scraping on the plate. I turned to him, dragging my eyes away from his wife. 'One of my patients is missing,' I said. 'The woman in room three?'

Dr Wakefield swallowed down his mouthful of food and reached for his wine. 'She's away at the moment.'

'Yes, I know. I assumed away and not released, else her name wouldn't still be on the blackboard outside her door. I wondered where she is, that's all.'

'She's in a sanatorium on the coast. She had a slight chill on her chest and it was thought the sea air would be beneficial.'

'Thought by whom?'

'By her relatives, Dr Cowdrey,' Mrs Wakefield said sharply. 'Who else?'

'You allowed her to be removed?' I was surprised. 'Was it safe to do so?'

'We advised against removing her, but when the client insists, there's really nothing to be done but comply,' Dr Wakefield snapped. He had finished eating and almost threw his knife and fork onto his plate. They clattered unpleasantly.

Understanding this removal of Miss Hebron from Flete House was a sensitive subject, I asked nervously, 'When will she be back?'

'Soon enough,' Dr Wakefield said, picking up his wine glass and taking a large mouthful. 'And then, Cowdrey, she's all yours.'

11

SUNDAY WITH THE BUTES

Mrs Wakefield's last words to me as I left the lodge that night were a reminder to be at church the next morning. She made a point of telling me not to be late.

Not wishing to incur her wrath, I made sure I was ready and waiting in plenty of time in the entrance hall on the morrow. I watched as most of the inmates were herded together and flanked by the attendants before setting out to walk to the church in the nearby village. Two male inmates had been left behind as being too unmanageable for an excursion outside the asylum, as had one of the women.

Knowing the villagers disliked the asylum, I was curious as to how our arrival would be received. The Flete House inmates were the first to arrive at the church, and the patients were quickly prodded into the pews on the right-hand side nearest the door, filling them up from the rear forward. The Wakefields didn't sit with their patients but settled into the front pew on the right side, and after a moment's hesitation, I decided I should too, taking a seat beside Dr Wakefield. The coldness of the wooden bench soon began to seep through my clothing, and I started to fidget just as the villagers were filing in.

I turned to watch and saw various expressions of disgust and distrust upon the villagers' faces as they gave the inmates a wide berth and made their way to the pews opposite. There really was no excuse for their doing so; all the patients were behaving themselves. So much for Christian charity, I thought.

Reverend Bute stepped out of the vestry a minute later, his cheeks rosy, his white hair flopping over his forehead, exactly as he had appeared on the train. He swept his eyes over the congregation, his smile deepening as he caught sight of me. I was glad of the recognition.

I have never been fond of sitting for hours in a cold church at the best of times, and was rather concerned that a lengthy service would make the inmates restless and justify the villagers' dislike, so I was glad Reverend Bute's sermon was short. When it came to the singing of hymns, these were sung with gusto by the congregation and with fervour by Mrs Wakefield, but I noticed that few of the inmates joined in.

When the service was over, the attendants hurried to get the inmates out of the church while the villagers hung back, watching and waiting their turn to exit. The Wakefields followed the inmates. I had ascertained from Dr Wakefield the previous evening that the day was my own. I was glad of the opportunity to be free of Flete House for a little while and approached Reverend Bute, standing in the church doorway, bidding his congregation goodbye one by one.

He grabbed my hand with both of his. 'Dr Cowdrey, how good to see you again.'

'And you,' I said. 'I enjoyed your sermon.'

'You mean you appreciated its brevity,' he said with a smile. 'Now, now, don't go blushing. My wife would agree with you. She can't stand long sermons either.'

'Some churchmen can say more in ten minutes than others can in two hours,' I said.

He chuckled. 'What a kind young man you are. Now, I seem to remember inviting you to tea? Is that right?'

'You did,' I said, glad he had remembered.

'Then tea you shall have. In fact, let us make it luncheon and tea. My wife has been asking after you and will want to interrogate you for hours.'

I thanked him with a laugh.

'Excellent,' he declared. 'Then you wait here while I disrobe and we'll walk round to the vicarage together.'

The vicarage was situated behind the church, and it took a walk of only a minute to reach the front door. It was a lovely little place, and I felt at home as soon as I walked into the hall. The decoration here was very different to our houses in London, and different again to the Wakefields' lodge. The Wakefields favoured dark colours for the walls and furnishings, as indeed did we Cowdreys, but the Butes preferred softer hues, and oh, what a difference it made. The small sitting room felt light and airy, and the sofa Reverend Bute pointed me to was soft and deep. I made a mental note to tell Clara about the vicarage in my next letter. She always liked to know how other people decorated their homes.

'Mrs Bute won't mind me turning up for luncheon unannounced, will she?' I asked.

Reverend Bute lit the pipe he had taken from a rack on the mantel and threw the spill into the fire. 'Good Lord, no. There's nothing Emma likes more than company. She's used to me bringing people back.'

'You're a picker up of waifs and strays, are you?'

He grinned. 'If that's how you like to view yourself, yes. Ah, here she is.'

A plump woman with a large floppy cap and white flour dappling her rounded pink cheeks came into the sitting room, wiping her hands on a cloth. She looked straight at me with enquiring but kindly eyes.

'Who's this, then?' she asked her husband. Before he could reply, she had looked me up and down and found her own answer. 'No, don't tell me, I can guess who you are. You're the new young doctor from Flete House Timothy told me about.'

'Got it in one,' Reverend Bute said as I bowed to his wife. 'I brought him back to partake of both luncheon and tea, my dear, but young Dr Cowdrey here is worried he's imposing. What do you say to that?'

'I say stuff and nonsense,' she said, giving me a broad smile. 'Don't you go thinking such a thing, young man.'

'I won't,' I promised her, liking her immensely already.

Mrs Bute told me to sit back down, and left her husband and me to chat while she finished up in the kitchen.

'Never happier than when she's helping in the kitchen,' Reverend Bute said, puffing on his pipe. 'And I know it's not the done thing, but how say we tell Emma she can call you Felix when she comes in?'

'Of course,' I said, 'and you must, too, sir.'

'Thank you, dear boy. Can I prevail on you to call me Timothy?'

I admitted it would feel odd to call a man of his years and position so, but promised I would try. That satisfied him and he sank back into the soft cushions of his armchair.

'So, Felix, tell me. How are you getting along at Flete House?'

'It's quite a change from what I've been used to,' I said. 'The pace is much slower, for one thing.'

'Is that welcome or not?'

'Welcome, I should say. I'm hoping it will give me a chance to study the patients. I would like to get a paper out of my time at Flete House, if I can.'

'Very good,' he said approvingly, sounding rather like my old schoolmaster reading my end of term report. 'And how are you getting along with the Wakefields?'

I looked down and studied my hands.

'There's hesitation in your manner, Felix,' he said, pointing his pipe at me. 'Is all not well?'

'I can complain about nothing,' I said. 'But I must admit, I had hoped Dr Wakefield would prove to be more of a companion for me. I had thought that when the working day was over, we would settle down for some intelligent conversations.'

'And you have been disappointed?'

'He is so very busy during the day, he has no time for me, and when the day is done, he retires at once to the lodge. Mrs Wakefield expects him home, of course, but…' I shook my head. 'I expect I'm just being selfish.'

'No, no, dear boy, not at all,' Reverend Bute said. 'You've left your family and your home, and you quite naturally feel a little lonely. But you need never feel so, Felix. You can come here for some mildly intelligent conversations whenever you wish.'

'You're very kind,' I said with heartfelt gratitude. 'I will certainly take you up on that.'

'See you do. A-ha.' He put his hand to cup his ear, then pointed at the door. 'Emma declares luncheon is ready. Come along, Felix. You're in for a treat, I promise.'

We went through to the dining room, and the smell of roast beef filled my nostrils, making my stomach rumble in delighted anticipation.

'Help yourself, Dr Cowdrey,' Mrs Bute instructed as I took a seat. 'Don't stand on ceremony.'

'Thank you, Mrs Bute,' I said. I caught Reverend Bute's eye. 'And please, call me Felix.'

She smiled broadly and sat as Reverend Bute carved the beef. 'So, what have you two been talking about?'

'Felix's first week at the asylum,' Reverend Bute said, forking two large slices of the beef onto my plate. 'He's a little disappointed, my dear.' He explained to his wife what I had told him.

'Well, I can't say I'm surprised,' Mrs Bute said when he finished. 'It's not exactly a cheery place, is it? And the Wakefields.' She made a face.

'What do you mean, Mrs Bute?' I asked, intrigued.

'Now, Emma,' Reverend Bute said warningly.

She gave him an exasperated look. 'Don't you 'now, Emma' me, Timothy. I shall say what I like about them. Felix is a doctor. He's trained to be discreet.'

I assured her she could tell me anything in complete confidence. 'You don't like the Wakefields?'

'Dr Wakefield can be very agreeable,' she said. 'He's charming and handsome, and that always helps. There are plenty of women in this village who gave him the eye when they first arrived, I can tell you.'

'Yes,' Reverend Bute said with a smile, 'a great many old maids had a spring in their step when they thought he was going to doctor them.'

'And he enjoyed the attention,' Mrs Bute said, 'until Mrs Wakefield got wind of it. Then Dr Wakefield rather had to behave himself and we didn't see him so often. Tell me, Felix, what do you think of her?'

I considered before answering as I didn't want to

sound ungentlemanly. But the Butes invited frankness, and I felt my reply would be safe with them. 'I can't say I care for her a great deal, Mrs Bute. I've found her a little unapproachable. Very defensive. Whatever I say to her, she takes as an insult.'

Mrs Bute and her husband shared a knowing glance.

'It's not just you she's like that with, if that's what you're thinking,' Reverend Bute said. 'Cedric said much the same.'

'Cedric?' I frowned, unfamiliar with the name. Then it came to me. 'Oh, you must mean Dr Dennison.'

'Yes, dear Cedric never got along with Mrs Wakefield,' Mrs Bute said wistfully. 'Do you know him, Felix?'

I shook my head. 'No, I've never met him. But you and your husband were friends?'

'Oh yes, he used to come to tea practically every Sunday. It's a shame you don't know him. I was hoping you could tell me how he is.'

'You've lost touch with him?'

'Completely,' Reverend Bute said. 'And to be honest, we're a little upset about it. Emma was very fond of him.'

'Perhaps his illness has prevented him from writing to you,' I suggested, hoping this idea might cheer Mrs Bute a little.

She looked up at me, frowning. 'Illness? Cedric's ill?'

I looked from her to her husband. 'So Dr Wakefield

told me. That was why he left Flete House. A sudden illness. You didn't know?'

'No, we had no idea. Oh, Timothy,' Mrs Bute said in a pained voice, and I realised I had only managed to increase her concern.

'Poor Cedric,' Reverend Bute mused. 'Well, yes, that would explain his silence.' He banged his hand on the table, making the cutlery jangle. 'Why on earth could the Wakefields not tell us he was ill? Why keep that from us?'

'You did enquire then of the Wakefields about Dr Dennison?'

'Of course we did,' Mrs Bute said, 'when we realised he had gone from Flete House. Cedric left on the Friday, you see, and told us he would be away for the next two days or so, but when we hadn't heard from him for over a week, I grew concerned. After church on the Sunday, I stopped Mrs Wakefield and asked her what had happened to Cedric. Oh, the look she gave me, Felix. You would have thought I'd asked the most impertinent question. Asked what business it was of mine. It was all I could to stop myself from striking her.'

'Emma has quite a temper,' Reverend Bute said in a theatrical aside.

'I insisted on knowing. So, very reluctantly, she told me that Cedric had left their employ.'

'Nothing more than that?'

'Not a word more.'

'Perhaps she was being discreet,' I suggested, not

really believing that. 'If Dr Dennison's illness was something not fit for discussion.'

'He would have told you, wouldn't he, Timothy?' Mrs Bute asked.

'I feel sure he would,' her husband agreed, 'whatever it was that ailed him. He knew I would make no judgement on him or that he need be embarrassed.'

'His illness could not have been apparent, I suppose?' I asked.

'He certainly didn't look unwell,' Reverend Bute said. 'In fact, I would have said he was hale and hearty. But then, I suppose illness can come on quite suddenly or lie hidden within the body. Such a pity we never found out where he lives, though. I would like to write to him.'

Mrs Bute nodded and ordered me to help myself to more beef, for I had quickly finished the slices I had been given. The luncheon was delicious – it reminded me of home – and the tea more than filling. The afternoon passed very pleasantly indeed, so pleasantly I was reluctant to return to Flete House.

As I walked back to the asylum a little before six, I couldn't help wondering at Dr Dennison's sudden disappearance and why Mrs Wakefield had been so unwilling to discuss it.

12

A PATIENT TO STUDY

I awoke the next morning with a new conviction: not to waste time. I reasoned my appointment at Flete House might not be of long duration, either because I would decide it wasn't for me and leave, or because Dr Wakefield would find a more qualified doctor to do my job. I was determined to make as much of the experience as I could, knowing it could only stand me in good stead for my future career. And so, as I sat in the dining hall at Flete House that morning, I studied the female inmates, trying to decide which one I would make a particular study.

They were all so interesting in their different ways, but I felt I had to base my decision on which female was most likely to be amenable to my study. All of them had demonstrated an initial wariness towards me, and while that wariness had diminished a little over the course of the last week as they became used to my presence, some were still intent on ignoring or avoiding me. Only Miss

Bonamy had shown any actual interest in me, and knowing her history, I was determined not to make her the subject of my study. After some deliberation, I settled upon Mrs Blake, who, because of her peculiar affliction, had not been at church the previous day. After breakfast, I took her file from the cabinet and refreshed my memory of its contents.

She had been admitted to Flete House almost a year earlier when she had been discovered in an emaciated and perilous condition by her brother, Mr Worrell. Mrs Blake had been widowed and taken in by her brother, but he had been absent for prolonged periods due to his business, and her mental condition had deteriorated in his absence to the point where her moods became extreme and the servants unable to manage her. The housekeeper had written to her master to inform him that his sister was acting oddly and was melancholic, and Mr Worrell had told her to do what she must to keep order within the house, adding that he would return home as soon as his business allowed.

When Mr Worrell returned home several months later, he discovered his sister locked up in her bedroom and chained to the bed. Horrified, he had released her and demanded to know what was going on from the housekeeper. The housekeeper told him that Mrs Blake had become difficult, breaking ornaments and hitting servants, and had to be restrained for her and the household's safety, reminding him that he had given her permission to do what was necessary to maintain order. Mr Worrell was not appeased. His sister had been sorely neglected, and that could not be excused. The housekeeper had left Mrs Blake imprisoned in her bedroom with the shutters permanently closed so no sunlight entered, and had left her to lie in soiled sheets with only meagre rations of food. Mr Worrell had promptly dismissed the hard-hearted housekeeper, refusing to give her a character.

Try as he might, Mr Worrell had not been able to make his sister better. He felt extraordinary guilt over having left her to her fate, but as Dr Dennison noted, he really had not had any choice. His business took him away far too frequently to assuage his fear of something similar happening again should he leave his sister in the care of another, and indeed, his remaining servants voiced their disinclination to care for a lunatic. Mrs Blake's increasing agitation and his inability to understand her mental condition had led Mr Worrell to seek a sanctuary for her, somewhere she would be looked after properly. And so, Mrs Blake had come to Flete House.

She had been delivered to Flete House in a closed carriage and under the effects of morphia so that she didn't become distressed during the journey. When she awoke, she had found herself in a strange room, and her mental malady had exhibited itself most profoundly. Dr Dennison had written of screaming and violent outbursts, so much so that Mrs Blake had had to be put under restraint until her mind calmed. That had taken several days, but she had calmed to the extent that the restraints could be removed.

Under Dr Dennison's care, Mrs Blake's physical

health had been somewhat restored. Her bed sores had been treated, and she had regained some weight so that she was no longer emaciated. But though her outbursts had diminished and though she was free to venture into the grounds of Flete House, she absolutely shrank from doing so, shaking uncontrollably and her respiration increasing dangerously. Dr Dennison concluded she had a fear of unenclosed spaces, that she felt safe only when surrounded by four walls. He had made several attempts to encourage her to take a few steps outside Flete House, but to no avail. He seemed to have tired of Mrs Blake quite quickly, for here his notes stopped.

I felt that I already had an understanding of her lunacy. Being locked up and abandoned to her fate had undoubtedly and quite naturally contributed to her fear of the outside world. I felt that if I could cure her of that fear, or at least lessen it, that would be a significant achievement.

And so I sought Mrs Blake out. I discovered her in the library, in the corner of the room, where bookshelves bound her in on either side. I nodded to the attendant who had taken up her post by the French doors, then moved towards the table at which Mrs Blake sat. She had taken a book from one of the shelves and I saw as I drew near that it was an illustrated volume of birds.

'Mrs Blake?' I said quietly, not wanting to alarm her.

She didn't look up. She froze, her head bent over the book.

'Would it be all right for me to sit down and talk with you, Mrs Blake?'

'I'm reading, Dr Cowdrey,' she said after a long moment.

Undeterred, I pulled out the chair opposite and sat down. She shrank back in her chair, her hands disappearing beneath the table into her lap. 'Perhaps you could stop reading for a little while so we can talk?' I suggested.

She still hadn't looked at me. 'What do you want to talk about?'

'Whatever you would like to talk about. You choose a subject.'

'I don't want to talk about anything. Do I have to talk to you?'

'No,' I said, foolishly reaching out across the table to her. She grabbed the book and shrank even further from me. I moved my chair back, increasing the distance between us. 'Not if you don't want to. But would you not like to speak to me? Just for a change?'

She shook her head. 'I want to read my book.'

I wasn't going to push her any more. 'Then please, do read.' I sat there while she tentatively replaced the book on the table, watching me warily from beneath her lashes. Her fingers began to trace the outline of the bird in the illustration. 'Do you like birds, Mrs Blake?' I asked, thinking to encourage her into talking with a subject she was obviously interested in.

She nodded.

'Which bird is that?' I pointed at the illustration. 'Is

it a goldfinch? It's very pretty. Have you ever seen one?'

'We had one in our garden.'

I had got her talking. 'Did you feed it to get it to stay?'

She nodded. 'It would stay on the bird table for quite a while. It gave me an opportunity to draw it.'

I leaned forward. She didn't shrink from me this time. 'Do you like to draw, Mrs Blake?'

'I was very fond of drawing.'

'If I were to get you some paper and paints, would you like to do some drawing?'

There was the faintest glimmer of interest, the sutblest of changes, in her expression. 'What would I draw?'

'You could copy from that book,' I suggested, then took a deep breath. 'Or you could draw from life?'

She looked around the room. 'There aren't any birds in here.'

'No, not in here. But out there,' I pointed towards the French doors, 'I'm sure you would see some beautiful birds—'

'No,' she said, her voice breaking. I saw her throat tighten. 'Not out there.'

I saw at once that I had been too hasty. 'Very well,' I said, patting the air to calm her. 'Copying from books. Would you like that?'

She stared down at the book. 'I think I would.'

'Then I shall fetch you paints and paper,' I said decisively, glad that I had had the foresight to investigate the cupboards beneath the bookshelves and discovered painting materials there. I went to them now and retrieved them. 'Here you are,' I said, pushing them across the table to Mrs Blake. 'I would very much like to see your representation of a goldfinch, Mrs Blake. Will you paint one for me?'

She opened the paintbox and examined the dried lozenges of watercolour paints. The paintbox had evidently not been used for some time and I was a little worried the stiff paintbrush would be unserviceable. But she looked up at me, the first time she had done so.

'Yes, if you wish it, Dr Cowdrey. I will paint for you.'

'Excellent, Mrs Blake,' I said. 'I shall look forward to seeing it.'

I rose, pushing my chair back beneath the table. I left the library feeling exceedingly pleased with the progress I had made.

I spent the rest of the day occupied with my other female patients, but when it came to time for tea, a ritual only the women took, it being an occupation believed to be necessary for their peace of mind, I looked around for Mrs Blake, curious as to how she had employed her day. Had she pushed aside the paintbox as soon as I left the library or had she dabbled with the paints, even a little? I was excited and pleased, therefore, when she came into the dayroom, a sheet of watercolour paper held in both her hands. She saw me watching her, and her eyes dropped away shyly as I approached.

'Mrs Blake,' I said. 'Do you have something to show me?'

She scanned the room behind me, as if worried we were being watched. I moved to block the other inmates from her view so that she felt as if only she and I were present. She held out the paper to me, blank side up.

I took the paper and turned it over. The most beautiful painting of a goldfinch I had ever seen confronted me and I was struck by how accomplished an artist Mrs Blake evidently was. That such talent should lie within a damaged mind was saddening.

'This is astonishing, Mrs Blake,' I said with genuine admiration, which I believe she could distinguish in my voice. A small smile broke her grave expression. That, I remember feeling, was a victory in itself. 'This is immeasurably better than the illustration in the book. This bird has such life.'

'That's very kind of you to say so, Dr Cowdrey,' she said.

An attendant came up to us and told Mrs Blake to come and have her tea. Mrs Blake followed the attendant to a table where tea things were set out.

I retired to my office and placed Mrs Blake's painting on top of the cabinet where I could see it from my desk. I took out a clean sheet of paper from my drawer and began to write up my notes from the day regarding Mrs Blake. The first sentence I wrote was: Progress has been made.

I continued to make progress with Mrs Blake.

My study of her became all-consuming, though I was careful not to neglect my other patients. That first painting of the goldfinch seemed to have unlocked a passion inside her, for she soon used up the watercolour paper I had provided, so that I had to apply to Mrs Wakefield for more. Mrs Blake painted swallows and sparrows, kingfishers and woodpeckers, thrushes, wrens and any other pictures of birds she could find in the illustrated book she had been reading. All her paintings were quite wonderful, and I soon ran out of room for their display in my office, so I began placing them on the empty sections of bookshelves in the library. I caught Mrs Blake looking at them once with pride shining out of her face and I was pleased it had been my intervention that had been the initial cause of that pride.

My next step was to work at reducing her fear of the outside world. I felt sure this could be achieved; she just needed my encouragement and especially my assurance that nothing terrible would happen to her. I knew I had to tread carefully and not try rushing her into leaving the house, as I had during our first conversation. I had seen the terror on her face and was determined not to provoke it again.

I began by encouraging her to sit nearer to the French doors in the library, explaining the light was better for her painting. She saw no deception or ulterior motive in my words and took a seat at a table I had dragged to the doors the previous evening when all the patients had been locked in their rooms for the night. I allowed her a few days to grow used to this new position, observing her bending over a book of fish we had discovered together. Over the next few days, she presented me with paintings of salmon, mackerel and trout, all of which took their place on the shelves.

I then suggested that instead of copying from books she paint what she could see out of the doors. Alarm flashed across her face, and I assured her the doors would not be opened. After a moment's consideration, she agreed, and she began to paint the view of the garden with its sweeping lawn. Mrs Blake apologised for the lack of objects in the painting she produced, but I was rather glad that, as a composition, there was nothing of much interest in it. If Mrs Blake recognised the view was not that inspiring, she might be prevailed upon to seek a more interesting landscape beyond the confines of the house.

When I felt emboldened to believe Mrs Blake could cope with a suggestion, only a suggestion, that she might want to leave the house in pursuit of inspiration, I made it. She did not immediately dismiss it as she had that first day. Instead, she stared through the doors and studied the lawn, her eyes rising towards the dull grey sky.

'I don't think I can,' she said, turning her head away.

'Why don't you think you can?' I asked gently.

'I'm safe in here.'

'There isn't any danger out there, Mrs Blake,' I assured her. 'I would be with you. No one will hurt you. You will come to no harm.'

'I'm safe in here,' she repeated.

I tried a different tack. 'Did you know there is a stream at the end of the garden? I thought I might have a wander down there. I've seen it from my bedroom window. I'm sure there is some interesting wildlife to see.'

She was interested, I could tell. Her bottom lip curled into her mouth, and her uneven teeth nipped at the delicate skin.

'Why don't you think about whether you would like to see the stream?' I said, rising from the table. I was being so careful about not pushing her into something that would set her back to how she had been before I arrived at Flete House. 'Will you do that for me, Mrs Blake? Will you think about it?'

'I will, Dr Cowdrey,' she promised.

And she did think about it. The next day when I said good morning to her, and before I could ask, she said she thought she would like to take a walk down to the stream, but only if I went with her.

I was delighted and said so. Of course I would accompany her. I opened the French doors and felt the cold air hit me at once. I instructed the attendant to fetch a shawl or cloak for Mrs Blake, for I was mindful of her frail condition and did not wish her to catch cold. We said nothing as we waited for the attendant to bring the cloak. I watched Mrs Blake out of the corner of my eye, my heart beating fast as I realised what an important moment this was for both of us, and I was desperate to do nothing that would scare her out of taking this momentous step.

The attendant returned, and I placed the cloak she brought around Mrs Blake's shoulders. I could feel her whole body trembling as I helped fasten it at her neck. She was terrified, and I wondered whether I should be pushing her towards this step. Was I being selfish? For whose good was I doing this? Hers or mine? Was I so anxious to prove that a damaged mind could be mended that I was willing to terrify this very fragile woman? I didn't have an answer for any of these questions, and they were put out of my mind when Mrs Blake slid her bony arm around mine and her hand gripped my wrist. She wasn't having second thoughts, and I told myself that neither should I.

'Ready?' I asked.

She nodded.

And I stepped outside. She stumbled out after me, and I sought to steady her. She turned wide, frightened eyes up to me.

'I can't, I can't,' she gasped, and wrenched her arm free. She scrambled back into the library and ran to the furthest corner of the room, pulling an armchair before her so she could hide behind it.

'It's all right,' I cried, closing the French doors and hurrying towards her, my hands held up to her in pacification.

'I can't go out there,' she whimpered.

'Please,' I said, trying to hide my disappointment. 'Please, come out from behind there, Mrs Blake. Let us sit down. Come, come.'

I held out my hand to her, and with more entreaty,

she placed hers in it. I felt the wiry strength in her grip, the shaking of her very bones as I gently pulled her out from the corner and guided her into the armchair.

'You did very well,' I assured her. 'To even contemplate leaving the house was remarkable.'

She began to cry and buried her face in her hands. 'I am so weak. What is the matter with me?'

'You've suffered a great deal,' I said, her self-recrimination upsetting me greatly. 'It's only natural that you should be scared. But we can make you better, Mrs Blake. I promise.'

She cried for quite a while, so long I felt unable to cope with her tears, and transferred her to the care of the attendant.

I was despondent, thinking that we might progress no farther and resolved to give Mrs Blake a little time to herself after this incident. So I was rather surprised when Mrs Blake sought me out one morning a few days later and asked if she might try again. I was on the point of suggesting we just sit by the open doors for a few days to get her used to the feel of the cold air and the smells of the outside when she said she really would like to see the stream. As it was her idea, I thought it best not to refuse, but prepared myself for a repetition of her running away screaming.

She was indeed frightened when she took my arm and I lifted my leg and took the first step outside. But I murmured reassuring words to her in what I hoped was a soothing manner, and she managed to place a foot on the ground before stopping. Her breath was coming fast, and I asked her if she wanted to return to the library. Her lips tightened and she shook her head.

'No, I must try,' she said, and brought her other leg out.

We stood there for a long while. I wanted to allow her all the time she needed to grow used to this new sensation, something I imagined she had not experienced for quite some time. I was not expecting more from her, but she was, it seemed, expecting a great deal of herself. She was determined to do all she could, and she haltingly began to place one foot in front of the other until we had moved a full yard from the French doors.

That was enough for her on this day. She told me so, and I turned her around and walked her back into the library.

We repeated this each day for the next week, and each day we moved a little farther from the house. Mrs Blake never relaxed entirely – she still gripped me with a strength I had not thought possible for her – but she certainly seemed surer in herself. By the middle of the second week, we had reached our goal and Mrs Blake could see the stream. The sight of it cheered her greatly and for only the second time in our brief acquaintance did I see her smile. Her smile made all my endeavours, and my decision to come to Flete House, worthwhile. I had succeeded where others had not even tried. I felt vindicated, triumphant. Was this not a sign that the career of an alienist was the one for me?

13

ABSENCE AND ATTENDANTS

'It is truly extraordinary, Cowdrey.'

It was the end of the day and I was in Dr Wakefield's office, briefing him on the condition of the female patients. I had nothing of any note to report. All the patients were physically well and their mental maladies remained unchanged. I had been about to tell him of Mrs Blake when he had caught sight of her at the stream. Another week had enabled her to not only approach the stream, but to sit down beside it. A few more days and I arranged for her paints and drawing paper to be brought to her. There she sat now, sketching the stream.

I sensed a compliment in Dr Wakefield's words and thanked him.

'How did you manage it?' he said, turning back to me and refilling his glass. He had offered me a glass of whisky when I had first come in, but it was a little early for me and I had declined.

'By perseverance,' I said, 'and reassurance that she would be safe. I saw she had an interest in nature and used that to encourage her to take the first step outside. As you see, she actually enjoys being out of the house, and her paintings are quite exquisite.'

'Yes, I've seen them in the library,' Dr Wakefield said, almost falling into his chair. I suspected he had been drinking even before I entered his office. 'A very talented woman. She could probably make some money from them if she were not mad.'

'Maybe one day she will,' I said. 'If she can become this better in only a few weeks, we can but hope she will, given time, recover entirely and be able to return home.'

He barked a laugh. 'Hold hard, old man. That kind of thing's not good for business.'

I frowned. 'I don't understand you.'

'As much as I like to make people better,' he said, leaning across his desk towards me, 'I would prefer it if they don't get too much better. We can't afford to lose clients.'

'But surely—'

He waved me silent. 'No, no, none of that 'but surely'. Do you have any idea how much Mr Worrell pays to have his sister here? Mrs Blake has one of the second-best bedrooms. That incurs a fee of two hundred pounds per annum. We can't afford to lose her. You may not like it, Cowdrey, but this is a business, not a free hospital. You have to understand that.'

I understood, of course I did, but he was right, I didn't like it.

'So,' he said, emptying his glass, 'who do you have in mind for your next project?' He grinned. 'Miss Bonamy?'

'I'm not sure even I could cure Miss Bonamy,' I said, not wanting to catch his eye and give him the satisfaction of seeing he had embarrassed me. 'I haven't actually considered any other project. I mustn't get ahead of myself. Mrs Blake isn't cured. She still refuses to go to church, as you know. She will need careful handling, I think, but I think too that it might be best to let her be for a while. Let her enjoy the stream and her painting.'

He shrugged. 'That's all very well and good, but you're going to get bored without something to study. Pick another to occupy you, Cowdrey. You won't be doing Mrs Blake a disservice.'

'Perhaps I will,' I said, to appear conciliatory more than anything else. I considered asking him for a recommendation, but remembering his suggestion of Miss Bonamy, decided to work that out for myself.

He nodded. 'Oh, and before I forget, we have a new attendant starting in a day or two to replace Alison Byrne.'

Mrs Byrne was one of the female attendants, and I had heard she had been complaining the work was getting too much for her (though I had not seen any evidence of her struggling) and had given notice.

Dr Wakefield peered at a scrap of paper on his desk.

'Byrne recommended the new woman, a Miss Harriet Frayn. Nora's interviewed her, said she seemed capable. Make yourself known to her when she arrives, tell her what's what. Yes?'

I assured him I would.

He sniffed and leaned back in his chair, eyeing me up and down. 'Isn't it about time you tripped back home to see the wife, Cowdrey?'

I loathed the way he said "the wife". He made Clara sound of no greater importance to me than a pet. 'Yes, I suppose it is. Clara has been asking me to pay her a visit.'

'Then go on Friday, when the day is done. Come back Sunday evening.'

'You'll be all right without me?'

He poured himself another drink and narrowed his eyes at me, almost caressing his glass. 'Think I can't manage without you, do you?'

'I didn't mean that—,' I hurried to say, embarassed by the implication I had unthinkingly made.

'Well, I can,' he interrupted me. 'And don't you forget it.'

I wrote to Clara, informing her I would come home on Friday, arriving in time for dinner and that I expected a fatted calf. I told her not to think about opening up our house just for two nights but that I would stay with her at my parents. I also wrote a short note to Reverend

Bute, excusing myself from not spending Sunday with him and his wife, as had become my habit.

When Friday morning came around, it occurred to me Mrs Blake might wonder where I was over the next two days and become distressed by my absence. I decided to inform her I would be away and sought her out at the stream where she was busy with her sketch-book and pencil. An attendant was sitting a few yards away, keeping one eye on her, the other on her book. Thinking it would be a good idea to also inform the staff of my absence, I walked towards her, realising as I drew nearer that her face was unknown to me.

'Good morning,' I said, 'I'm Dr Cowdrey. You're new here, aren't you?'

The attendant had got to her feet at my approach. There was no sun, yet she wore green-tinted spectacles, and I supposed she must suffer from some affliction of the eyes. Her skin was rather dingy and there were deep lines around her mouth. Dark brown hair streaked with grey peeped out from the edges of her cap and her rather portly frame made me think her age to be forty at least.

'I started yesterday, doctor,' she said in a rather deep, unfeminine voice.

'Of course,' I said, cursing myself for my slowness, 'you're Harriet Frayn. Forgive me, I should have sought you out sooner. I meant to.'

'That's all right, doctor. I know what I've got to do. Been told to keep an eye on 'er.' She jerked her head at Mrs Blake.

'Good. It is very important that you are especially

vigilant in regard to Mrs Blake over the next two days. I will be away until Sunday evening and Mrs Blake may fret at my absence.'

'Very good, doctor,' she said and sat back down, her attention returning to her book. I moved to Mrs Blake and told her I would be away. Disappointingly, she did not seem unduly concerned. I doubted if she would miss me at all.

14

A VISIT HOME

I had barely stepped inside my parents' front door when I heard Clara squeal, 'Felix!', and felt the full force of her body thump against mine. Before I could take another breath, her arms were tight around my neck.

I laughed and squeezed her to me, grinning at Mother, who was watching indulgently from the drawing-room door. 'You've missed me then,' I said, disentangling myself.

'We've all missed you,' Mother said as she angled her cheek for a kiss. 'Are they working you so hard at that place that you couldn't come home sooner than this?'

'Oh Mother, I've been away no time at all,' I said, putting my arms around both their waists and steering them inside the drawing room. 'But yes, I have been busy.'

I heard footsteps in the hall and a moment later, my father appeared.

'Is that Felix? So, you're here at last. Well, how's it been? Interesting. Exhausting?'

'Adam, let Felix sit down,' Mother admonished, but she looked at me expectantly, wanting to hear.

'It is interesting, Dad, and not at all exhausting,' I said, taking a seat. 'I certainly worked a great deal harder at St Eustace's.'

'And you've made friends there,' Clara said. 'You wrote of the Butes. They sound nice. I'm so glad you have company, someone you can talk to.'

'And the work?' my father asked, a little impatiently.

'Absorbing. I've made a particular study of one patient. A sad history of mistreatment that causes her to be frightened of leaving the house. Dr Wakefield and my predecessor made no progress with her at all, but I have.'

'How clever of you, Felix,' Clara said, and my mother echoed her sentiment.

'So, you have found your calling,' my father said, and I wondered if I had heard a note of disappointment in his voice or whether I imagined it.

'I don't know if it's my calling, but I find it more agreeable than the hospital, certainly.'

They asked for details of my life at Flete House, and I did my best to satisfy their curiosity. After a while, we moved to the dining room, and I was so pleased to discover Clara had done as I asked, though I had asked in jest, and ensured a hearty meal awaited me. I ate until my stomach felt stretched at the seams and a great blanket of tiredness wrapped itself around me. It must have been evident, for Mother said I must be weary after travelling and suggested an early night. I did not argue, and I went up to my old bedroom that Clara now occupied, she at my heels.

I sank into the familiar bed and held my arm wide for Clara. It was a great comfort to have her at my side and I realised how much I had missed her presence at Flete House. But I didn't have time to ponder this long. My eyes soon closed, and I slept soundly until the morning.

'So, you're doing well,' Father said when he and I retired to his study after breakfast the next morning to smoke.

I nodded, scraping out the bowl of a pipe. 'I rather think I am. It bodes well, at least.'

'This success you've had with this female patient. You think you can cure this woman of her madness?'

'I'd like to think she is curable. Although, Dr Wakefield would rather I didn't.'

'Why do you say that?'

I paused before answering. 'Tell me, Dad, do you think it right to put money before a woman's peace of mind?'

My father's eyes narrowed as he lit his pipe. 'Explain.'

'Dr Wakefield has tried to dissuade me from

attempting to cure this woman. He doesn't mind me making progress, but he says he can't afford for her to be made so much better that she can leave the asylum. It just seems a little callous to me.'

'It is his business, Felix.'

'But he and I, we're in the business of making people better, aren't we, not making money?'

My father was wearing his patient expression. 'I can see why you think so, Felix, but you're not a child. You're old enough to understand that money does matter. I imagine this Dr Wakefield has invested a great deal in his asylum. He needs to make money. And,' he held up his finger to stop me as I made to interrupt, 'just think. If he doesn't have enough patients, he may have to close the asylum, and then where will those who are left go? Their relatives may not wish to commit them to a public asylum, but there may not be another convenient private asylum where they can go. They would have to be cared for at home, and the care there may not be adequate.'

I thought of Mrs Blake and the mistreatment she had suffered in what should have been a safe place for her, the home of her devoted brother. She had indeed been treated badly at home and was better off at Flete House. 'You're right, Dad,' I conceded. 'I've been foolish.'

'Not foolish, Felix, just over-concerned with principle. You do what you can for this woman, and the others in your care. If they are insane, then Flete House must be the best place for them.'

'*If* they are insane,' I agreed with a smile. 'Although

I can only think that if a person were sane, it would be a veritable torment to be lodged at Flete House. The food, for one thing.'

We both laughed and puffed on our pipes until they were spent, then joined Mother and Clara in the drawing room. When I left on Sunday afternoon, I was quite sorry to go.

Night was coming down as I stepped off the train onto the platform at Chelmsford Station. I had not thought before I left Flete House to ask for Danby to meet me, and as I walked out of the station, I looked in vain for him and the trap. I chided myself for my omission. Of course, the Wakefields would not have enquired into which train I was likely to arrive on and so would not know when to send Danby for me. I hailed a cab, resenting a little the cost of it made necessary by my lack of foresight, and had it take me to the gates of Flete House.

The gates were locked, as was usual, and I had to ring the bell to get the attention of Danby, who slouched out of the small hut he occupied almost hidden in the trees opposite the lodge.

'I would have liked to see you at the station,' I said as he dragged the heavy gate open. 'I had to get a cab.'

'I wasn't told to fetch you,' he said without any hint of apology or sympathy. He had opened the gate barely wide enough for me to squeeze through, and closed it after me with a clang.

'I forgot to send word when I was arriving,' I said, foolishly trying to make conversation.

He turned the key in the lock. 'Don't moan about me not being there, then.'

'I wasn't—,' I began to protest, but he was already on his way back to his hut. I looked to the lodge and saw light shining from behind the curtains. I wondered whether I should inform the Wakefields I was back, but rather suspected they wouldn't care one way or the other, and Danby had put me off speaking to anyone at that moment.

Rain began to fall, quite a gentle rain, but I pulled my coat collar a little tighter as drops slipped down my neck. The sky had grown very dark without my even noticing it, and I found myself hurrying along the drive, sending gravel skipping before me. The house loomed up ahead of me, and its outline looked rather ominous, for the full moon was behind it and only one room was illuminated. It was the left-hand window on the first floor.

I stopped and stared up at the window in some confusion, wondering why there was a light there. As I stared, a figure moved to stand at the window. I could make out nothing of the person's features or clothing, for the light was behind them, but I could discern the unmistakable shape of a woman.

I moved nearer, never taking my eyes off the figure.

Even though I could not see any feature upon her face, I could tell – no, I could feel – her watching me.

And then she closed the shutters and I saw her no more. The spell had been broken, and I hurried into the porch and took out the key Mrs Wakefield had given me on my first day. As I turned the key in the lock, one thought ran through my mind. The woman who occupied room three had returned.

15

MISS HEBRON

I had decided that I would change a few things at Flete House for myself during the train journey back. No longer would I take every meal in the dining hall. I'd been told I could dine alone in my office if I wanted, and I found that I did want to. I left a note before retiring that night of my return in the kitchen saying I wished to be served my breakfast in my office from now on. I also left a very polite note for the cook as to whether it would be possible for me to have more interesting meals than the inmates if I were to provide the food. This had been my mother's suggestion, and I took to it readily. I hoped the cook would be agreeable – I told her I would give her a little something for her trouble – and saw no real need to inform the Wakefields of this new arrangement. I wasn't doing anything underhand, but I didn't want to have to face Mrs Wakefield's disapproval if it wasn't necessary.

I was sitting at the small round table in my office,

Edith having brought in my breakfast and confirming that the cook was happy to provide what I wanted, when Mrs Wakefield entered without knocking.

'You're breakfasting in here,' she declared, staring at my plate.

'Yes,' I said, determined not to quail before her. 'Dr Wakefield said I could take my meals in here if I preferred. I find that I do. Good morning, Mrs Wakefield.'

She closed the door, her eyes registering disdain. 'I've come to tell you that Miss Hebron returned while you were away in London.' She managed to make this sound as if I had been playing truant.

'Yes, the woman in room three. I saw her at the window last night.'

She nodded. 'Showing herself off, I expect. That's the kind of woman she is, Dr Cowdrey. I advise you to take very little notice of Miss Hebron. She craves attention, and it is best not to give it to her.'

'I shall look up her history,' I said, a little annoyed Mrs Wakefield should presume to tell me what I should do in regard to my female charges. 'I trust she is fully recovered?'

'She is recovered enough to be back here,' she said stiffly.

'You and Dr Wakefield must be very relieved,' I said. 'She is your highest-paying patient, isn't she?'

As soon as I spoke those words, I wished I'd kept my mouth shut. Mrs Wakefield's face turned purple, and her dark eyes glared at me. 'I don't think that's any of your business, Dr Cowdrey,' she snarled and, yanking the door open, strode out, her heavy footsteps ringing in my ears.

I finished my breakfast, cursing Mrs Wakefield. I found I truly disliked her, as I had disliked nobody before, not even Abigail. Her warning against me having too much to do with Miss Hebron was not only foolish, for it had aroused rather than stifled any interest I had in the lady, but it was contrary to my duty as a doctor. Miss Hebron had been ill, ill enough for her to spend almost two months at a sanatorium, and it was my duty to assess her current condition. She would probably still be rather weak and perhaps in need of medication. To ignore or avoid her was simply not possible nor ethical.

I drank a mouthful of coffee and went to the cabinet of case files, pulling out the drawer marked H. I retrieved Miss Hebron's file and returned to my desk to read her file while I finished my breakfast.

Rachel Hebron had been admitted to Flete House by her legal guardian and stepbrother, a Mr Ralph Hawke. The Lunacy Order, signed by two doctors, stated Miss Hebron was believed to be a danger to others, citing a rooftop incident with a family friend that had almost resulted in the friend falling to her death.

I flicked through the file. Dr Wakefield had made copious notes in the first few months of Miss Hebron's residency at Flete House. He had noted her intelligence and her genteel qualities, and expressed a regret that madness should have manifested in so obvious a lady.

He had also made special note of her belief that her family was unfairly persecuting her, that they had put her in Flete House not because she was mad but because they viewed her as a nuisance and wanted to get her out of the way. Dr Wakefield had dismissed this persecution belief as a common accusation made by asylum inmates.

Dr Wakefield's notes ended after five months, and Dr Dennison's handwriting appeared. However, Dr Dennison seemed not to have found Miss Hebron interesting because he had recorded far fewer interviews with the lady. Indeed, I could find none dated later than September of the previous year, despite Dr Dennison's last note stating she might prove an interesting subject for study.

I pondered on this. Although I was still interested in seeing what further progress could be made with Mrs Blake, I wanted to give her a little time to become used to her new, if somewhat restricted, freedom. She seemed perfectly content sketching by the stream, and I remembered Dr Wakefield's assertion that I would need a new patient to study. I must confess that Mrs Wakefield's advice may have been a factor in my deciding to try a series of interviews with Miss Hebron in much the same way as I had with Mrs Blake. In short, I was determined to thwart Mrs Wakefield.

Before I went in search of Miss Hebron, I checked over the night log to see if any patient needed particular attention. Confirming nothing was required, I left my office to see Mrs Blake and make sure she was still doing well. She had gone straight out to the stream after breakfast and was busy sketching when I approached. She looked up.

'Good morning, Mrs Blake. You look very well this morning.'

'Thank you, doctor,' she said, returning her gaze to her sketchpad. 'It's very kind of you to say so.'

'What are we drawing today?' I said, peering at the sketch but seeing only a mass of lines without definite form.

'The bank of the stream,' she said, pointing with the end of her pencil, and resumed drawing lines.

I could see she was not in the mood for conversation. I spied the new attendant sitting a little way away and moved towards her. 'Good morning, Miss Frayn. How was Mrs Blake in my absence?'

'She was well enough, doctor,' Miss Frayn said. 'Never fretted for a moment.'

'Good,' I said, not entirely meaning it. It would have been just a little flattering if Mrs Blake had missed me. 'Then I shall leave her to sketch. Tell me, do you know if Miss Hebron is in the dayroom?'

Her mouth twitched as she looked at me, as though my question amused her. 'She's there, doctor.'

I thanked her and returned to the house, making my way to the women's dayroom. I immediately detected a change in the atmosphere in the room. The women still occupied the tables as they normally did, but it seemed that there was a distance between them and the returned inmate.

Miss Hebron lay stretched out on the sofa in the bay window. Although there were several affluent patients at Flete House, it was clear at a glance why Miss Hebron had the very best room. She was undoubtedly a lady. Her bearing, the very way she had positioned herself, not only declared this but positively made a virtue of her gentility. Then there was her clothing; soft silks, brocade. Tasteful, not overdone. Her hair hung over her shoulders, a few strands pulled back and tied at the back of her head. Her hair, to be honest, was a disappointment. It was abundant but not glossy. In colour it was dark brown, rather dull and very frizzy. As for her face, well, it was pleasant enough, but there was something about it that prevented me from calling her pretty. Perhaps her brown eyes were too close together, or perhaps her nose was a little too wide, I cannot say. In her face were the signs of recent illness. There was a paleness beneath the dusting of freckles across her cheeks and purplish tinges to the undersides of her eyes.

'Miss Hebron? Allow me to introduce myself. I'm Dr Cowdrey.'

She raised her eyes to me, then looked me up and down. 'I saw you from my window last night.'

'And I saw you,' I said, pulling up a chair. 'You surprised me. I didn't know you were returning.'

'I wish I hadn't come back,' she said. 'I wish I had died at the sanatorium. Then everyone would be happy.'

Her words rather took me aback. 'You cannot mean

that, Miss Hebron. I'm sure a great many people would be very upset if you were to die.'

She slid her gaze away from me. 'How can you be sure? You've never met my family. If they cared about me, they wouldn't have locked me up in here.'

Here then was the first indication of Miss Hebron's persecution mania Dr Wakefield had noted in his very first entries. I was about to speak when she said, 'Where is Dr Dennison?'

'Dr Dennison has left Flete House,' I said.

'Huh,' she snorted. 'Nora got rid of him, you mean.'

'I beg your pardon?' I said tartly. I thought it highly impertinent of her to refer to Mrs Wakefield so familiarly.

She looked at me disdainfully. 'I suppose you think Mrs Wakefield a saint. All her good works and her reading the Bible to us morning, noon and night, what else could she be?'

'I think nothing of the sort,' I said rather irritably.

She sat up, suddenly animated. 'Don't tell me you've seen her for what she is? She hasn't fooled you, then.'

'No one has fooled me, Miss Hebron. No one can,' I assured her.

She sank back and smoothed out her skirts. 'Is that right, Dr Cowdrey?'

I stood and replaced the chair from where I had taken it. Miss Hebron's manner was as irritating in its way as Mrs Wakefield was in hers, and I found I was not in the mood to suffer it. 'I shall leave you, Miss

Hebron. Perhaps you will feel inclined to speak to me about your history some day soon. I should like to hear it from your own lips.'

'Perhaps I will,' she called after me, 'and perhaps I won't. It will all depend upon whether you are willing to believe me.'

By that, I supposed she meant whether I would believe in her family's persecution of her. I thought it best not to reply and went about my business.

'I met Miss Hebron today,' I said to Dr Wakefield as I sat in his office, my notebook upon my knee, informing him of my day's observations.

He didn't look up from his desk. 'And what did you make of her?'

'A rather difficult young lady. Combative in her manner. I've read your notes upon her admission here, her belief that she has been persecuted, and am certain you were right. That is where her lunacy has its roots.'

Dr Wakefield grunted. 'I wouldn't pry too deeply into Miss Hebron's mania if I were you. You won't get very far.'

'That's quite the coincidence. Mrs Wakefield warned me off her too.'

He grimaced. 'Just leave Miss Hebron be. It's safer.'

I wondered at his use of the word 'safer'. What on earth could he mean by that?

'I had thought to make a study of her,' I said. 'Now that Mrs Blake seems to be managing by herself.'

'She's not worth the effort, believe me.'

'You said I should find a new subject.'

'I didn't mean her,' he retorted.

'But it is an interesting lunacy,' I persisted, yet even as I said so, I wondered why I was being so obstinate. Miss Hebron had certainly not endeared herself to me to give me cause.

Dr Wakefield sighed. 'It seems you are determined not to pay me or Nora any mind, so if you insist, by all means try what you can with her. But she is our highest-paying patient, Cowdrey, and her residence here must not be put in jeopardy. Have I made myself clear?'

'Completely,' I assured him.

I approached Miss Hebron the very next day in the music room. She was playing at the piano, a delightful tune I didn't recognise, and I sat down near the door to listen. She played for perhaps a minute more, then stopped and slammed down the lid.

'What is it you want to know, Dr Cowdrey?'

She had quite taken me aback with this direct question. 'I want you to talk about yourself,' I said, floundering a little with my answer.

She twisted around on the piano stool and looked at me quizzically. 'Is that what Mrs Blake did?'

'No,' I replied carefully, wondering at this interest in her fellow inmate. 'What I know of Mrs Blake's history I know only from her case notes. She is disinclined to discuss what happened to her and I have not pressed her.'

Miss Hebron turned her head towards the windows and looked out into the garden. At the very edge of my line of sight, I could see Mrs Blake sitting on her folding stool with her drawing apparatus by the stream, and a little to her right, the plump, ever-watchful figure of Harriet Frayn.

'Well, whatever you did to her, it's done wonders. She wouldn't so much as step a foot out of the door before.' She turned back to me with a smile. 'You must have the magic touch, doctor.'

It was tempting, but I tried not to feel flattered by this remark. 'No magic, Miss Hebron, just patience.'

'Ah, patience. I'm afraid I lack that particular virtue.' She lifted the piano lid and began pressing one key at a time.

'If you would rather play, I will leave you,' I offered.

'I'm thinking about what I can tell you,' she said.

'Do you need to think before you speak on that subject?'

'I need you to believe me.'

'All I can promise you is that I will listen.'

She turned back to me. 'Maybe that will be enough. Well then, where shall I start?'

I consulted her file. 'The incident on the rooftop,' I

suggested, knowing it was that event which had led to her being put in Flete House.

She tutted. 'That was nothing.'

'Your family didn't think it was nothing. Nor did the parents of the friend involved. According to your case notes, they thought you and she were planning to jump to your deaths.'

'They misunderstood the situation,' she said with a sigh. 'We weren't going to jump.'

'What, then?'

Miss Hebron twirled a strand of her hair around her finger. 'We were looking at the view.'

I frowned, doubting her.

She glared at me. 'We were looking at the view,' she insisted.

'From the very edge of the roof?'

'We were never in any danger of falling. I would go on the roof of Kessell Court all the time and stay up there for hours. No one bothered me, they let me alone. It was so very peaceful up there.'

Was it possible? Could the witnesses to that event have misconstrued what Miss Hebron and her friend had been doing? A thought occurred to me and I voiced it.

'Did your friend say the same thing? That you were looking at the view?'

'Felicity tried to,' Miss Hebron nodded, 'but no one would listen. Her parents were screaming at me, and at her, too.'

'They wanted you prosecuted for endangering their daughter,' I pointed out.

I quickly realised I shouldn't have said that. Miss Hebron's eyes blazed, and she started off the piano stool towards me.

'Felicity's parents were hateful,' she cried, the veins on her neck standing out. 'They would say anything to hurt me.'

I stood and held out my hands. 'Calm down, Miss Hebron, please.' Her breath was coming fast. 'You must not excite yourself or become violent, or you will need to be put under restraint.'

She suddenly moved backwards and fell down onto the stool. She shook her head submissively. 'No restraints,' she pleaded.

Unnerved by her anger and just as sudden capitulation, I decided to call a halt to our interview. 'I think we've had enough for today,' I said, putting my notebook away in my jacket pocket. 'I'll let you continue with your piano playing, but perhaps we could resume our conversation another day?'

She didn't answer me, and I left the room.

16

A STRANGE CHANGE

The next morning, I sought out Mrs Blake to resume our conversations. I was feeling more than a little miserable, for my brief interviews with Miss Hebron had disappointed me more than I would have thought possible. I had been looking forward to examining her history to see if there was more to her lunacy than a persecution mania. Mrs Blake, for all the success I had had with her, presented a far less interesting case, as I believed her lunacy was perfectly understandable when one considered what she had suffered.

Mrs Blake was sitting by the stream. I nodded a greeting to Miss Frayn a few feet away, and drew nearer to Mrs Blake, wondering why she had not looked up and smiled at me as she usually did.

'Good morning, Mrs Blake,' I said.

'Good morning, Dr Cowdrey,' she replied, keeping her head down.

'How are you today?'

She didn't answer me straight away. Instead, she looked around her, at the stream, at the trees, at the grass, at Harriet Frayn. And when she did reply, she still didn't look at me. 'Much as I was, I think, Dr Cowdrey.'

I bent down to look up into her face, but she turned it away. 'Is something wrong, Mrs Blake?' I asked.

Her hands were trembling. 'I'm just feeling a little strange today, Dr Cowdrey. Please leave me alone.'

'If you're unwell—'

'I'm not unwell. Just leave me alone. Please.'

I straightened and took a step back, perplexed. 'If that is what you wish, Mrs Blake, of course I will leave you. But you must tell me if you are ill so I can make you better. Yes?'

Her jaw tightened. She nodded.

I walked over to Miss Frayn. 'Has something happened to Mrs Blake?' I asked quietly. 'She's seems rather unsettled.'

Miss Frayn pupped her lips. 'The patients have their moods, doctor. You shouldn't pay any attention.'

'It's my duty to pay attention, Miss Frayn,' I said, a little testily.

She looked up at me through those tinted spectacles of hers. 'I'll keep an eye on 'er. If I see anything untoward I'll let you know. But it's best not to push when they get like this. It only makes 'em worse.'

A little irritated, I left her to return to the house. When I reached the French doors of the library, I looked back to the stream and saw Miss Frayn approach Mrs Blake. It looked as if Mrs Blake was talking to her, I noticed a little resentfully. So why wasn't she prepared to talk to me?

'You seem rather down in the dumps, young Felix,' Reverend Bute observed as he poured me out a glass of port. 'What is the matter?'

I took a sip. 'It's the patient I've told you about, the lady who was frightened of the outdoors.'

'Oh yes, the one who has taken to drawing God's most beautiful creations with such skill. What's happened? I thought you had high hopes for her improvement.'

'I did. Before I went to London, she was doing so well. But I've come back, and this past week or so…,' I sighed and shook my head. 'It's almost as if she has reverted to how she was before. She received a letter the other day from her brother and I took it to her, thinking she would be glad to receive it, but it seems to have had the opposite effect. She's lost all interest in sketching. She just sits in the dayroom, staring at the floor. I've tried talking to her to find out what's wrong, but she turns her head away and refuses to speak with me.'

'Does she speak to anyone else?'

'Why do you ask that?'

'Because if she speaks to other people but not to you, then that would suggest her problem, if you will forgive me, Felix, lies with you.'

I considered. 'She talks to the attendant, Miss

Harriet Frayn, or rather Miss Frayn talks to her. But then that is Miss Frayn's job. She has to keep an eye on her. And Mrs Blake will talk with Mrs Wakefield, but I suppose she dare not ignore her.'

Reverend Bute chuckled at the face I made. 'Well, I suppose these things happen, Felix.' He reached out and patted my arm. 'You mustn't let it distress you. You're dealing with people who have fractured minds, not limbs. I imagine it is simple with a broken leg. You mend the fracture and you can see the person growing stronger each day. But with a lunatic, you simply cannot tell what is going on in their head.'

'But what did I do wrong?'

'Perhaps you did nothing wrong.'

'I went home to London,' I reminded him. 'She was well enough before then.'

'Her manner had altered by the time you came back?'

I thought hard. No, that wasn't quite right. Mrs Blake hadn't seemed any different when I saw her my first morning back. It had been a day or two later she had seemed disinclined to speak with me. 'It was her brother's letter,' I said decidedly. 'There must have been something in his letter to upset her.'

'Didn't she and her brother get along?'

'He was the one who put her in Flete House. I suppose she may harbour a resentment towards him, but she has never said so, and neither Dr Wakefield nor Dr Dennison recorded any such antipathy in their notes.'

'Then the reason is beyond us, Felix,' Reverend

Bute said as Mrs Bute entered, bearing a well-stocked cheese board. 'Ah, replenishments. Thank you, my dear.'

'Well,' Mrs Bute said as she sat down, 'have you asked Felix what's wrong?'

'I have,' Reverend Bute confirmed, 'and it's his work. A patient has regressed and Felix cannot put his finger on why. He thinks it may be his fault.'

Mrs Bute gave me a pitying look. 'I'm sure you've done nothing wrong, Felix. You're such a kind boy.'

She always thought of me as a boy. It was really rather endearing, but her words failed to convince me. It was a platitude she uttered, a kindness to make me feel better. My mother and Clara would have done the same had they been there.

I returned to Flete House later that evening, grateful to the Butes for their company and kindnesses, but determined to discover what had made Mrs Blake so very unhappy once again.

I awoke to the sound of screaming.

It took me a few seconds to realise what my ears were hearing. When understanding set in, I threw back my bedcovers and rushed to the window. I quickly found the source of the screaming. It was the Wakefields' maid, Judith. She was standing beside the stream, pointing at the water, her shoulders jerking with each scream.

Her screaming had roused others; figures were running from the house towards her. I grabbed my dressing gown from the end of the bed, pulling it on even as I dashed along the corridor and hurtled down the two flights of stairs, skidding at the bottom, and hurrying down into the kitchen and out through the kitchen door.

'What's happened?' I yelled to the crowd gathering around Judith, who had stopped screaming by this time.

They parted a little as I hurtled into them. I looked down into the water. A body floated on the surface, face down. Long dark hair spread out frond-like from the head, as did the white nightgown, exposing the lower legs.

I felt someone knock against me. 'What is it?' Dr Wakefield demanded breathlessly.

He must have run up from the lodge. Either he had heard the screams or someone had run to tell him something was wrong. Over his shoulder, I could see Mrs Wakefield in her nightgown hurrying over the grass.

Dr Wakefield stared down into the stream. 'Oh, dear God,' he cried, running his hand over his face. 'Who is it?'

'Miles?' Mrs Wakefield asked, grabbing her husband's arm. She, too, looked into the stream. Her face paled. 'Who is it?' she gasped.

'I don't know,' Dr Wakefield said.

Danby had come up and was standing by Mrs Wakefield. 'Shall we get her out, Mrs Wakefield?'

She looked at him in bewilderment and gave no answer.

'Yes, get her out,' Dr Wakefield said, moving his wife out of the way. 'Carefully,' he added as Danby and one of the male attendants waded into the water and took hold of the body's arms. They floated the body to the bank where two other men hauled it up onto the muddy grass.

'Turn her over,' Dr Wakefield instructed.

I saw Mrs Wakefield grab his hand and squeeze it so tightly the skin over her knuckles turned white. Danby leant beside the body and pushed it over onto its back. The sodden hair stuck to the face, and he pinched the tresses away to reveal the face of Mrs Blake.

17

A SUDDEN DEATH

Danby carried Mrs Blake's body into the stable, holding her while Dr Wakefield hastily set two planks of wood upon barrels to create a makeshift table. Danby laid Mrs Blake down without ceremony. The floor beneath quickly became damp with the water that dripped steadily from her clothing and hair. A horse blanket was thrown over her and I was glad. I didn't want to have to look at her lifeless body.

'How did she get out?' Mrs Wakefield asked.

'She must have got hold of a set of keys somehow,' Dr Wakefield said. 'One of the attendants being careless.'

'But why did she do this… this evil thing?' she cried, clutching the cross that hung around her neck.

Dr Wakefield turned to me. 'What did you do?' he demanded.

I took a step back. 'What did *I* do?'

'You must have said or done something to her. Frightened her in some way to make her do this.'

'I... I,' I began to protest, but then broke off. Was he right? Had my trying to get her to talk to me frightened her so much that she had decided the only way to avoid me was to take her own life?

Dr Wakefield grew tired of waiting for my reply. 'See to the women,' he ordered me. 'They won't have seen anything because the shutters are closed, but they might have heard Judith screaming. Oh, damn her. Why couldn't she have kept her mouth shut? Make sure they are all right and keep them in their rooms. If any of them are agitated, administer a sedative.'

'No, Miles, they must have their breakfast,' Mrs Wakefield said. 'They will be worse if their routines are upset. We should—'

'Yes, all right, Nora,' he snapped, and I saw Danby glower at him. 'Once the breakfast is ready, the patients can be brought down. But they will have to stay in the dining hall. If they go into other parts of the house, they will be able to see the police arriving. Nora, give them a Bible reading or something to keep them occupied. Cowdrey, say nothing to any of them about what has happened. Is that clear?'

I nodded, and he waved me away. I returned to my room, washed and dressed as quickly as I could, then left to begin my tour of the female bedrooms. All the attendants, male and female, had gathered on the first floor landing. They were talking in whispers amongst themselves, but stopped when they saw me.

‘Is it true, doctor?’ one of them asked. ‘Is one of ’em dead?’

‘Mrs Blake has taken her own life,’ I said, a lump in my throat as I spoke those awful words. ‘The police will be coming. Dr Wakefield wants the patients kept in their rooms with the shutters closed. When breakfast is ready, you are to take the patients straight to the dining hall and act as if all is normal. We will keep them there until the police have been and gone. Let me make one thing very clear. The patients are not to be told anything, not a word. For them to be told of Mrs Blake’s death will only upset them. Dr Wakefield was very insistent upon this point.’

The attendants muttered their agreement with these instructions and dispersed. As they went their separate ways, I noticed that one of them, a young woman with whom I had spoken on a few occasions, Mary Turnbull, had red, puffy eyes. She had been crying, and I wondered why. Had she been close to Mrs Blake?

But I had little leisure to wonder further. I needed to follow in the wake of the female attendants and see to my patients.

———

Fortunately, most of the inmates seemed to be unaffected by the incident. Those whose rooms were closest to the stream had indeed heard the screaming of the maid, but though they asked about it, they were satisfied when I told them it was noise made by children playing nearby.

I left Miss Hebron to last as she was at the front of the house and, I thought, the least likely to have heard Judith screaming. She was dressed but had her silk dressing gown on over her frock. She lounged on her chaise longue by the large window where I had seen her the night of my return from London. She looked around almost lazily at me.

'What is going on, Dr Cowdrey?' she said. 'There have been screams and shouts, men charging up the drive—'

'How do you know that?' I demanded angrily, and pointed at the closed shutters. 'You shouldn't have been able to see out of your windows.'

Her mouth curved in a smile. 'How very alarmed you sound, doctor. Are the Wakefields so fearful of us seeing what is happening that they've ordered our shutters to remain closed?'

'How do you know?' I asked again.

She pointed to the shutter above her. 'There are gaps, Dr Cowdrey. One need only press one's eye to the gap to see all.' She swung her legs to the ground. 'You can tell me, doctor. I'm not going to faint. What has happened?'

She already knew something was wrong, and it would only increase her interest if I were to deny it. 'Mrs Blake has had an accident,' I said, stretching the truth only a little.

'I see. Is she dead?'

'Yes, I'm afraid she is,' I said, appalled by the cold way she asked.

Miss Hebron nodded thoughtfully. 'Poor Mrs Blake. You worked so hard with her, didn't you? You must feel rather disappointed that all your time has been wasted.'

'My time was nothing,' I said, a little angrily. 'What is my time compared to the loss of her life?'

'Forgive me,' she said. 'That was cruel of me. I'm sure you did all you could. She did seem happier than before.'

'She *was* happy,' I said, falling into a chair by the door. 'I don't know why that changed.'

'Perhaps you will never know, doctor. Perhaps what you thought was an improvement was just a show, a pretence to make you happy.'

'You mean she was just—,' I broke off, unable to say the words.

Miss Hebron nodded. 'Yes, she was showing you what you wanted to see.'

I stared at her, wondering if what she said was possible. Had it all been for my benefit? Had Mrs Blake not improved at all?

'I think that must have been so because I could hear her crying at night.' Miss Hebron pointed to a curtain that hung in the corner of the room.

I had not noticed this curtain before and rose to move towards it. 'You could hear her?' I grabbed the curtain and tugged it to one side. There was a door behind it. I tried the handle. It was locked. 'Where's the key?'

Miss Hebron shrugged. 'The Wakefields have it, I suppose. It's never been opened.'

'Did you hear Mrs Blake say anything?'

'Nothing I could make out. It was mostly sobs I heard. She must have been terribly unhappy. But then, aren't we all, all of us who are kept here?'

I let the curtain drop back into place and turned to her. 'You are unhappy, Miss Hebron?'

She raised an eyebrow at me. 'How can I be anything else, Dr Cowdrey?'

'You are safe and well looked after here.'

'But I am not free,' she said, lifting her legs back up onto the chaise longue.

'For a very good reason.'

'For no reason at all, save for my stepmother's hatred.' She turned her head to me. 'How deeply have you looked into my history, doctor?'

I shrugged. 'I've read your case notes.'

'And what use are they? They are notes made by doctors who, shall we say, appreciated the generosity of my stepfamily.'

I took a step towards her. 'What are you saying?'

'What I am saying, doctor, is that I am not mad. What I am is angry and frustrated, and I admit, I have at times an ungovernable temper. But that does not make me mad. You say Mrs Blake had an accident, but I will hazard a guess that that accident was of her own making. Am I right? You don't answer, so I see that I am. She was unhappy and has killed herself. I can understand that.'

Her words alarmed me. 'You're not thinking of harming yourself, Miss Hebron?' I asked worriedly.

She looked at me for a long moment, then turned her head away. 'When will breakfast be ready?'

———

The rest of the day passed in a blur.

The inmates had to be kept in the dining hall for rather longer than I think Dr Wakefield had anticipated, and this did indeed cause some of the patients, the men mostly, to become a little unruly. Dr Wakefield had those men taken to their rooms and sedated to keep them quiet. The women were far more willing to sit at the dining hall tables and listen to Mrs Wakefield reading from the Bible, and this being so, my presence there was not needed. I would have preferred to shut myself away in my office, but I felt I ought to be on hand should Dr Wakefield need me, and so waited in the small sitting room next door to his office.

There was no police presence in Flete, so they had to be sent for from Chelmsford, and this took a little while. When they did arrive, it was a police sergeant who asked to see the body. He made his observations, then left, saying he would arrange for a mortuary vehicle to come out as soon as possible to take Mrs Blake away. This didn't happen until the early afternoon, and all the patients were by this point growing restless at being confined to the one room. The decision was made to release them into their dayrooms, but Danby was told to stop the vehicle at the gates to give him time to send word to the house so we could get the patients back in the dining hall and out of the way.

It had been a long day by the time the patients were returned to their bedrooms and locked up for the night. There had been so much activity and yet so few answers or information had come my way. Dr Wakefield had barely spoken a word to me since the morning, so before I retired for the night, I knocked on his office door. He shouted a weary, 'Yes,' and I entered.

'What do you want?' he said, pouring himself a large measure of whisky.

'I wondered what the police said,' I replied, ignoring his tone.

He sank back in his chair and gulped down the whisky. 'The police said nothing. They've logged it as a suicide, but there will be an inquest which we shall all have to attend.'

An inquest would make Mrs Blake's death public, something, I was sure, the Wakefields would rather have avoided. 'I'm so very sorry, Dr Wakefield. I should have seen this coming.'

He banged his empty glass down on the desk, making me jump. 'This is what happens when you interfere, Cowdrey. What did I tell you on your very first day here? Don't try to cure the patients. You ignored me, and this is the result.'

'With respect, Dr Wakefield,' I said, my ire up, 'you knew what I was doing with Mrs Blake. You even congratulated me on my success. Whatever went wrong with her happened when I wasn't here.'

'Oh, so it's my fault, is it?'

'I'm not saying that.'

'Then what are you saying?'

I took a deep breath and voiced what had been on my mind all day. 'That in view of what has happened, perhaps I should leave Flete House.'

He tugged his earlobe. 'Don't think I haven't considered firing you. But how would that look now? The fact is, regardless of any ill-advised treatment you may have engaged in, it wouldn't have made any difference if Mrs Blake hadn't managed to get out of her room and out of the house.'

I had forgotten about this seemingly impossible feat of hers. 'Yes, how did she manage that?'

'Nora has her suspicions.'

I had no doubt Mrs Wakefield did have her suspicions. 'Which are?' I pressed.

'That the night watch was negligent. They didn't lock Mrs Blake's door and so Mrs Blake was able to leave her room and take the key for the kitchen door.'

'Mary Turnbull was on watch,' I said, remembering her reddened eyes.

'Yes, Mary Turnbull. I've spoken with her, but she says she didn't see anything, that she did lock the doors, etcetera, etcetera. She doesn't know how Mrs Blake could have got out.'

'But she must have seen her if she had been at her

station. Mrs Blake would have had to pass her to go downstairs.'

'Exactly. Mary's lying, which is lucky for us.'

'How do you mean lucky?' I asked, perplexed.

'Because if she was negligent,' he said, 'which she obviously was, then she is to blame and we are in the clear.'

I understood his meaning. Mary Turnbull was to be made the scapegoat at the inquest. She would be blamed entirely, and the Wakefields and myself cleared of any suspicion that we had neglected our duty of care.

'You will back us up on this, Cowdrey,' Dr Wakefield said, his eyes hard upon me. 'I don't want you telling the coroner any nonsense about your treatment and that you should take full responsibility. You understand?'

I nodded. 'Yes, Dr Wakefield, I understand.'

'Now, get out of here.' He waved me to the door. 'I have to write to Mrs Blake's brother and tell him she's dead.'

I closed the door upon him, hearing him pour more whisky into his glass.

18

THE INQUEST

The inquest into Mrs Blake's death was to be held at The Black Dog public house in the village. I had been to The Black Dog a few times with Reverend Bute and had found it a rather comforting place. Not today, though. The pub had a very different atmosphere. The prospect of an inquest afforded entertainment for the village; everyone seemed to have turned out for the show.

Mrs Blake's brother, Mr Worrell, came to Flete to attend the inquest. He arrived the day before and came to Flete House to see the Wakefields and take tea. I had not been invited to take part; indeed, Dr Wakefield as good as told me to stay out of the way. Part of me wished to talk with Mr Worrell, to tell him how sorry I was, but another part of me was glad I didn't have to face him. The Wakefields invited Mr Worrell to stay with them at the lodge while the inquest was held, but he declined, saying he had taken a room at The Black Dog.

The first time I saw him was at The Black Dog on the day of the inquest. He came down the stairs slowly, holding on to the rail tightly as if worried he might fall. And well he might, I thought as I studied him. His face was ashen, his cheeks hollow, and his eyes had a blank look to them. He was a man who looked utterly broken, and I turned away before he found me in that room, my conscience pricking me.

Judith and Mary Turnbull were already seated when I took a seat in the front row of chairs that had been set out for the participants and spectators. It wasn't long before the Wakefields joined me, saying nothing but glancing uneasily around as the villagers settled into their seats. There were so many present, however, that the chairs ran out and some had to stand at the back. The coroner banged his gavel to get everyone's attention and ordered the jurors to be sworn in.

The jurors were all from the village. Once they had made their oaths, they sat down behind several small tables which had been pushed together to make one long one. The crowd grew quiet, expectant, as the coroner cleared his throat.

'We are here to inquire into the death of Mrs Elizabeth Blake, a mental patient at Flete House Private Lunatic Asylum. The body of Mrs Blake has been viewed by the jurors, who are assembled to deliver a verdict on the nature of her death. I call the first witness, Miss Judith Benn.'

Judith looked extremely nervous and conscious of

all the eyes upon her as she took the seat indicated by the coroner.

'You are Miss Judith Benn?' the coroner asked.

'Yes, sir.'

'And you found the body of Mrs Elizabeth Blake on the morning of the third of April of this year?'

'Yes, sir.'

'Describe how you came to find the body.'

Judith took a deep breath. 'I had gone up to the house for a loaf of bread for the breakfast table. I like to feed the fish in the stream of a morning, so I took the stale bread Cook always leaves out for me and walked across the lawn to the stream.'

'Which door did you enter and exit the house by?'

'The kitchen door, sir.'

'Was the door locked or unlocked?'

'Unlocked and open, sir.'

'Was that usual?'

'No, sir. I usually have to unlock it.'

The coroner made a note. 'Continue.'

'When I got to the stream, I saw something white floating there. I couldn't think what it was, so I looked closer. And then I realised it was a body, face down in the water. I started screaming, I was that shocked. I'd never seen a dead body before. Then the others arrived and one of 'em made me come away.'

'Did you make any attempt to pull the body out of the water?'

'No, sir.' Judith shuddered. 'I weren't going to touch it.'

'Is there anything else you wish to tell us?'

Judith shook her head, and the coroner told her she could return to her seat. She seemed rather disappointed now it was all over.

The coroner called Dr Wakefield next. 'You are the proprietor of Flete House Private Lunatic Asylum?'

'I am,' he said, crossing his legs.

'Mrs Blake had been a patient for how long?'

'For almost a year.'

'What was the nature of her mental illness?'

'Mrs Blake had suffered mistreatment at the hands of a housekeeper who was supposed to look after her.'

I heard a sob from behind and half turned to see Mr Worrell with his head in his hands. Dr Wakefield cleared his throat and continued.

'This neglect had left her physically fragile, suffering from malnutrition, a variety of skin complaints and minor ailments, and had left her with an extreme fear of the outside world.'

'Was she a danger to others?'

'Only when she felt threatened. If anyone attempted to physically move her, for example, she would lash out. But at all other times, she was more docile than otherwise.'

'Was she ever considered to pose a danger to herself?'

'No.' Dr Wakefield was emphatic. 'There was never any evidence of a tendency towards suicide. If there had been, we would have taken extra precautions to keep her safe.'

'I see.' The coroner nodded and made a note. 'To return to Mrs Blake's death. Her death occurred either during the night of the second or the early hours of the third of April. How is it that Mrs Blake was out of bed at such an hour, presumably unattended?'

'That is a question I would like to know the answer to myself,' Dr Wakefield said, nodding. 'The patients are locked in their rooms at eight o'clock every night and the doors remain locked until they are opened at seven o'clock the next morning. The only reason for a room to be unlocked during the night would be to attend to the patient if they were ill, and that was not the case with Mrs Blake.'

'I understand attendants are posted on both the first and second floors of Flete House throughout the night to tend to any patient should they need help.'

'That is correct.'

'Was an attendant stationed on the female corridor during the night of the second to the morning of the third?'

'Yes, Mary Turnbull was on duty.' Dr Wakefield pointed at Mary, who tried to make herself small at the end of the row.

The coroner asked Dr Wakefield if there was anything he wanted to add. I saw Dr Wakefield look behind me to where Mr Worrell was sitting. When he spoke, his voice was a little louder than before, as if he didn't want anyone to miss his words.

'I would like to say that I am extremely saddened by the death of Mrs Blake. That it should have happened while she was in my care is a matter of great grief to me and to my wife. Mrs Blake had of late shown encouraging signs of making some recovery, but it is undeniable that in the last few days of her life, she had regressed somewhat.'

'What was the cause of that regression?' the coroner asked.

'Unknown,' Dr Wakefield said, then pointed to me. 'Dr Cowdrey, my colleague there, had made a particular study of Mrs Blake and had been highly successful in reducing her fear of the outside.'

'But you say that changed although it is not known what caused the change?'

'Correct, but that is often the way with lunacy. Unfortunately, we simply do not know what goes on in a lunatic's head. If we were able to understand that, there would be far fewer lunatics than there are.'

The coroner nodded understandingly, and I could see Dr Wakefield's concerned expression morph into one of undisguised relief as his account was accepted.

The coroner thanked him and said he could step down. Then he called me to the stand.

'Dr Cowdrey,' the coroner began, 'Dr Wakefield has told this court that you had made a particular study of Mrs Blake and that you had succeeded in moderating her fear of the outside world. Would you agree with that statement?'

'I would.'

'What form did your particular study take?'

I could guess what the coroner was trying to discover, whether my treatment had been harsh, and that it had led Mrs Blake to her death. I would be careful with my answer.

'I talked with her,' I began, 'and found that she had an interest in wildlife. She was also a highly accomplished painter. When I first began my study of her, I suggested copying illustrations from books. When she had become used to that, I suggested she might like to paint from life instead. Mrs Blake resisted this suggestion at first. By degrees, I would talk with her, each time moving her closer towards the French doors of the library so that she could, in effect, see what she was missing. When I felt she was ready, I suggested we take a walk in the garden. Again, this was at first resisted, but then she insisted on trying, and we began, by degrees again, to walk down to the stream. She became so enamoured of the stream and the insects and other animals she could see there, that she would go there every day and paint and sketch. She even had to be told when to come in.'

'And this is the success of which Dr Wakefield spoke?'

'Yes. I believe, and so does Dr Wakefield, that such behaviour was an improvement in Mrs Blake and could be considered a success.'

'But there was a reversal in this improvement that neither you nor Dr Wakefield can account for?'

'That is true. I had been away in London for a few days, and when I returned, I found Mrs Blake to be rather subdued in her manner. I noted it at the time but found nothing to particularly concern me at that point. I assumed my absence had a negative effect upon her and that it might take a little while for her to feel comfortable enough for us to resume our conversations.'

'But the resumption of your talks did not take place?'

'No, despite my trying to engage her in conversation. She seemed averse to talking with me at all. I began to think that my absence was not the cause. Quite the reverse, in fact, as she seemed to desire my absence. I was perplexed. Even more so when a few days later she received a letter from her brother, Mr Worrell. I would have expected the receipt of such a letter to please her but it seemed to make her worse.'

'Were you aware of the contents of this letter?'

'I was not. It was a private letter, and Mrs Blake had become uncommunicative and did not confide in me.'

'But despite this reversal in her manner, you had no reason to suspect Mrs Blake was capable of or considering taking her own life?'

I shook my head. 'No reason at all. Her death came as a complete shock to me, to all of us at Flete House.' I caught Dr Wakefield's eye. There was an expectation in his expression which I understood entirely. I took a deep breath and obliged him. 'And it must be noted that had she not been able to leave her room, Mrs Blake would not have had the opportunity to end her life.'

The coroner made a note of this last and thanked me. I resumed my seat, accepting the almost imperceptible nod of approval Dr Wakefield gave me.

Then the coroner called Mr Worrell. Mr Worrell took the stand with tears in his eyes, wiping them away with a crumpled handkerchief. The coroner expressed his condolences, then asked what had been in the letter Mr Worrell had sent to his sister.

'All I wrote was that I was looking forward to seeing her again and how pleased I was that she was so much better,' Mr Worrell cried, his voice breaking. 'There was nothing in my letter to upset her, there couldn't have been.'

'Did you write to your sister often?'

'Not as often as I should. My business takes me away a great deal, and it is not always easy to write.'

'So, despite its innocuous contents, it may be possible that your letter gave her cause, however inexplicable, for alarm?' the coroner asked.

Mr Worrell gave an enormous sigh. 'I suppose it's possible, if the doctor says that was when he noted a change. But I didn't mean it if it was. I loved Elizabeth, I would never have done anything to deliberately upset her.'

He began sobbing into his handkerchief and the coroner sighed, realising he was unlikely to get anything more. He thanked Mr Worrell and said he could stand down. He then called for Mary Turnbull. Mary looked terrified as she took the witness chair.

'Miss Turnbull,' the coroner began in a tone that

lacked the deference he had shown Dr Wakefield and me. 'You were on duty on the women's floor of Flete House on the night of the second to the third of April?'

'Yes, sir.'

'And it was your job to ensure all the female patients' doors were locked?'

'Yes, sir,' Mary said, her voice small and quiet.

'Speak up,' the coroner barked.

'Yes, sir,' Mary almost shouted, making the spectators laugh.

The coroner banged his gavel and ordered quiet. Only when the room had settled did he return to Mary. 'Did you lock the door of Mrs Blake on the night of the second to the third of April?'

'I thought I did, sir.'

'What do you mean?'

'Well, I remember going along the corridor, locking and then trying the doors. I seem to remember they were all locked.'

'So, how do you account for Mrs Blake being able to leave her room?'

'I can't account for it, sir,' Mary said miserably, and burst into tears.

The spectators immediately began muttering amongst themselves and the coroner was forced to call for silence again.

'Miss Turnbull, please compose yourself,' he said irritably. 'Now, did you see Mrs Blake leave her room?'

Mary wiped her nose and sniffed noisily. 'No, sir. If I had, I would have turned her about.'

'But you were on duty in the corridor all night?'

'Yes, sir.'

'You didn't leave it at any time?'

'No, sir.'

The coroner huffed and leant his elbows on the table before him. 'I cannot then comprehend how Mrs Blake was able to leave her room without being seen by you. Could she have climbed out of her window?'

'No, sir. The windows are all locked and shuttered. And Mrs Blake's window was still like that when I went to look in her room after she was found in the stream.'

'Then how did she pass you without you seeing her?'

Mary looked around the room. Everyone was waiting for her answer. She began to cry again, silently this time, the tears running down her cheeks.

'I fell asleep, sir,' she wailed, and buried her face in her hands.

There was a collective gasp from the spectators. Dr Wakefield looked at his wife and she gave him a tight, wintry smile.

'You fell asleep on duty?' the coroner asked in a disgusted tone.

Mary looked up and nodded. Her face had become a mess of blotchy skin and mucus. 'I ain't never done so before, sir, I swear it. I don't know why I fell asleep then.'

'Had you been drinking?'

She wiped her nose with her sleeve. 'I had a mug of

beer with me. But only the one, sir. It wouldn't have felled a child, it wouldn't, not that one mug.'

'Are you a habitual drinker, Miss Turnbull?'

The word was not familiar to her, and the coroner had to rephrase his question. 'Do you have a drink of beer regularly?'

She shrugged one shoulder. 'Every now and then. Ain't no harm in it.'

'Do you always drink on duty?'

'It gets thirsty during the night.'

'I see,' the coroner said disapprovingly. 'Then I think that explains how Mrs Blake was able to leave her room without being seen. You may step down, Miss Turnbull.'

Mary scurried back to her seat. Mrs Wakefield shifted away as she sat down, distancing herself from her.

So, now we had the answer to Mrs Blake's death. Mary had been drunk and not locked the door, as she believed. Taking advantage of this, Mrs Blake had left her room, discovered the sleeping Mary, and taken her keys to open the kitchen door. It was all ridiculously simple.

The coroner seemed to have heard all the testimony he required and called upon the jury to agree their verdict. It didn't take them long. They muttered amongst themselves for perhaps half a minute, then the foreman stood up, cleared his throat and returned a verdict of suicide. The coroner said it would be so recorded and declared the inquest at an end.

Dr Wakefield breathed, 'Thank God,' and rose, holding out his hand to his wife. 'Come on, Nora. Let's get back.'

Mrs Wakefield took his hand, and without a word to me, they both made their way to Mr Worrell to exchange a few words of sympathy and discuss how Mrs Blake's belongings that were still at the house would be dealt with. This, they concluded quickly, and walked out of The Black Dog before anyone could prevent them. Mr Worrell returned to his room.

I was left with Mary Turnbull. What was her position now? She had been proved negligent in her duty and the Wakefields had not told her to get back to work. It was unlikely they had forgotten her. Their walking away without a word could only mean one thing, that Mary Turnbull no longer had a position at Flete House.

Awkwardly, I turned to her. 'I'm very sorry for you, Mary.'

She pinched her nose with her handkerchief and turned her red eyes up to me. 'No, you're not. You blamed me just like everyone else.'

'But I never said—'

'You didn't have to, did you? You just said that if Mrs Blake hadn't been able to leave her room, she wouldn't be dead. What else did you mean but that it was my fault?'

'Well, you did fail to lock her room and fall asleep at

your post, Mary. You must take some of the blame, you know.'

She stuffed her sodden handkerchief into her bodice. 'I locked her door, I know I did. I remember turning the key and trying the door. It were locked. And that weren't no natural sleep I fell into neither. I don't never sleep that sound.'

'What are you saying?'

'I'm saying summink was put in my beer, that's what.'

'But who would do such a thing?' I laughed at the ridiculousness of what she was suggesting.

'That's it, laugh at me. You're all the same, you lot. Well, between you all, you've done for me. I hope you're satisfied.'

She shoved me out of the way and strode out of the inn. I stared after her, appalled at her rudeness, but also confused by her words.

'Felix?'

I turned to see Reverend Bute.

'Did you see that?' I demanded, pointing after Mary.

'I'm afraid I did,' he nodded. 'I suppose the Wakefields have dismissed her?'

'They didn't say so, but what else can they do? This was all her fault.'

He frowned at me disapprovingly. 'Not *all* her fault, Felix. She wasn't to blame for the state of mind that led Mrs Blake to take her own life.'

'Are you saying I am?' I demanded. His expression of affront shamed me immediately. 'Forgive me,' I begged. 'I'm not myself. This has been very upsetting. And Mary said something very odd just now that, well, frankly, I don't understand at all.'

'What did she say?' he asked.

'She said something had been put in her beer that night to make her sleep.'

'How very peculiar. I can't see why anyone would do that. An excuse, possibly, trying to blame someone else. It's understandable. Now,' he clapped me on the shoulder. 'Come with me to the vicarage and forget all about this sorry affair.'

It was a tempting offer, but there was something I wanted to do. 'If you'll forgive me, Timothy, I rather thought I would go to your church. To pray for Mrs Blake,' I explained, 'and to ask for forgiveness.'

Reverend Bute patted my arm. 'I shall come with you, Felix, and we shall pray together.'

'Thank you,' I said.

'But,' he held up a finger, 'I want you to remember one thing as you pray. What you did with Mrs Blake you did with the best of intentions. You wanted to make her better. You failed in that endeavour this time, but that is not to say you will do so again. You will learn from this, I do not doubt. Please do not stop trying to help people, I implore you. You have a good heart, Felix. You must always use it.'

19

RALPH HAWKE

There was an increased vigilance at Flete House from that moment onwards. Mrs Wakefield checked all the inmates' doors of a night to ensure they were locked and the attendants were lectured daily on the perils of drink.

For his part, Dr Wakefield would poke his head into the women's dayroom, take a quick look around to content himself that all was well before leaving to see to the men. He gave me the distinct impression that his faith in me, such as it had been, had diminished sorely, and I was not to be trusted.

It was an odd set of emotions that was churning within me at this time. The Wakefields were not my friends, as I had imagined them to be; their attitude made it clear I was an employee, and this was a blow to my vanity. But I also felt that I owed them my loyalty. Dr Wakefield had not made me the scapegoat for Mrs Blake, even though he could easily have done so, and he had refused to accept my resignation. I kept remembering my father's words that the Wakefields had a business to run, and that viewed in that vein, their behaviour was entirely reasonable. I should not judge them too harshly. Still, a part of me wanted to leave Flete House, but another part of me felt a strong duty towards the women in my care, and I would not allow myself to contemplate abandoning them.

And though in the immediate aftermath of Mrs Blake's death, I had decided to heed Dr Wakefield's advice and simply tend to the daily needs of the patients and not try to make them better, as the days wore on, I grew bored with such dull routine, and thought I might try talking with Miss Hebron once again. But before I got the chance, Dr Wakefield came into my office.

'Cowdrey, Miss Hebron is expecting her guardian to visit today. Around three o'clock, I think, so Nora's arranging for them to have tea together in the small sitting room. I'll be around to greet Mr Hawke when he arrives, but then I'll leave them alone. He may ask to see you. Make sure you are available and be polite.'

'Of course,' I said, a little affronted he felt he needed to say this to me.

'And be careful what you say to him,' he continued, wagging his finger at me. 'Don't mention Mrs Blake. Hopefully, Miss Hebron won't tell him of it, but if she does and he brings the subject up, say as little as possible and be sure to tell him that the person responsible has been dismissed.'

I assured Dr Wakefield I would follow his instructions to the letter. Indeed, I had no desire to discuss Mrs Blake with anyone.

When three o'clock approached, I left my office and made my way to the women's dayroom. Dr Wakefield only wanted me to talk to Mr Hawke if asked for, but I hoped to catch a glimpse of him at the very least, visitors at Flete House being a rare occurrence. I saw a carriage coming along the drive, and a few moments later, heard footsteps in the hall that told me the Wakefields had also become aware of its approach and were readying themselves to greet the relative of their most prestigious client.

I opened the door of the dayroom a little and put my eye to the crack. Dr Wakefield and Mrs Wakefield were in the hall, he tugging at his cuffs and adjusting his tie, Mrs Wakefield patting her hair and tucking stray strands beneath her cap. They were nervous, I could tell.

'Is it him?' a voice behind me called, and I turned to see Miss Hebron standing by the fireplace, staring at me. Her voice sounded strained and she kept clutching at her skirts.

'It's your guardian, yes,' I said. 'You knew he was coming to see you today?'

Miss Hebron nodded. 'Mrs Wakefield told me. I wish he wouldn't come.'

I moved towards her. 'Why? Surely you are pleased to see your stepbrother?'

Her right hand went to her throat. 'You don't know him,' she said so quietly I had to lean closer to make out the words.

'But he cares for you,' I said. 'He took you to a sanatorium when you were ill.'

Her eyes widened as they shifted to over my shoulder, towards the door. There were voices in the hallway, those of the Wakefields and an unfamiliar male voice that could only belong to Mr Hawke.

Miss Hebron suddenly grabbed my wrist. 'Don't let him hurt me.'

I put my hand over hers. 'He won't hurt you,' I assured her. 'He's come to see how you are, that's all.'

I turned again as the dayroom door squealed on its hinges. Dr Wakefield was in the doorway. His eyes dropped to my hand on Miss Hebron's. I snatched it away.

'Miss Hebron,' he said, 'your guardian is here to see you. Please come with me.'

I stepped aside for her to pass, and she did so haltingly, her reluctance evident. She passed through the doorway and Dr Wakefield closed the door. I heard Mr Hawke say, 'Rachel,' and then the sound of retreating footsteps.

I lingered for what seemed an age in the dayroom, wondering what there was in Miss Hebron's and Mr Hawke's history to make her so frightened of him. Was it linked to her persecution mania? Or had he really mistreated her in some way?

I was on the point of returning to my office when the dayroom door opened and Harriet Frayn waddled in. 'You're wanted, doctor,' she said, and turned back the way she had come without waiting to see if I would follow.

But, of course, I followed. I was pleased Mr Hawke had asked to see me. I entered the small sitting room. Mr Hawke was sitting on one side of the settee, Rachel was huddled at the other end. Miss Frayn closed the door behind me and settled herself on a stool in the corner of the room.

Mr Hawke rose. He was taller than me by a couple of inches, and broader. His hair was so dark it was almost black and he had a dark, brooding countenance. He didn't give me his hand. Instead, he looked me up and down. 'Dr Cowdrey, I believe,' he said.

'Yes, I am Dr Cowdrey,' I said. 'You wanted to see me?'

He resumed his seat and gestured at the armchair by his side. I obediently sat down.

'You have the care of the female patients, Dr Wakefield tells me. How has Rachel been since her return from the sanatorium?'

I glanced at Miss Hebron. She wasn't looking at either of us, but staring out of the window. 'Miss Hebron has been well, on the whole,' I said. 'She was rather wan when she returned, but as you can see, she has recovered some of her colour.' Although, I noted, she looked rather pale at the moment.

He looked at her, then turned back to me. 'She seems rather subdued.'

'Yes,' I said carefully. 'Your visit seems to have

caused her great anxiety. Why would that be? Do you know?'

His frown deepened. 'I cannot say. Has she said anything about me?'

I had to tell him of the fear I had witnessed in his stepsister. 'She thinks you mean to harm her.'

Mr Hawke's jaw tightened. 'She spoke of a Mrs Blake, a woman who died here recently. Could that have upset her?'

'I suppose it could,' I nodded, wondering exactly what Miss Hebron had told him. Had she told him Mrs Blake had killed herself or implied it was a natural death? 'But we did our best to shield all the inmates here from that sorry incident.'

'I see,' he nodded and leaned a little closer. 'How do you feel her mental state to be? Stable? I mean, she's not getting worse?'

It felt odd, uncomfortable, to be talking about Miss Hebron as if she wasn't sitting only a few feet away. 'I have seen no worsening,' I said, 'but I have not yet had the opportunity for any lengthy interviews with your stepsister, Mr Hawke. She seemed disinclined to talk with me. I am hoping that will change.'

'Now, wait a moment,' he said, holding out his hand. 'What do these interviews involve? I don't want you putting ideas in her head.'

'I would do nothing of the sort, sir. I would simply endeavour to discover the cause of her lunacy and try to alleviate it if possible.'

'That's all?'

'Yes, that's all.'

'I'm not sure I approve of that. Having our family's private affairs discussed with a complete stranger.'

'Such matters as would be discussed would be for mine and Dr Wakefield's ears only. Notes would be made in her case file, and nothing more. I would never break my patient's confidentiality.'

Mr Hawke studied me for a long moment. Then he spoke decidedly. 'If I have your word that it will be so, then you may talk with Rachel, but I don't think it will do any good.'

I cleared my throat. 'Forgive me, Mr Hawke, but you cannot know that.'

'No, but I have known Rachel for many years and let me tell you, Dr Cowdrey, everything that comes out of her mouth is either wicked or a downright lie.'

I was shocked by the vehemence of his words, as well as by him saying so before his stepsister. Indeed, I saw Miss Hebron start, and glare at his back as he spoke, and I would not have blamed her if she had railed against him for speaking so hatefully of her. But she simply turned her head away.

It seemed Mr Hawke had said all he wanted to say. He rose and said he was ready to leave. He bid his stepsister a farewell which she did not return, and I walked with him to the front door. Mrs Wakefield was already there. She apologised for her husband not being present, explaining he had been detained elsewhere in the house, and wished Mr Hawke a good journey. Her smile remained only as long as Mr

Hawke was in view. Then it vanished and she turned on me.

'What did he speak to you about?' she demanded.

'He asked how his stepsister has been since her return,' I said.

'Did he ask about Mrs Blake?'

'A word only. He was worried her death had upset Miss Hebron.'

She gave a contemptuous snort. 'As if she could be upset by such a thing. Where is she now?'

'We left her in the sitting room.'

'Alone?'

'The attendant, Miss Frayn, is with her.'

'Get her back in the dayroom. I will not pander to her by letting an attendant wait on her pleasure all day.'

She strode off into the back of the house where she had a small office, and I returned to the sitting room. Miss Hebron was still sitting on the settee, but Harriet Frayn had moved to sit beside her and they were quietly talking. They broke off as I entered, and Miss Frayn rose, her hands clasped in front of her expectantly. I made a mental note to have a word with her later not to become overfamiliar with Miss Hebron.

'Has he gone?' Miss Hebron asked, looking up at me.

'Yes,' I said. 'I'm sorry if his coming has distressed you. His words were a little unkind.'

'A little?' she said mockingly. 'Oh, I wish he wouldn't come. Or if he must, that he brings Aunt Bea with him.'

'Who is Aunt Bea?'

She gave me a contemptuous look. 'She's my aunt, of course.'

Miss Frayn sniggered, and angrily, I told her she could leave the room. I didn't speak again until I heard the door close behind her. Then I sat down by Miss Hebron, deliberately deciding to ignore Mrs Wakefield's instruction to return her to the dayroom.

'Your aunt on your mother's or father's side?' I said, determined to prove my question hadn't been so very foolish.

'My father's. Aunt Bea never married, so she lived with us at Kessell Court.'

'And you are fond of her?'

'I'm very fond of her. She's the only one who loves me.'

'Your stepbrother must love you too,' I said, though certainly he had not demonstrated his love before me. 'Why else would he visit you?'

She leaned forward, a smile playing on her lips. 'You think Ralph comes here out of love? Don't be fooled, doctor. He comes here to keep an eye on me and for no other reason.'

'No, I'm sure you're wrong. After all, he had you removed to a sanatorium when he knew you to be unwell. Why would he do that if he didn't care for you?'

She shrugged. 'Guilty conscience?'

'What do you mean by that?'

She leaned back in the chair. 'Have you seen any

signs of madness in me, Dr Cowdrey? I mean, true signs and not just me losing my temper?'

I could see where she was trying to lead me, and I was anxious not to indulge her persecution mania. 'I don't think that is a pertinent question, Miss Hebron,' I said carefully.

'It's very pertinent, doctor, to me, at least. But perhaps not to people who have something to gain by my being in here.'

'Convince me,' I said, deciding that playing along with her delusion might be the best way to get her to talk. 'Tell me about your family.'

She slid her gaze to me. I saw consideration and intelligence in her eyes.

'Are you sure you want me to talk, Dr Cowdrey? You've been warned against it, and not just by my step-brother, I think.'

Miss Hebron could only have been referring to the Wakefields. Had she heard them talking about me?

'There is no harm in just talking,' I said.

'Well, if you're sure you want to hear my story.' She smoothed her hands over her skirts. 'Where shall I begin?'

20

RACHEL'S STORY

'Let's begin with your parents,' I said.

'Very well.' Miss Hebron paused to collect her thoughts. 'My mother died when I was six years old. My father died when I was fourteen.'

'Were you close to them?'

'Yes, at least I thought so. I know I was close to my mother. I have many memories of her. Aunt Bea used to say I was like her.'

'In what way?'

'Aunt Bea didn't elaborate. But I remember how she used to shake her head and say, "Just like your mother".'

'And what were you doing when she said that?'

'I expect I was being naughty.'

'Your mother was naughty?'

'It's not called naughty when you're grown up, is it? It's called spirited or daring, or something like that.'

'So, when she said, "Just like your mother", your aunt was speaking approvingly?'

Miss Hebron smiled. 'Aunt Bea never found fault with me.'

'And what of your father?'

'He never found fault with me either. We were very happy before he went away to Italy. We were always together at Kessell Court, and it was lovely then.'

'What happened in Italy?'

She drew in a deep breath. 'His doctor sent him there for his health. Said there was a problem with his chest, I think, and that he wouldn't be well if he stayed in England over winter. I remember I asked to go with him, but he wouldn't take me. He said Italy was no place for a young girl.'

'Were you upset about being left behind?'

'Not really. I love Kessell Court, you see. I miss it so very much. And I had Aunt Bea with me, of course.'

'You said you were happy before your father went to Italy. What happened to change that?'

'What happened?' she said sourly. 'He brought Lucinda back with him, that's what happened.'

'Lucinda is your stepmother,' I clarified, recalling the details of her case notes. 'You didn't like her?'

'Oh, yes,' she said, startling me with this admission so contrary to what I had expected, 'I did. That's what makes what happened later so horrid.'

'Tell me about your stepmother,' I said. 'Why was she in Italy?'

'Because she couldn't afford to live in England. Her

first husband had died and left her with practically nothing, so she said, and living in Italy was the only way she could maintain herself in a respectable manner.'

'Was Mr Hawke with her in Italy?'

'Oh, call him Ralph, won't you? And you may call me Rachel, at least while we're alone.'

I told her I would do as she asked and bade her continue.

'Ralph was at school over here, at a cheap one, apparently, all she could afford. Anyway, Lucinda managed to convince my father that she loved him and got him to marry her.'

'You don't think that your father did love her and that was why he married her?'

'He loved my mother,' she said with emphasis.

'But he may have been lonely,' I pointed out.

'Why would he be lonely?' she declared. 'He had me and Aunt Bea.'

I chose not to pursue this point. Her vehemence told me she had no comprehension that possessing a wife was very different to having a sister and daughter.

'And he brought Lucinda home to Kessell Court?'

'Yes, he brought her to our home, where she had the perfect right to sleep in my mother's bed and walk where she had walked.'

This made sense, her believing that Lucinda had been trying to replace her mother. 'But you said you liked her.'

'She fooled me, as she fooled my father. She would fuss over me, and I was her little darling, then.'

'But that changed?'

She nodded. 'As soon as little Emily came along.'

I knew who Emily was. She was Rachel's half-sister who had died in a tragic accident when she was only five years old. 'Emily died,' I said carefully.

Rachel played with her ribbons. 'Yes.'

I sensed a reluctance to talk about Emily, and I was anxious not to force her. I changed the subject. 'When did you first meet Ralph?'

'When he came home from school for the holidays. He was twelve then.'

'Did you become friends?'

She nodded. 'I liked having a brother.'

'When did that liking cease?'

'When he put me in here,' she said, thumping the arm of the settee.

'But up until then, you had been happy together?'

She didn't answer me at once. She tapped her fingers upon her knee, then said, 'I don't want to talk about Ralph at the moment.'

'Who do you want to talk about?' I asked.

'Emily. I'll talk to you about Emily.'

This was a surprise. I had been wrong earlier thinking she wasn't ready to speak of her half-sister. I waited, my pencil hovering above my notebook. I checked the clock on the mantel and saw that it was past five o'clock. I mentally urged Rachel to talk quickly, for I was eager to learn something of her feelings about Emily before the dinner bell went.

'Emily was perfect,' she said. 'The perfect little doll,

with pretty blond ringlets and bright blue eyes. Everybody loved her.' She looked up at me from beneath her eyelashes. 'Even I loved her. There, that has surprised you, hasn't it?'

'Not especially. Children are easy to love.'

'Do you have children, Dr Cowdrey?'

'No,' I said before I realised I had broken one of Dr Wakefield's rules and told an inmate a personal fact. 'But I know they are easy to love.'

'Not all of them. Some are noisy and naughty, some are ugly and dirty. But Emily was beautiful and well behaved, so yes, she was, as you put it, easy to love. That's what Lucinda never understood. She thought I hated Emily, but I didn't. Do you want to hear about the accident?'

I did, but I said, 'Only if you want to tell me.'

'It had been such a lovely day. It was Emily's birthday, her fifth. Father and Lucinda had given her their presents in the morning – a brand new white dress with a big pink ribbon around the waist, ribbons for her hair and a big doll that was almost as tall as she. Then, in the afternoon, we had a lovely tea in the garden. That was when Ralph brought out the pony.' She sniffed and held her hand up to her mouth.

'If it's too painful for you to continue,' I said, holding out my hand to her.

'No, I want to tell you.' She gave one last sniff and let her hand drop. 'Ralph wasn't with us and Emily was calling for him. She loved him so, she couldn't bear for him to be away from her. But Ralph had gone to get her last present. Huh,' she laughed bitterly, 'her last in more ways than one. I remember, we were sitting around the table on the lawn, Father, Aunt Bea, Lucinda, and me, and Lucinda pointed towards the fence at the side of the garden where there is a pathway. I couldn't quite see what she was pointing at, but Emily started waving and jumping up and down, and then I saw why. Ralph was leading a pony into the garden, a lovely chestnut pony with pink ribbons for reins. I would have loved to have had such a pony when I was five, but I was never given one. Everyone was laughing, and Emily was running backwards and forwards, so very excited.

'Father lifted Emily onto the pony's back. He shouldn't have done that, really. He wasn't strong enough to lift her, but Lucinda let him. Ralph began to lead the pony around in a circle, and Emily was holding on tight, laughing.' Her brow creased, and I saw tears in her eyes.

'The pony suddenly reared. Emily tumbled backwards over its rump and fell. She fell on her head. I heard her neck crack. And then Lucinda was screaming and Father… well, he was just staring, his mouth open, not knowing what to do. Ralph was picking Emily up and cradling her, and Aunt Bea was rushing me back into the house. Oh God, that day.' Rachel put her hand to her forehead and shook her head. 'That was really when all the trouble started.'

'What do you mean by trouble?'

'I mean that everyone suffered from that point on. Lucinda blamed everyone else for Emily's death. Ralph was shouted at for leading the pony around, Aunt Bea was to blame for having started to pour the tea when he was doing that and so distracting Lucinda, and Father…' She sniffed heavily and put her hand to her throat. 'Lucinda screamed at Father that he should never have bought the pony for Emily, that if he hadn't done that, then Emily would still be alive.'

I frowned. 'But the way you have told me this story, your stepmother was as pleased as anyone with the pony.'

'Oh, she was, that's why she was being such a hypocrite. In fact, I remember her suggesting buying the pony for Emily's birthday. Aunt Bea had shaken her head and said she didn't think that was such a good idea. "Animals have minds of their own, Lucinda," she said. "Won't it be terribly dangerous?" But Lucinda pooh-poohed Aunt Bea's concerns.'

'So, you're saying the pony was your stepmother's idea, but she blamed your father for it all the same?'

'That's exactly what I'm saying. That gives you an idea of the woman she is, doesn't it?'

There was a look of triumph in her eyes that I didn't quite like. She was becoming excited, and I decided to steer the conversation off her stepmother's hypocrisy. 'And were you in trouble, too?'

'Oh, I came in for the worst. Lucinda said I had wanted Emily to die ever since she was born and now I had my way.'

I was shocked. 'She said you had wished your half-sister dead?'

‘That’s what she said. As if I could ever wish for such a thing.’ Rachel shook her head. ‘Can you imagine what it felt like to be accused of something so monstrous?’

‘No, I cannot,’ I admitted. ‘And your father allowed your stepmother to rail at you in this way?’

‘Poor Father, he was broken by Emily’s death. He didn’t need Lucinda’s accusations, he felt enough blame of his own.’ Rachel’s jaw hardened. ‘And I will never forgive her that. She killed my father, Dr Cowdrey. Lucinda hounded him over Emily’s death, day in, day out, until my father could take no more. His heart gave out seven months after Emily died. So, I lost him too.’

‘That must have been awful for you.’

She nodded. ‘It was awful.’

Just then, the door opened and Miss Frayn entered to say dinner was about to be served and that Miss Hebron should go into the dining hall. As Rachel walked out of the door, I found myself wondering what incidents other than the one on the roof of Kessell Court had led her family to conclude that Rachel Hebron was mad.

Because to be perfectly honest, I was beginning to think she was the sanest lunatic I had so far encountered.

I talked with Rachel again the next morning in the music room. Upon reflection, I had decided it was best not to ask her to talk about the reason for her incarceration at Flete House. Instead, noting her almost dreamlike smile when she had spoken of Kessell Court, I decided to ask her about her family home.

'I have this hanging in my room,' I said, showing her the painting I had taken down from above my chest of drawers. 'It has your signature here in the right-hand corner.'

Rachel took the picture and stared at it. 'Yes, I painted that when I first came here.' She ran her fingers over the canvas.

'It's Kessell Court, isn't it?' I said. 'You must have painted it from memory. That's quite an achievement.'

'I know every stone,' she said, 'every pane of glass. I do love it so. I miss it.' She handed the painting back to me.

'It's a beautiful house. Elizabethan, isn't it?'

She nodded. 'Gervase Hebron demolished the original medieval house to build it. It took him three years.'

I examined the painting. 'Have you employed any artistic licence?' I didn't think it possible that the painting reflected true life; it was too perfect a vision.

'None at all,' she said indignantly. 'That is exactly how Kessell Court is, to the very trees and flowers.'

'It must be wonderful to possess such a place,' I said, a little wistfully, setting the painting against the leg of my chair. 'I've always lived in London and sometimes dream of a country home. Nothing as grand as Kessell Court, of course.'

'Yes, well, it would be wonderful if I were in

possession of it,' she said, and my heart sank a little as I realised the sullen, persecuted Rachel had returned.

'Your aunt has called it home all her life?'

'Yes, dear Aunt Bea has always been there. Hardly ever leaves it. I think it would be good for her to get away every now and then, to go to London perhaps, spend a little money on herself, but she won't. She's so selfless.'

'But she must be happy there.'

'I suppose,' she said, pulling at a thread on her dress. 'Even if she does have to put up with Lucinda.'

'Do they get along well together?' I ventured.

Rachel sighed as if she was bored with my questions. 'Aunt Bea gets along with everyone. It's in her nature. She doesn't argue, she doesn't complain. She just does whatever makes other people happy.'

'Some people are like that,' I said, thinking fondly of my mother.

'I suppose some people are. I'm not, in case you're wondering.'

'I've gathered that.'

Her lips pursed, as if she was trying not to smile. 'So, you do have a sarcastic streak, Dr Cowdrey. I was beginning to wonder if you were quite the prig you seemed.'

'You'd be surprised,' I said.

'Would I?' she asked, a gleam in her eyes.

Her brazen stare embarassed me and I flicked through my notes to make the moment pass. I looked up and saw her smiling at Miss Frayn who was sitting by the door. I grew annoyed as I realised both women found me amusing.

'I think that's enough for today.' I rose, knocking against my chair and making the painting fall over with a bang.

'Careful, doctor,' Rachel said as I picked it up. I had chipped the frame in my clumsiness. 'That took me hours to paint.'

'I'll return it to my wall,' I said. 'Unless you would like to hang it in your room?'

She studied me for a long moment. 'No, you can keep the picture. I have it up here,' and she tapped her right temple. 'Maybe one day I'll get to see it again.'

I left Rachel to sort through the scores on top of the piano. I returned to my bedroom, and hooked the string at the back of the painting over the nail in the wall. I set it straight and stepped back to study the picture. Rachel didn't have the artistic skill of Mrs Blake, but the painting was still very accomplished. She had captured the beauty of Kessell Court, so much so that a desire grew within me to see the original.

On my next trip home to London, I decided I would make a detour and do just that.

21

KESSELL COURT

Kessell Court lay on the outskirts of a village called Alderley, twenty or so miles from Flete. I took the train to the nearest station, then it being a pleasant day and Kessell Court not all that far, decided to walk to the house. The road to the house was lined with trees, the leaves only lately having started to grow, and it led me to the gates of the drive. I pressed my face between the iron bars to try and see the house. I could see only the corner of the building from there, and as I had no intention of presenting myself at the front door, decided that I would continue walking, hoping the road would bring me around to the rear and that the rear would be less obstructive to my view.

I was fortunate. Much like Flete House, the rear of the property was bounded by trees and no attempt to wall the land in had been made. I could walk through the trees and yet remain hidden from view. I should have felt some qualms about trespassing in this way, but

I wanted to see the house, to see the roof from where the incident that had led to Rachel's incarceration had occurred.

Looking upon the house, I could see why Rachel had such a deep affection for the place. It was beautiful with its deep red bricks contrasting with black diamonds and white stone window jambs, and the round decorative chimneys rising into the clear blue sky. A wide lawn sloped away from a paved verandah, and to the right was a low fence bordering a path that led to a series of outbuildings. If I ever left London to live in the country, Kessell Court would have been the house I would wish to own, though I knew such a place was far out of my financial reach, and always would be.

So carried away was I by such daydreams, I had not noticed I had wandered out of the trees and onto the lawn. A cry of alarm brought me back to myself, and I turned in its direction to find myself a few yards away from an elderly lady in a mop cap who had one hand pressed to her heart and was staring at me with wide, pale blue eyes.

'Forgive me,' I cried, taking a step towards her with my arm outstretched. Her eyes widened, and I halted. 'I didn't mean to startle you.'

'Who are you?' she gasped.

'My name is Felix Cowdrey. I'm a doctor at Flete House. Are you Miss Beatrice Hebron?'

'Yes, I am,' she said, surprised at my knowing her name. 'You look after Rachel?'

'She's in my care, yes. She and I were talking about

Kessell Court the other day. She spoke so fondly of it, I had a desire to see it for myself. Most impertinent of me. I realise I'm trespassing.'

'Well, yes, you are,' she said, looking back towards the house worriedly. 'But if you know Rachel, I suppose it is all right.'

'I can leave,' I offered.

Miss Beatrice shook her head. 'No, now you're here, you must come in and have tea. Dr…?'

'Cowdrey,' I reminded her. 'Are you sure? I realise you weren't expecting me and I don't want to put you out.'

'You must come into the house,' she said. 'Lucinda and Ralph aren't here and… well, I'd like to hear about Rachel.'

Was she not allowed to talk of Rachel when Mrs Hebron and her son were present? I wondered as we walked over the lawn to the house. I made favourable comments about Kessell Court as we walked, but she hardly spoke at all, listening intently to my words instead. As we reached the verandah, I looked up at the roof, trying to imagine Rachel standing up there with her friend. It was high, at least forty feet, and I was certain that anyone falling off the roof would be killed when they hit the ground.

Miss Beatrice took me through to the drawing room, ordering tea from a maid on the way. She bid me sit and waited until I was settled before taking a seat herself in a very upright armchair.

'How is Rachel, Dr Cowdrey? Is she better?'

'She's recovered from her chest complaint, yes,' I assured her. 'You could visit her at Flete House, you know, Miss Hebron. It is allowed.'

'I know it is,' she said, fiddling with her lace cuffs. 'But I don't like to. The very idea of entering a madhouse…' She shuddered.

I gave a little laugh. 'It's really not like you think. You'd be surprised by how pleasant it is.'

'Maybe, but I don't think I could. And…' she sighed, 'I'm not sure Ralph and Lucinda would like me to visit Rachel.'

'They can't stop you,' I said. 'You're Rachel's aunt.'

'Oh, they wouldn't stop me,' she hurried to say, 'not if I really wanted to. Ralph would take me there, I know, if I asked him. But they wouldn't like it, and I wouldn't want to upset them.'

I was seeing what Rachel meant by her aunt being considerate to everyone but herself. It didn't feel right that Miss Beatrice should feel so constrained, but it wasn't my place to say so. Just then, the maid arrived with the tea tray and set it down on the table beside us. The maid left and Miss Beatrice poured.

'I understand,' I said as she added milk to my cup, 'that there is some animosity between your sister-in-law in particular and Rachel. Forgive me, I realise this must sound as if I am prying, but it would help me to help Rachel if I could have your perspective on their relationship.'

She didn't like the idea of talking about Lucinda behind her back, I could tell, but she nodded and began.

'They are both such strong characters, Dr Cowdrey, that's the problem. Rachel was always used to getting her own way that when my dear brother brought Lucinda home, and he began to, quite naturally, consider her before Rachel, Rachel felt rather pushed to one side.'

'But I understand that Mrs Hebron treated Rachel very well to begin with.'

'Yes,' she said, 'that's true.'

I waited for her to continue, but when she didn't, I said, 'But then Emily came along.'

Miss Beatrice's expression grew sad. 'Poor little Emily,' she said. 'Her death broke all our hearts. And Lucinda… well, hers has never mended.'

'But Mrs Hebron did neglect Rachel from the moment of Emily's birth?' I pressed.

'She made sure Rachel had everything she needed,' Miss Beatrice said emphatically. 'Rachel was never neglected, Dr Cowdrey.'

'Not materially, perhaps. But emotionally?'

Miss Beatrice sighed. 'Rachel could be difficult. She has moods, doctor, and quite a temper. Lucinda found her rather tiresome and didn't bother to hide it.'

'So, Rachel might be justified in feeling that her stepmother didn't care for her?'

'She might,' Miss Beatrice admitted reluctantly. 'I tried to make up for Lucinda, but I'm not sure I succeeded.'

'Rachel speaks very fondly of you.'

She smiled. 'Does she? I do miss her. I go into her

bedroom sometimes and just sit for a while, remembering her in there. Nothing's been touched since she went away, you know. All her things are still up there.' She raised her eyes to the ceiling.

'Could I see her room?' I asked, thinking it might be useful.

'Oh, if you would like to. Yes, I'll take you up if you've finished your tea.'

I told her I had, and we both rose. She led me up the wide wooden staircase, the treads creaking loudly beneath our feet, and along a narrow corridor to an oak door with a black iron latch. Miss Beatrice lifted the latch and pushed the door open.

'After you,' she said.

I entered a very feminine bedroom. Floral patterned wallpaper hung on the walls and pale yellow curtains framed the diamond-leaded windows. The bed was a four poster with a canopy that matched the curtains, and was covered with a white bedspread. There was a chest of drawers and a large wardrobe on the opposite wall, a washstand in the corner and a window seat heaped with cushions. On the windowsill was a quite staggering array of objects, from books and dolls, to seashells, pine cones and the skeletons of birds. There was even a catapult such as I had had when a child sitting alongside a small bow, complete with a quarrel of arrows.

I examined the room, opening the drawers and wardrobe, peering at the paintings on the walls and reading the titles of the books. I moved to the window and looked out. The lawn was below with the verandah over to the left, and I could see the tops of the trees where I had trespassed. 'It's quite a view,' I said over my shoulder to Miss Beatrice.

She joined me at the window. 'Yes, it is lovely. Rachel would always sit here,' she indicated the window seat in front of her, 'and look out, calling down to us when we were sitting on the verandah.'

I wondered who the 'us' was, whether it included Lucinda, or just Miss Beatrice and Rachel's father. Miss Beatrice headed back towards the door. She looked a little worried at my lingering.

'Lucinda and Ralph will be back soon,' she said. 'I don't think they'd like to find us up here.'

I didn't want to cause her any trouble, so I joined her at the door, pulling it shut behind me. 'Where are they?' I asked.

'They went to visit the Polkes, our neighbours. On the way back, they will have stopped at the graveyard. Lucinda likes to put flowers on the children's graves.'

'The children's graves?' I asked. Emily was obviously one of the children, but who was the other Lucinda remembered with flowers?

'Yes, Lucinda always puts flowers on little Ned's grave when she visits Emily. He was a stable boy here.' She gave a little laugh. 'Ned idolised Ralph. Followed him around everywhere when he came home from school until Ralph grew quite irritated. Ned ate some yew berries from the tree in the churchyard. They're poisonous, as I'm sure you know, and he died. Such a pity. He was a very happy little boy.'

We were halfway down the stairs by this time when the front door opened and Miss Beatrice halted, causing me to do the same. I heard her breath catch in her throat.

Ralph Hawke and an older woman dressed in black were standing in the doorway.

'What the devil are you doing here?' Mr Hawke cried, glaring at me.

'Who is it, Ralph?' the woman, who could only be Lucinda Hebron, asked without taking her fierce eyes off me. She must have been an attractive woman in her youth, but she appeared gaunt and grey-skinned to me.

'He's the new doctor at Flete House, Mother,' he said, and stepped forward. 'Has something happened to Rachel?'

'No, nothing,' I said, hurrying down the stairs toward him, desperately trying to think up a good reason for my being at Kessell Court. To say that I had simply had a desire to see the house would sound ridiculous to a man like Ralph Hawke, I felt sure.

'Then why are you here?' he demanded.

'Dr Cowdrey was passing, Ralph,' Miss Beatrice said. 'So, he thought he would pop in.'

'Why was he upstairs?' Mrs Hebron glowered at Miss Beatrice.

Miss Beatrice quailed. 'I was showing him Rachel's room, Lucinda. He thought it might help Rachel if he could see her room and the things she had.'

'How could that be helpful?' Mr Hawke demanded scornfully.

I floundered for an answer and my delay cost me dear.

'Why are you bothering trying to help Rachel?' Mrs Hebron cried furiously, her breath coming fast as she took a determined step towards me. 'You should leave her to rot.'

Mr Hawke put his hand on her shoulder, but she shook it off. He tried again, this time murmuring, 'Mother' in her ear.

'I won't have it,' she said in a cracked voice to him. 'I won't have her back here.'

'She's not coming back,' Mr Hawke said, and he gave a warning look to Miss Beatrice, I suppose not to contradict him. 'Beatrice, take Mother through to the drawing room, will you? Don't worry, I'll see Dr Cowdrey out.'

I gave Miss Beatrice what I hoped was an understanding smile as she passed by me. Mrs Hebron cast gave me the severest of scowls as she was gently steered toward the drawing room.

'I didn't mean to upset Mrs Hebron,' I said to Mr Hawke as the drawing-room door closed.

'Then what did you mean to do?' Mr Hawke sneered. 'Why are you really here?'

'Miss Beatrice told you why.'

'I don't believe it. Just passing? We're not on the way to anywhere here. And as for looking around Rachel's bedroom because it might be helpful, that's nonsense. Dr Wakefield never felt the need to see Rachel's bedroom, and he's a far more experienced doctor than you. Are you just prying, is that it? Or did Rachel put you up to this, hoping my mother would see you, knowing it would upset her?'

'Your stepsister knows nothing of my being here,' I assured him, feeling my cheeks grow red.

Mr Hawke studied me for a long moment, his dark eyes peering into mine. Then he moved to the front door and opened it. 'Time you were on your way, Dr Cowdrey.'

I picked up my hat from the chair where the maid had placed it. 'I apologise for any distress I have caused, Mr Hawke. It wasn't my intention, I assure you.'

'Maybe not,' he said, thawing just a little, 'but my mother won't see it that way. Don't come here again.'

I nodded and said goodbye.

He closed the door behind me and I made my way down the drive, wishing I had never made the detour to Kessell Court, but that I had gone straight on to London and home.

22

DOUBT

I spent a happy two days with Clara in London, then returned to Flete House.

After breakfast on the Monday, I sought out Rachel. I had decided not to tell her of my visit to Kessell Court. She was in the dayroom with the other women, reading a magazine.

Rachel closed her magazine at my approach. 'What do you want me to talk about today, doctor?' she asked, her lips curving in a smile.

Determined to examine her feelings towards Emily, I asked her to tell me about the five years they had had together. She told me she had many stories about Emily, and began recounting a few. This continued over the following days and I noted that although Rachel spoke of Emily with some affection, her comments were always tinged with a certain bitterness as soon as she mentioned her stepmother. If she continued talking about Lucinda, Rachel grew heated and animated, and one day talked to me of a specific incident wherein she judged her stepmother to have treated her most unfairly.

The Hebrons had been invited to a neighbour's house, the Polkes, for afternoon tea. As a treat, Rachel had offered to curl Emily's hair, and the two girls had gone to the kitchen to heat the curling tongs on the kitchen range. Without supervision, and not really knowing what she was doing, Rachel said she had left the tongs too long on the range, and when she curled a great handful of Emily's golden tresses around the metal, the metal was so hot it immediately singed the hair, filling the kitchen with a dreadful smell. Lucinda had come into the kitchen to look for her daughter and caught Rachel just at the moment when the hair crisped up. Emily's beautiful head of hair had been irreversibly marred, and the singed tress hung black and brittle against the untouched blond. The only remedy was to cut off the damaged hair. An accident, so easily done, I knew from Clara's own experience with curling tongs, and yet Lucinda immediately took the attitude that Rachel had ruined her daughter's hair deliberately. She had vented her fury on the undeserving Rachel by striking her across the face. Rachel showed me the small scar beneath her left eye where one of Lucinda's rings had broken the skin.

Seeing her mother rage at Rachel had made the little Emily cry so greatly that the visit to the neighbours had to be abandoned, thereby spoiling everyone's day, something that Rachel had, according to Lucinda, wanted all along.

It did indeed seem to me that Lucinda had blown the matter out of all proportion, and this was just one of many such arguments between Rachel and her step-mother of which I learned. It was easy to understand why Rachel had come to hate her stepmother and accuse her of persecution.

During our talks, I was careful not to ask Rachel about Lucinda too often, as I didn't wish for her to become overexcited. One day I asked instead about Ralph Hawke.

'You got along well with Ralph at this time. What was your relationship like?'

'We were very good friends,' she said, 'and I would look forward to Ralph coming home to Kessell Court. Lucinda was so much nicer when he was there, and if she started on me, he would plead with her to leave me alone, and she usually did, at least when he was in the room. She would get the odd gibe in when he had gone out, of course.'

'He is quite a bit older than you,' I said. 'Did you have much in common?'

Rachel shrugged. 'Brothers and sisters don't need to have things in common. They have to get along with one another, even if they wouldn't choose their siblings as friends.'

Her words made me think of Theo. He was my brother, and I loved him, but Rachel was right. Had we not shared a bloodline, I doubted we would have been friends.

'So you were friendly right up to the time you were committed here,' I said.

'Now I think about it,' she said slowly, 'he changed before then.'

'Changed how?'

'It was when he finished school and came home for good. He was a young man then, and had no time for a girl like me. He began to take an interest in Kessell Court.'

'What sort of an interest?'

'Making improvements, repairs, managing the estate and the tenants, that sort of interest.'

Her sneering tone intrigued me. 'What was wrong with that?' I asked.

'Because he had no right to enquire into those things,' she said, staring hard at me.

'No right?' I repeated. 'But surely, it was his duty as heir—'

'Heir?' she spat the word at me, her eyebrows arching. 'Dr Cowdrey, Ralph wasn't my father's heir. Kessell Court belongs to me.'

I stared at Rachel. 'Your father made you his heir?'

She nodded, the corners of her lips turning up as she tried not to smile. 'You're surprised. You think a woman shouldn't be given a house and estate to run, don't you? You don't think a woman could manage them properly.'

'It's not that,' I protested.

'Liar,' she said, smiling at me. 'Don't worry, you're not the first to think so, and I'm sure you won't be the last. The truth is Ralph hasn't a penny to his name. He is what Lucinda would politely term 'impoverished'. She would be too had Father not left her an allowance and the right to live in my house.'

My mind was racing. 'But if he has no money, how can Ralph afford to put you in here?'

She snorted. 'Ralph can't. I pay for my imprisonment.'

'You pay?' I was incredulous.

'Father made Ralph my legal guardian, which means he has access to my money and can use it as he thinks fit.'

'But… but that's monstrous,' I spluttered.

She lowered her eyes and said nothing. I stared at her. The sheer unfairness of her situation made my blood run hot. Her own money was being used for her incarceration. It was cruel, it was unfair… Wasn't it?

I ended our interview, leaving Rachel to be watched over by Miss Frayn. I decided to take a walk in the garden when I encountered Dr Wakefield coming out of the stables.

'Dr Wakefield,' I called out to him, 'could I have a word?'

He nodded impatiently, and we walked towards one another. 'What is it? Problem?'

'About Miss Hebron,' I said.

He groaned. 'Oh really, Cowdrey, must we? I've told you not to bother with her. If she's causing you problems, it's your own fault.'

'Not at all,' I replied indignantly. 'My interviews with her have been very satisfactory, in fact. But I've just learned that she pays for her fees here. Were you aware of that?'

Dr Wakefield frowned and shrugged. 'Why should that be of interest to me? As long as the fees are paid, I don't care where the money comes from.'

'But…,' I began, struggling to know how to make him understand my concern, 'doesn't that cause a conflict of interest?'

He put his hands on his hips. 'You're going to have to explain, Cowdrey. I don't know what you're getting at.'

'I mean, if Rachel—'

'Rachel?' a woman's voice behind me cried out.

I whirled around to look into the outraged face of Mrs Wakefield.

'Who is Rachel?' she demanded.

I looked back at Dr Wakefield, who had his eyes fixed on the ground. I would receive no help from him. 'I mean, Miss Hebron,' I explained to Mrs Wakefield.

'Then you must call her Miss Hebron, Dr Cowdrey,' Mrs Wakefield declared. Her pupils were like pinpoints. Her face had gone white.

'Of course,' I said, cursing myself for my mistake. It

was just my luck she had crept up behind me as I said Rachel's name.

'It seems to me that you are forgetting your position,' she said, moving to stand by her husband. 'I will not have it, do you hear? You are her doctor, not her companion or her friend. Her doctor, sir.'

'I know that,' I said impatiently. 'But she's asked me to call her by her first name in our interviews and—'

'I don't care what she says to you,' she snarled.

'Dr Wakefield,' I pleaded.

'You must listen to Nora, Cowdrey. No good will come of talking with Rachel Hebron. Believe me.' He took her hand and led her away in the direction of the lodge.

It started to rain, and I headed back into the house. I barked at the attendants who got in my way, sending them scurrying and casting hateful looks over their shoulders at me, but I didn't care. I banged into my office, kicking the door shut behind me.

Dr Wakefield hadn't answered my question as to whether there was a conflict of interest in Ralph Hawke using Rachel's money to pay for her own incarceration. I knew that it wasn't legally wrong, but was it morally so? And there was another question going round in my head. Quite apart from the question of money and who paid for what, there was also the feeling I had and could not seem to shake off. The feeling that Rachel Hebron was not insane.

The idea that Rachel Hebron was not a lunatic kept going round in my mind.

So much of what Rachel had told me could have been lies, as I'd been warned, and I tried to view her words from this perspective. I did not care for Ralph Hawke but that didn't make him a villain. I disliked Mrs Wakefield but my dislike didn't mean that she was not right to view Rachel with suspicion. But then, why was Dr Wakefield so reluctant to discuss Rachel with me? And I had another question, seemingly unrelated to Rachel Hebron, but feeling strangely pertinent as though it was connected. Why had Dr Dennison not been in touch with the Butes?

I would have liked to discuss my worries with my father, but he was in London and busy with affairs of his own. So, late one morning, when the female patients were quiet and had no need of me, I made my way into Flete to pay a visit to the Butes.

Mrs Bute was tending her roses in the front garden when I walked up the paved pathway. 'Why Felix,' she said with a wide, welcoming smile, 'what are you doing here at this time of day?'

'I wanted to talk with your husband, Mrs Bute.'

'Oh, he's pottering in the back,' she said. 'Go around. He'll be pleased to see you. Are you staying to lunch?'

'I'd love to,' I said with enthusiasm as I retraced my steps and made my way to the garden. I knocked on the side of the wooden shed and poked my head through the open doorway.

‘Felix, my boy,’ Reverend Bute cried as he saw me. He showed me his hands, dirty with earth. ‘You’ve caught me potting. What can I do for you? No, first things first. Has Emma asked you to stay for lunch?’

‘Yes, she did, and I’ve accepted, thank you. But I wanted to ask you something, something you may not want to answer.’

He frowned at me and, reaching for a cloth, wiped the dirt from his hands. ‘That sounds ominous. Would I be breaking a confidence if I did answer you?’

‘I don’t think so,’ I said, ‘just that you might think I was prying into things I had no right to.’

‘I cannot say I approve of prying, Felix, but you may ask. Don’t be offended if I choose not to answer you, though.’

‘I won’t,’ I promised, and took a deep breath. ‘You said before that you didn’t know Dr Dennison was ill and that you would have expected him to tell you if he was.’

‘Yes, that’s right.’

‘And you haven’t heard from him since leaving Flete House?’

‘Not a word. Why are you asking?’

‘It’s been playing on my mind,’ I shrugged. ‘Is it possible that he wasn’t ill at all, but that he was made to leave Flete House?’

Reverend Bute sighed and threw the dirty cloth on the wooden bench. ‘It’s possible. As I understand it, his relationship with the Wakefields was fractious. Let us go into the house and have lunch. I think Emma may be able to tell you more than I.'

'Felix thinks there might be more to Cedric leaving Flete House than the Wakefields have admitted, Emma,' Reverend Bute said to his wife as we sat down at the dining table.

Mrs Bute looked up at me excitedly. 'What have you found out?'

'Nothing,' I said. 'It's just a feeling I have.'

'Tell him what you saw and heard that time in the church, Emma,' Reverend Bute said.

She frowned at him. 'But you said I wasn't to repeat—'

'Oh, I think we can trust Felix to be discreet, my dear.'

Mrs Bute beamed, pleased to be given permission to reveal a previously forbidden subject. 'I was in the church one afternoon, in the Lady Chapel, throwing away the dead flowers. I was quite tucked away in there, so I suppose Mrs Wakefield didn't see me when she came in. She often comes in on her own. But she had only got a little way in when she stopped and turned back to the door. She went back out, and I wondered if there was something wrong, so I went to follow her when I heard Cedric's voice.'

'That is when you should have made your presence

known, my dear,' Reverend Bute reproved her with a smile.

She shook her head at him. 'Oh, hush now. Anyway, I could hear them talking in the porch, and it, well, it sounded rather heated, so I tiptoed back to the Lady Chapel, but I could still hear them. Cedric said to Mrs Wakefield, "You can't stop me talking to her," and Mrs Wakefield said, "We pay your salary, Dr Dennison. My husband can instruct you in any way he thinks fit". So, Cedric says back, "What are you so worried I will discover?" Well, that made my ears prick up, I can tell you, and I listened hard for her reply.'

'What did she say?' I asked excitedly.

'She said, "You are a fool. I shall speak to my husband. He will know how to deal with you." And then Cedric said, and really, I can't condone him speaking to her like that, even though I know he was provoked, he said, "And he will do exactly as you tell him, Mrs Wakefield. I pity your husband being married to a woman like you."' Mrs Bute made a face of extreme disapproval. 'He shouldn't have said that.'

'Do you know what they were talking about?'

She shook her head. 'I'm afraid not. I heard Cedric's footsteps going away, and I expected Mrs Wakefield to come back into the church, but she didn't. So, I went to the door and peeked out. The conversation must have upset her and put her off coming in because she was walking towards the gate where that Danby fellow was waiting. She walked off with him back to Flete House, I think.'

‘But didn’t you ask Dr Dennison about the argument when you next saw him?’

‘Well, that’s just it, we didn’t see him again,’ Mrs Bute said. ‘He was gone without a word.’ She sighed. ‘But get on and eat your food, Felix, before it grows cold.’

I did as she told me, my mind racing.

23

SUSPICIOUS LETTERS

So Dr Dennison and Mrs Wakefield had quarrelled, and immediately after that quarrel, Dr Dennison had disappeared. That sounds melodramatic but the fact is he *had* disappeared. He had left Flete House suddenly, and his good friends the Butes had not heard from him since. They didn't think him to be the kind of man who would forget his friends, so why had he not been in touch?

I must confess, terrible thoughts entered my head. We accuse women of reading too many novels that stimulate their nerves and make them hysterical. Perhaps I was guilty of that too because I was imagining Dr Dennison locked up in one of the empty bedrooms at Flete House, at the bottom of the stream, and oh, a dozen other terrible ends for him. The truth, I tried to tell myself, was almost certainly more prosaic. He had probably found he could no longer work with the Wakefields and simply taken himself off, perhaps to go abroad and work, and that explained why he had not been in touch with the Butes. That certainly seemed more likely, and yet, I could not shake the feeling that there was more to the matter.

I returned to my office after lunch with the Butes and sat down at the desk, wondering what I should do next. I looked around my office and saw all the pictures Mrs Blake had drawn for me, the beautiful coloured drawings of birds and fish she had copied from books before I had persuaded her to go outside sitting next to the pencil sketches of the stream and garden of Flete House that had made me so happy to receive because they had been proof of my success. What a hollow victory that had proved to be.

I jumped up from my desk, pushing my chair back and making a terrible screeching sound as the legs dragged across the floor. I snatched down the drawings. When I had a good handful, I made to rip them in half, then stopped myself. These were beautiful drawings. Mrs Blake had been a poor, mentally wounded woman who had suffered so much, and yet despite all that, she had created things of such beauty. What right had I to destroy them because I had failed her?

I laid the drawings on my desk and smoothed out the creases I had made. I would not destroy them; I would treasure them instead. I looked at the bookshelves to find two heavy books that I could lay the papers between and so flatten them out. Finding two suitable books together, I carried them to my desk and lifted one off of the other. As I did so, a piece of paper fell out and floated to the floor.

I bent down to retrieve it. There was writing on the paper, and I realised with a start that it was the writing of Dr Dennison, recognising it from the case files. I hurriedly put Mrs Blake's drawings on top of the bottom book and placed the other on top. Then I resumed my seat and began to read what turned out to be a letter.

My heart began to beat faster. Dr Dennison began his letter, *Dear Mr Hawke*. It ran thus:

> Dear Mr Hawke,
>
> You will forgive me for writing to you unsolicited, but I have the care of your stepsister, Miss Rachel Hebron, and I have concerns in regard to her residency here at Flete House.
>
> I have talked with her at great length and have discovered no signs of mental illness in her. On the contrary, I have found her to be a very intelligent young woman, fully aware of her actions and their consequences, which I can inform you are not the norm amongst women troubled with a mental malady. I am aware of the reasons for her committal, the incident on the roof at Kessell Court being the catalyst, but her explanation of that event has impressed me by its soundness. It is my very great concern that Miss Hebron should not be committed to any asylum on the grounds of lunacy. I do not believe her to be lunatic, merely an impassioned young woman who has, on occasion, made errors of judgement.
>
> I am sure I need not impress upon you the very

great anguish that a sane person being forced to live amongst lunatics can cause, and I fear for her health, both physical and mental, were she to remain here without good reason. I would, therefore, suggest that Miss Hebron is re-examined by two independent doctors with no connection to either yourself or Dr Wakefield to ascertain whether she is insane or the contrary.

Yours sincerely,
Cedric Dennison (Dr)

I sank back in my chair, open-mouthed at this letter. Here, written by my predecessor, were the very thoughts that had been going through my own mind. Dr Dennison had been convinced Rachel Hebron was not mad, and he had written to Ralph Hawke to tell him so!

Had this letter actually been sent? Was this a copy I held in my hand or the original? And had it been hidden between those two books, or had it simply got lost there? Did the Wakefields know Dr Dennison had written this letter? Had this been the cause of the quarrel?

I grabbed Rachel's file, determined to reread every word it contained to see if I could spot some clue that would support me in my, and seemingly Dr Dennison's, suspicions that she should not be locked up in Flete House. I would start at the very beginning and make note of anything I deemed important or suspicious.

The first item was Ralph Hawke's letter of enquiry to Dr Wakefield. It ran thus:

Dr Wakefield,

I am writing to you in regard to my stepsister, Miss Rachel Hebron.

She has exhibited several signs of lunacy in the opinion of our doctor and has become a danger to others. It is my belief that it would be safer for my family and our neighbours if she were to be committed to the care of an establishment such as yours.

Kindly furnish me with details of the care your asylum provides and your fees.

Yours sincerely,

Ralph Hawke

There was nothing of particular note in that letter. I set it aside and moved on. Dr Wakefield had replied to Mr Hawke and there was a copy of his letter in the file.

Dear Mr Hawke,

Further to your enquiry, I have enclosed a list of our fees for your perusal.

We provide a modern approach to insanity at Flete House. Our patients are provided with their own rooms, the size and quality according to the fee paid. Male patients have the second floor, female patients the first. Rooms are locked during the night and an attendant is on watch throughout.

During the day, patients are continually supervised on the ground floor of the house where they have access to a music room and library as well as their dayrooms. Patients are also encouraged to spend time in the grounds where they benefit from fresh air and gentle exercise.

We view our patients almost as guests rather than inmates, and our clients find that their loved ones are far happier at Flete House than they have been with their families, who are often ill-equipped to deal with their madness.

I trust this reply answers any questions you have and that we can be of service to you in the care of Miss Hebron.

Your servant,

Miles Wakefield (Dr)

I could find no fault with Dr Wakefield's reply. I set it aside and came to Ralph Hawke's second letter.

Dr Wakefield,

I would like to commit my stepsister to your care, engaging your best and largest room for her use.

My doctor informs me that the written testimony of two doctors is required to confirm insanity and to have that person committed to an asylum. He is willing to sign such a testimony and suggests you as the second signatory.

Would you therefore visit us at Kessell Court to interview my stepsister for yourself and confirm her lunacy?

Yours sincerely,

Ralph Hawke

I had read this letter weeks before when I had first opened Rachel's file and nothing then had struck me. Rereading it now, I noted down several things. Firstly, that Ralph Hawke had begun his letter by confirming that he wanted Rachel to take up residence at Flete House, implying he was convinced of her lunacy. It was only in the second paragraph that he addressed the practicality of having her insanity confirmed. Surely that should have been the first item in his letter? Only once her insanity had been confirmed should he have engaged the Wakefields.

My second note was that Mr Hawke referred to the doctor as '*my* doctor'. Again, nothing particularly wrong in that, I supposed; it just seemed on this second reading a little suspect. If the doctor referred to was Mr Hawke's own physician, then it might imply the doctor had something to gain from agreeing that Rachel was insane. Before arriving at Flete House, I would never have even considered that a doctor might be so mercenary, but not now.

My third note was that Mr Hawke asked and expected Dr Wakefield to provide the second certifying signature. Surely, the second doctor should have been entirely independent, a man who had no vested interest in confirming a woman to be insane?

Dr Wakefield's reply to Ralph Hawke's second letter was missing. Perhaps he had not bothered to make a copy, but that he had replied was obvious, for the next item in the file was the Lunacy Order bearing his signature and that of a Dr Blamey, presumably the doctor of whom Ralph Hawke had written. Together, their signatures ensured that Rachel took up residence at Flete House in the best room available at a cost of two-hundred and fifty pounds per annum.

I fell back in my chair. Stop, I told myself, think. You read this file before and saw nothing amiss in it. Now, a snippet of information spoken by a certified lunatic and gossip about a quarrel is leading you to see a conspiracy to wrongfully incarcerate a perfectly sane woman so that her impoverished stepbrother and stepmother can have the use of the family home and benefit from its estate.

I closed the file and pushed away from the desk. Going to the window, I pressed my forehead against the glass, feeling the cold seep into my skin. I closed my eyes and tried to still my mind, staying that way for a minute, perhaps longer. When I opened my eyes, my breath had misted the pane, but my mind was clear.

So far, I had nothing but my own suspicions, accusations made by Rachel and a series of letters that may or may not suggest something underhand. What I needed was proof that what Rachel had implied was true, that she had been the victim of a conspiracy to rob her of her liberty, her home and her fortune.

To get the first part of that proof, I needed to go to London.

24

TURNING DETECTIVE

I travelled to London on the following Friday. I let the Wakefields assume I was simply paying a visit home, not that I was on a mission to investigate Rachel Hebron's claims.

Clara was naturally disappointed when I arrived home and told her I had come on business and, as such, could spend little time with her. Her face fell and my conscience pricked me a little, but it couldn't be helped. I couldn't take her with me. She would only ask too many questions and get in my way.

I intended to read Lawrence Hebron's will. Only then, once I had seen his last wishes set down in ink, could I tell whether Rachel had been telling me the truth or spinning me a web of lies. For though my feelings towards the Wakefields had grown decidedly cooler than they had been – not that they had ever been warm – I could not forget that they and Ralph Hawke had told me Rachel was an inveterate liar. Could they all be wrong? Or were they trying to deliberately mislead me? I had to find out for myself.

I made my way to St Paul's Cathedral. There, through the churchyard, I would find the entrance to Doctors' Commons. Many people know of Doctors' Commons as the place where marriage licences are issued, but it is also where wills are deposited in the department known as the Prerogative Office. I was familiar with the Prerogative Office through my short time at Cowdrey and Burkett, having often been despatched to view and order copies of wills for clients who wanted to contest bequests or research their family history.

It felt a little strange and oddly pleasurable to walk once more through the stone archway into the dark, dingy office. Nothing had changed. It was exactly as I remembered it with the reading stands in the middle of the room, the counter to one end where applications were made, and as usual, quite a number of people, mostly young men, no doubt sent by their employers as I had once been. I recognised none of them, which was not unsurprising after so long an absence. I did, however, recognise the clerk behind the counter. I recalled his name was Bostridge, and he was as much a fixture of the Prerogative Office as the reading stands, the musty smell and the dustmotes hanging in the air.

I joined the end of the queue at the counter, wondering if Bostridge would remember me. But there was no sign of recognition in his face as he looked up at me and called, 'Next.' I stepped up to the counter and laid my hands on the wooden board.

'I'd like to see the will of a Mr Lawrence Hebron of Kessell Court in Essex,' I said, wondering if I should acknowledge him as an old acquaintance, but deciding against it.

'Date of death?' he asked, barely looking up from his ledger.

I checked my notebook, wherein I had made a note of Lawrence Hebron's demise, and told it to Bostridge. I watched as he wrote Hebron, Lawrence, his county of residence and the date of his death, then handed this slip of paper to a clerk he called from a small room behind the counter.

'A shilling,' Bostridge said, and I deposited the requisite fee on the counter.

'I'll shout when it's ready,' he said, and before I could reply, he had looked over my shoulder and called, 'Next'. I moved out of the way and took a seat on one of the few wooden benches provided while I waited for Lawrence Hebron's will to be unearthed.

I had to wait nearly fifteen minutes before Bostridge called out 'Lawrence Hebron' to inform me the will had been retrieved. I stepped back up to the counter and took the long, vertically folded piece of paper. I took it to one of the central wooden reading stands and unfolded it. I was surprised at how short it was, only one page long, and began to read. I shall spare you all the legal jargon and cite only the main points of the will.

This is the last will and testament of me, Lawrence Hebron, of Kessel Court, Essex.

I leave the entirety of my estate, this forming Kessell Court, the grounds, farm, tenant housing and revenues, to my only living daughter, Rachel Hebron. I appoint my stepson, Mr Ralph Hawke, to be Rachel's legal guardian and to have the management of her affairs until she reaches the age of twenty-one or until she marries, whichever is the sooner.

To my beloved sister, Miss Beatrice Hebron, I bequeath the sum of £50 per annum, which she has told me is more than sufficient for her needs, and permanent residence at Kessel Court for the remainder of her life.

To my wife Lucinda, I bequeath an annual allowance of £150 to continue until her death or until she remarries.

To my stepson, Ralph Hawke, I bequeath the sum of £200.

In the event of my daughter Rachel Hebron dying before she marries, the estate in its entirety will pass to my sister, Miss Beatrice Hebron, assuming she is still alive at the time of Rachel's death. In the event of both my sister's and my daughter's decease, there being no Hebrons left, my estate is to pass to my stepson, Mr Ralph Hawke, in its entirety.

There were also several smaller bequests to servants and friends. I must confess to being surprised at the allowance given to Lucinda. It seemed rather measly, only one hundred and fifty pounds a year. I noted too that while Beatrice Hebron had been called 'beloved', no such term of endearment had been given to Lucinda. I recalled Rachel's words, that Lucinda had hounded Lawrence after Emily's death, and that might have been no exaggeration. Perhaps Lawrence had resented his wife blaming him for their little daughter's death and had had his revenge by making only a relatively small provision for her. He had been careful to provide for his spinster sister, ensuring Lucinda could not evict Beatrice from Kessell Court. A thought occurred to me. Had Rachel threatened to throw Lucinda out? Presumably as owner of Kessell Court, she would have been entitled to do that, and the treatment she had suffered at Lucinda's hands would certainly have made such a threat a possibility, I felt sure. After all, Lawrence had not made a provision in his will that Lucinda must be allowed to reside at Kessel Court as he had for Beatrice.

It seemed to me that Lawrence Hebron had done his best to protect Rachel and her financial interests, but he had not foreseen the events that would unfold after his death. He had not foreseen that he would need to protect Rachel from his stepson. For after reading Lawrence Hebron's will, I was convinced Rachel was not, as I had been assured by the Wakefields and Ralph Hawke, a wicked liar. In fact, quite the opposite.

As I returned to the counter and requested from Bostridge that a copy be made of Lawrence Hebron's will, sliding sixpence across the counter in payment, I was certain Rachel was the only person in this sorry affair telling the truth.

———

I returned to Milton Square and to my parents' house.

As I handed Jempson my hat and coat, I heard women's voices coming from the drawing room and amongst them, recognised Abigail's. A few months earlier, I would have groaned inwardly at such a sound, but Flete House had changed my feelings towards my family, even towards Abigail, so that now I rather, if not actually enjoyed, felt comforted by her company.

When I had confided this to Clara, to my surprise, she expressed the same sentiment, deducing that Abigail was much happier now Theo's career was in the ascendant. His promotion to full partner had widened their social circle considerably and had raised them in society too. Theo and Abigail were getting noticed, and this made both of them happy. I will not say that Abigail was a reformed character – Clara told me there were still occasional flashes of her old temper – but she was much pleasanter to be around. I entered the drawing room with a smile.

'Felix,' Clara said as I sat down beside her and Mother handed me a cup of tea, 'Abigail is inviting us to dinner tonight.'

I turned to Abigail. 'Just us?'

'Oh Lord, no,' Abigail said with a vigorous shake of

her head that made her pearl earrings swing. 'We've got fourteen coming. Sixteen if you come too.'

'I had no idea it was such a large party,' Clara said worriedly. 'Isn't that rather a lot for you to manage, Abi?'

It was so like Clara to find a large dinner party daunting. The most she and I had ever invited to dinner was six, and she had found that small number a great strain.

Abigail gave a slightly mocking laugh, and Clara coloured a little. 'Oh no, Clara dear. I've grown used to giving large dinner parties over the last few months. Really, you two extra will be no bother.'

She managed to make it sound as if she was doing us a great kindness by inviting us. Where I might have taken umbrage at this before I went to Flete House, I merely smiled now. I glanced up and found Clara looking at me expectantly. Perhaps she expected me to decline the invitation, but the truth was I felt so starved of agreeable company at Flete House that I welcomed this opportunity to socialise. I readily agreed and realised Clara was glad I did so. She evidently felt in need of a little entertainment, too.

Clara dressed with great care for the dinner party and she looked so very pretty in her green dress that set off her pale skin and red hair so well. This was the first time I had seen Theo since my return and he clapped me on the shoulder when we arrived at number eight and said it was good to see me. He introduced me to their guests, who were not, as I had expected, all fellow lawyers, but members of the new club Theo had joined. They were with their wives, so it was quite a jolly party. During dinner, Clara was sat at the far end of the table on Theo's right hand, and I was grateful to Abigail she had put her there. Clara would not have enjoyed being sandwiched between two complete strangers. For my part, and surprising me a little, Abigail had seated me next to her at the foot of the table. I had rather thought I was the last person she would want so close. She really had mellowed.

'Have you got a new cook?' I asked as I took a spoonful of the delicious *soup a la reine*. They had not had anything this good the last time I dined with them.

Abigail nodded. 'We had to get a new one. Our last one declared she couldn't cope with fancy dinner parties, as she called them.' She lowered her voice and leaned towards me. 'This new cook doesn't come cheap, though.'

'Well,' I said, doing the same, 'if this soup is anything to go by, I would say you've made an excellent investment.'

She smiled, pleased at my endorsement. Her gaze wandered down the table. 'Look at your wife, Felix, chattering away. She's really come out of herself lately. Time was when she wouldn't say boo to a goose.'

I looked down the table, and saw Clara deep in conversation with the gentleman beside her. He was about sixty years old, I reasoned, and affluent-looking. 'Who is she talking with?' I asked Abigail.

'That's Reginald Burnley,' she said. 'I'm glad

Clara's being nice to him. He's filthy rich and forever in the law courts. It could be very good for the business if he takes to Theo.'

'But that's not his wife, surely?' I asked, looking down my side of the table at the woman he had come with. She looked no older than Abigail.

'No, Mr Burnley's a widower. That's his daughter, Charlotte.'

'She's very pretty.'

'I suppose she is,' Abigail said, not sounding entirely convinced. 'Not that being pretty has done her any good, poor dear.'

'She's not married, you mean?' I said, understanding why she accompanied her father and not a husband. 'But if her family's wealthy, then surely, men should be queuing up to marry her?'

'Oh, she's not short of suitors. But she turns them all away.'

'I wonder why.'

'A terrible experience, if you ask me. She was engaged a few years ago, but it ended badly, by all accounts.'

'What happened?' I asked, intrigued.

'Well, it's quite a mystery,' Abigail said, her eyes twinkling. 'No one quite knows what went on at the end, from what I can gather. She was engaged to this chap, Ralph Hawke—'

'What?' I burst out. The conversations all around us stopped, and I felt the stares of everyone at the table fix on me. I smiled, embarrassed, muttered, 'Excuse me,' and they resumed their conversations. I leant closer to Abigail, who was looking at me in surprise. 'Did you say Ralph Hawke?'

'Yes. Why? Do you know him?'

'It's quite an extraordinary coincidence,' I said, shaking my head, marvelling at such serendipity. 'I met Ralph Hawke only a short while ago.'

Abigail moved her wine glass out of the way to lean even closer towards me. 'What was he like?'

I shrugged, not wanting to admit how unfriendly he had been towards me. 'I don't really know. We didn't speak at any length.'

'That's so like a man, never asking the right questions, never noticing anything.' She sighed dramatically, then frowned. 'Do you mean to say he was at your asylum?'

'He's not a patient,' I said quickly. 'He was visiting. I really can't talk about it, Abi. Client confidentiality and all that.'

'Oh, what a bore. I'm dying to know what he's like. All my friends say he must be an absolute devil.'

'Why do you say that?'

'Well, the story goes that Charlotte was absolutely dotty about him, even though he had no money and no one could understand how her father allowed her to accept his proposal. Then she went to meet his mother at the family home and something awful must have happened there because Charlotte came back early and declared the engagement was off. She refused to say why, she wouldn't even tell her father. Mr Burnley was all for going to Ralph Hawke and demanding an explanation, but Charlotte threatened to kill herself if he did, all very histrionic. And since then, she hasn't so much as looked at another man. Personally, I think he must have…' Abigail made a face, 'you know.'

I frowned. 'No, I don't know.'

'You're going to make me say it, aren't you?' she said irritably. 'Very well. I think he must have tried to force himself on her. Men can be such beasts.'

I said nothing to this. I was honestly rather shocked at Abigail's insinuation. I thought of Ralph Hawke and wondered if it could be true, if he was indeed that sort of man, if he had it within him to force himself on a lady.

After dinner, some of the party took to playing cards. I have never been fond of cards so settled instead into one of the deep settees with a glass of champagne and watched Charlotte Burnley as she played. Despite my curiosity, I had decided against trying to strike up a conversation with her. If she had resolutely refused to talk about Ralph Hawke with her father, she would certainly not do so with me, a complete stranger.

She was a very elegant woman with alabaster skin and wide blue eyes that often looked away to avoid making eye contact with her fellow card players. I thought this a little odd because I knew that being rich gives a person confidence, and according to Abi, the Burnleys had plenty. But maybe Charlotte Burnley was conscious of being the subject of gossip, and that made her nervous. I could understand that too. Or had what happened – whatever had happened – at Kessell Court left a far deeper impression on her than anyone would ever know?

Miss Burnley must have felt my eyes upon her, for she began to act very self-consciously, pressing fingers to her flushing cheeks and pawing at her pearl choker, pulling it away from her lovely long neck to reveal a small but ugly red scar. It hadn't been my intention to make her feel uncomfortable, and so I rose from the settee to find Clara, my mind racing with thoughts of Ralph Hawke and Miss Burnley, and an eagerness for the morning to come around.

For in the morning, I was hoping to meet Dr Dennison.

25

A LOST MAN FOUND

Half past ten the next morning found me on the doorstep of No. 9 Clifton Terrace in Hackney, the address that had been printed on the letter Dr Dennison had written to Mr Hawke. I had to hope Dr Dennison still lived there.

There was such a lengthy wait for my knock to be answered that I began to despair anyone was in. But then the door opened a fraction, and I saw half the face of a woman staring out at me.

'Yes?' she asked tartly.

'Good morning. My name is Felix Cowdrey. I'm looking for a Dr Cedric Dennison. I have reason to believe he lives here.'

The brown eyes narrowed. 'Are you a friend of his?'

'No, we've never met. But he once worked where I do now, and I wondered if I could have a word with him.' I grew impatient. 'Does he live here?'

'He lives here,' she said after a moment's consideration, and my pulse quickened. I had found Cedric Dennison. 'But I'm not sure if he can see you.'

'Would you be so kind as to ask if he will? Please, I really do need to speak with him.'

She looked me up and down, then said, 'Wait here,' and closed the door. A few minutes later, the door reopened, wider this time, and the lady said, 'Come in.'

'Thank you,' I said, and stepped over the threshold. The house was much smaller than mine in Milton Square and far less grand. Work needed to be done to the place — wallpaper was peeling and there were cracked tiles in the hall floor — and I wondered what financial condition Dennison must be in to have let his house deteriorate so.

'Are you Mrs Dennison?' I asked.

'Miss Dennison,' she said, putting her hand on the newel post. 'I'm Cedric's sister.'

I expected her to lead me into the back parlour, but she put her foot on the bottom step of the stairs and looked back at me. 'You'll have to forgive Cedric seeing you upstairs. He hasn't been well these past few days, and I told him he must stay in bed.'

'He's been ill?' I asked. My heart sank a little. Had the Wakefields not been lying after all?

'I wouldn't call it an illness,' she said, and I wondered at the venom in her voice.

We had reached the first floor landing, and she knocked on an open door, the rear bedroom, before pushing it open wider. She jerked her head at me to follow.

I entered and saw a single bed against the wall with a man lying in it. He had an ashen pallor and his hand shook as he held it out to me.

'Dr Dennison?' I said, shaking it gently.

He nodded and winced. 'I'm Cedric Dennison.' His sister put a chair behind me and bid me sit. 'Do you want tea?'

'No, thank you,' I said, not wanting to put his sister to any trouble. 'I wouldn't have bothered you if I'd realised you were so ill. Perhaps I had better go.'

'Please, don't. It's pleasant to have someone to talk to,' he said with a weak smile. 'It must be important. You have the look of a man who needs to know something. It's all right, Flora, you can leave us.'

Miss Dennison looked at me doubtfully, then instructed her brother not to tire himself. She closed the door behind her and I heard her footsteps on the stairs.

'She worries about me,' he said. 'Now, it's Cowdrey, isn't it?'

'Yes, Felix Cowdrey. I took over your position at Flete House.'

'Ah,' he said. 'And how are you finding it?'

'I don't like it very much,' I admitted. 'In fact, I am thinking of leaving.' I surprised myself by saying this. It had not been in my mind to leave Flete House at the present moment, but something about seeing him and being back in London had suddenly put the thought in my head.

'Best thing you could do,' he said. 'That place isn't right.'

I was pleased to hear him say this. It implied I hadn't been imagining things. 'I found a letter you wrote,' I said, 'or a copy of a letter, I'm not sure which. To a Mr Ralph Hawke.'

His tired eyes narrowed at me. 'It must have been a first draft if it's the letter I think it is.'

I delved into my jacket pocket and showed him the letter. 'A first draft,' he nodded. 'The one I actually sent had more details.'

'You thought Rachel Hebron wasn't mad, and you wanted her stepbrother to have her reassessed. Is that correct?'

'That is correct.'

'Was she reassessed?'

'Not to my knowledge,' he said with a shake of his head. 'I sent the letter, but I never received a reply. I came back to London to see Flora and never returned to Flete House.'

'Because you fell ill.'

His lips thinned into a smile. 'Because I was attacked and left for dead, Dr Cowdrey.'

'You were attacked? By whom?'

'I have no idea. I was hit on the head from behind. I went down and then I just remember being kicked repeatedly and feeling a great deal of pain. After that,' he raised his hands and waggled the fingers, 'oblivion.'

'Were you robbed?'

'No, nothing valuable was taken.'

'So, the motive was…?' I could barely dare to give voice to my newest suspicion.

'To keep me quiet?' he nodded. 'Yes, I think so.'

My fingers played with a loose thread on his blanket. 'Who…' I licked my dry lips, 'who wanted to keep you quiet?'

'Dr Cowdrey—'

'Felix, please.'

'Felix, all I can say is, both the Wakefields and Mr Hawke had a vested interest in stopping me. I didn't tell the Wakefields about my letter to Mr Hawke, but they found out about it. I can only presume Mr Hawke wrote to them rather than replying to my letter. Flora wrote to Dr Wakefield to tell him I had been attacked and couldn't return to Flete House, and he wrote back to tell me that he was sorry for my condition but that if I had returned to Flete House, he would have been compelled to dismiss me on the grounds of my improper interference in regard to Miss Hebron. The great hypocrite. He wrote that he would send on my belongings and that I was to have no further communication with anyone connected with Flete House.'

'What do you mean by calling Dr Wakefield a hypocrite?'

'Perhaps I shouldn't say…' he began, turning his head away from me to stare out of his bedroom window at a bird hopping from branch to branch on the tree outside.

'Perhaps you should,' I urged.

He turned back to me. 'Has Mrs Wakefield changed at all? Is she still very possessive of her husband?'

I frowned. 'I wouldn't say possessive. Rather

oppressive. He seems subdued when she is around. When I first met him, he was so open, so…' I searched for the right word, 'free.'

'There you have it. Dr Wakefield can't afford to upset his wife, not again.'

I sighed in irritation. 'I wish you'd stop hinting and tell me what you mean.'

Dennison laughed, then pressed a hand to his chest, wincing in pain. 'Sorry. I'll tell you the reason I call Dr Wakefield a hypocrite in accusing me of acting improperly with Rachel Hebron. When she first arrived at Flete House, Dr Wakefield took a great interest in her case. He spent a lot of time with her.' He gave me a meaningful look.

'You're not saying…?' I began, not quite able to believe he meant what I thought he meant.

'Yes,' Dennison nodded, 'he began a… well, I don't know quite what to call it. A flirtation? A liaison? You have to understand, Miss Hebron arrived at the house in a very vulnerable condition. She was frightened and alone, and when Dr Wakefield showed an interest in her, she was so desperate for a friend that she fell for him.'

'She told you this?' I asked, wondering why Rachel hadn't confided this to me.

'She did, very reluctantly. She was ashamed of herself for becoming romantically involved with a married man.'

'Forgive me, Dr Dennison—'

'Cedric,' he said with a smile.

'Cedric then, forgive me, but how do you know she

was telling you the truth? I mean, there is a woman currently at Flete House who is in there because of unbridled promiscuity—'

'She wasn't lying, Felix. Miss Hebron showed me the letters Dr Wakefield wrote to her. Love letters, little notes, wishing he could spend more time with her but that he couldn't get away from his wife, that sort of thing. She only showed me three or four, but there were many others that Mrs Wakefield had taken away and destroyed.'

'Mrs Wakefield discovered the liaison?'

Dennison nodded. 'And has been making her husband pay ever since. The money for Flete House is all hers. If he loses her, he loses everything.'

'I had no idea,' I said, sinking back into the chair. So many things about the Wakefields now made sense. 'Did you tell Ralph Hawke about this?'

'I was going to, but I never got the chance, as I've said. And judging by what happened to me, I rather came to think he wouldn't care that his sister was in danger of losing her virtue at the hands of the man supposed to be looking after her.'

'You suspect Ralph Hawke attacked you?'

'I doubt he actually wielded the weapon himself. He's a gentleman, Felix. Gentlemen don't venture into Hackney with heavy clubs to attack doctors. No, I suspect he hired someone to do the deed.'

'Dear God,' I breathed. 'He would have you silenced to keep his stepsister in Flete House?'

'To have the use of her house and fortune, yes, I

believe so. Miss Hebron told me the contents of her father's will and how greatly upset her stepmother and stepbrother were at how little they had been left. I was inclined to doubt Miss Hebron's accusations at first. I agreed with Dr Wakefield that persecution manias are common amongst committed lunatics. But when I failed to observe any signs of lunacy in her, I started to believe in her assertions.'

'I've read her father's will,' I said. 'It certainly doesn't favour her stepfamily. And I found out about Ralph Hawke's former fiancée, Miss Charlotte Burnley. She broke the engagement off after a visit to Kessell Court and all the society gossip points towards Mr Hawke having done something terrible. In view of what you're saying, I can now entirely believe it.'

Dr Dennison's eyebrows rose. 'You have been busy. So, you don't think Miss Hebron is mad, either?'

'No, I don't, especially not after what you've told me.'

He nodded. 'Tell me, do the Wakefields know you have come to see me?'

'I haven't breathed a word to them. I thought it best not to.'

'Then you've been cleverer than me. I told Dr Wakefield my concerns about Miss Hebron and I got told in no uncertain terms to leave well alone.'

'By Dr Wakefield?'

'By the dreadful Leonora.'

I remembered what Mrs Bute told me. 'You argued with Mrs Wakefield outside the church?'

He frowned. 'How the devil do you know that?'

'Mrs Bute overheard you. I've become very friendly with them.'

Dennison groaned. 'Oh, yes, the Butes. I've neglected them terribly. How are they?'

'They're very well. Concerned about you, though.'

'Yes, I haven't written. That's very remiss of me. Would you convey my apologies to them? Explain my situation?'

'Of course, and they will understand. Would you like them to visit you?'

'If they would like to, they would be very welcome.'

'I'll tell them.' I looked him up and down. 'What exactly is wrong with you?' I asked, thinking I could perhaps help.

'I haven't been right since the attack,' he said wearily. 'My ribs were broken, and the brute cracked my skull. The blow must have caused permanent damage there.' He pointed to the back of his head. 'I get terrible headaches. When I get them, I can't do anything. I get dizzy, I can't focus. Poor Flora. She has to look after me, and with so little money, that isn't easy. I really must get better soon for her sake.'

'Ralph Hawke must be made to answer for this,' I said through gritted teeth. 'He can't be allowed to get away with it. And I must see Rachel freed from Flete House.'

'Then you will need strong evidence. Have you any?'

'I have a copy of Laurence Hebron's will. I also

have your medical opinion that supports mine and the draft of your letter to Ralph Hawke. I have my own notes and opinion of her sanity as a doctor. At the very least, if I raise doubts about the validity of the original Lunacy Order assessment, then a new assessment must be made. Although I don't feel it's the act of a gentleman, I could also imply impropriety on the part of Dr Wakefield. If I have to, I will. His letters to Miss Hebron would be useful evidence. Does she still have them?'

'No,' he shook his head, 'she gave what she had left to me, and I kept them in my bedroom at Flete House. They must still be there, unless Mrs Wakefield has discovered them.'

'You hid them?'

'On top of the wardrobe, at the very back. I didn't have a chance to retrieve them. Take a look, they may still be there.'

'I will. Thank you.' I rose and lifted the chair to put it back from where Miss Dennison had moved it.

'Felix,' Dennison said, 'are you married?'

'Yes.'

'Then, for your wife's sake, be careful. I wouldn't want you to end up like this.'

I thanked him and left the room. I think he had already fallen asleep by the time I closed the door. I stepped as quietly as I could down the stairs. Miss Dennison was waiting for me at the bottom.

'He's sleeping,' I said, and moved past her to the front door.

‘Why are you here?’ she asked. ‘I don’t want him worried any more than he has been.’

‘I don’t want to bother him either,’ I assured her. ‘I just needed something confirmed and he’s done that. I shouldn’t need to come here again.’

‘I wish Cedric had never gone to that wretched place,’ she said. ‘He thought it was going to be good for his career. He had hopes of being a great alienist. Now see what that place has done to him. My brother is probably crippled for life, did he tell you that?’

I nodded as I stepped out onto the front step. ‘He thinks there is permanent damage to his head.’

‘That place has ruined his life.’ She was close to tears. ‘My advice is to leave it before it does the same to you.’

I went home to tell Clara I had to return at once to Flete House. I was desperate to find the letters Dr Wakefield wrote to Rachel and now I knew of their existence, I had the absurd notion that I had better get to them quickly before Mrs Wakefield. Stupid, I know, to imagine that she would suddenly think to look on top of my wardrobe after all this time, but that was how my mind was working.

I took the train straight back to Flete House, arriving very late and rousing Danby from his sleep to unlock the gates for me. I had grown used to his surly manner and made no attempt to thank him or apologise for disturbing his rest.

I headed on up to the house and made straight for my bedroom. I threw my coat and hat down on the bed, then placed the chair by the wardrobe and climbed on to it. Peeking above the top of the wardrobe, I could see a small packet of papers tied up with string beneath the bag I had thrown there on my first day. I reached for the packet, my fingers feeling dust on the paper, and tugged it free from the bag. I climbed down from the chair.

Ripping off the string that held the letters together, I sank onto my bed and began unfolding the papers, laying them side by side on the counterpane. Some were just one line, others were a paragraph or more, but they were all in Dr Wakefield's hand. I took up the first one.

> My darling Rachel, forgive me for not having had time for you today. The new patients have kept me so very busy. Tomorrow, I promise we shall be together. Miles.

So, it was true. Dr Wakefield had indulged himself in a love affair with Rachel. Sickened, I carried on reading.

> Rachel, you must be patient with me. I do what I can.

I had no idea what this short note might refer to, but the next one was clear enough.

My wife suspects. Be discreet, I beg you.

The next ran thus:

My dearest, darling Rachel. I know this is difficult for you, it is for me as well. But you must understand my position. If I leave Leonora, I have nothing. We must enjoy what we have and not wish for more. Please, do not make trouble for me.

I had read enough. I gathered up the notes and strode out of my bedroom, clattering down the stairs to the women's floor. Harriet Frayn rose from her station on the landing at my approach. I had acknowledged her on my way to my bedroom and she seemed surprised to see me again.

'Something the matter, Dr Cowdrey?' she asked.

'I want to see Miss Hebron,' I said.

'All the women have gone to bed,' she protested.

'I know the damn time,' I said, my voice rising a little, then realised I shouldn't be making such a noise and put fingers to my mouth. 'I know she will be in bed but I must see her at once.'

Miss Frayn stared at me from behind her tinted spectacles for a long moment, then reached for the keys on her desk, holding them tight so they wouldn't jangle. I followed her to room three and waited, jiggling on the balls of my toes in my impatience.

The door swung open, and I stepped inside. Rachel was in bed, and she roused herself sleepily, pushing herself up on one elbow. She wore no nightcap and her hair hung unbound around her face.

'Forgive me,' I said as Miss Frayn lit the candle on the bedside table from a box of matches she kept in her apron, 'but I have to talk to you about something.'

Rachel leant back against the pillows. She smoothed her hair, sighed heavily, and asked, 'What?'

I glanced at Miss Frayn. 'You can go.'

'That wouldn't be proper, sir,' she said. 'Miss Hebron is in her nightgown and you here, in her bedroom—'

'Yes, you're right,' I said, suddenly realising what a suspicious position I had put myself in. Dr Dennison had accused Dr Wakefield of impropriety; bursting into Rachel's bedroom in the middle of the night was hardly less improper. 'Please, don't be frightened,' I pleaded. 'Of course, Miss Frayn must stay.' I showed Rachel the packet of letters. 'Do you recognise these?'

She looked at them warily. 'I think I do. Where did you get them?'

'I found them where Dr Dennison told me I would.'

She swallowed. 'You've met with Dr Dennison?'

'I have, and he told me...' I dropped my gaze from hers and shook my head, embarrassed to have to speak of such matters. 'He told me of what happened between you and Dr Wakefield.'

'He shouldn't have done that,' Rachel said, drawing her knees up to her chest and wrapping her arms around them.

'He had good reason to tell me,' I assured her.

Her breath was coming fast. 'Dr Wakefield told me he loved me, but he lied. He didn't love me at all. Oh, what must you think of me?'

'The sin was Dr Wakefield's. He must bear all the blame for the way he took advantage of you.' Rachel's chin began to wobble. I didn't want to make her cry, so I hurried on. 'I have evidence that you are wrongfully incarcerated, at least, I believe I can raise enough doubt to insist on a reassessment of your mental state.' I saw disbelief in her eyes. 'You are not mad, Rachel,' I said, leaning forward and gripping her wrist. 'I have become convinced of that, just as Dr Dennison was. I have seen your father's will, I know how little money Ralph Hawke has, and how useful Kessell Court is to him. I know he mistreated his fiancée, Miss Charlotte Burnley, so much so that she broke off her engagement. And if I can contact Miss Polke, I am sure her testimony that the incident on the roof was a misunderstanding will be invaluable in securing your release.'

Rachel glanced at Miss Frayn, who had stepped nearer to the bed as I had taken hold of her wrist. Seeing her, I released Rachel, but she still hovered near.

'Do you really think so?' Rachel asked hopefully, grabbing my hand as I drew it away.

'I do,' I assured her.

'But her parents will not let you see Felicity,' she cried despairingly. 'She is not even allowed to write to me here.'

'There must be some way,' I insisted.

'Perhaps,' she said as she gestured irritably at Miss Frayn to step away, 'you could ask Aunt Bea to ask her.'

'Yes,' I said excitedly, 'I could.'

'Then write to Aunt Bea,' Rachel said. 'Ask her to make contact with Felicity and for Felicity to write down her testimony. Would a written testimony be sufficient?'

'I'm sure it would,' I nodded. 'I shall write to your aunt first thing in the morning.'

'Don't tell her why you want Felicity's testimony,' Rachel said as I made to go.

'Why not?'

Rachel sighed. 'I love Aunt Bea dearly, Dr Cowdrey, but she is not discreet. She will talk of it to my step-mother or to Ralph and then…', she shrugged help-lessly, 'your hopes for me will all come to nothing.'

She was right. I could picture the scene. Miss Beat-rice receiving my letter while the family was at break-fast, Mrs Hebron asking casually who the letter was from, and Miss Beatrice, incapable of telling a lie, telling her it was from me and what I was asking of her.

'I'll tell her it's for my case notes,' I agreed. I put my hand on the door knob and looked back at Rachel. 'You will be freed from here, Rachel. You have my promise.'

I left the room, waiting in the hall while Miss Frayn closed and locked the door. 'I must ask a favour of you, Miss Frayn,' I said quietly to her as we walked back to her station on the landing.

'What, doctor?' she said, tucking the keys away beneath her apron.

'I think you have grown fond of Miss Hebron and would not wish to do anything that may thwart our hopes. I ask that you speak of what has just happened to no one. It must be a secret.'

'I won't say a word to anyone,' she said with a determined nod. 'Besides, I won't be here.'

'You won't?' I asked, worried she was planning on leaving me without a confederate to watch over Rachel.

'I've got to go 'ome for a few days. Me sister ain't well and she needs me to help out with the little ones.'

'I see,' I said.

'Don't worry,' she said, seeing my concern, 'Miss Hebron will be all right. She's got you to keep an eye on 'er.'

I smiled a little uncertainly and bid her goodnight.

I climbed into my cold bed that night, tired in body but wide awake in my mind as I kept going over and over the huge step I would be taking in the morning when I wrote to Miss Beatrice Hebron. Once I had sent that letter, I knew there would be no turning back.

26

A LETTER AND A TESTIMONY

I wrote to Miss Beatrice Hebron the next morning, and received a reply with an enclosure five days later.

Miss Beatrice said I had timed my request well, for Felicity Polke had been visiting friends in Dorset for the past month or so and had only just returned home. She had paid a visit to Felicity at the Polke family home and managed to see the girl alone. Felicity had been very pleased by my request and wrote the testimony I asked for that very day. Miss Beatrice hoped it would prove useful in my study of Rachel and I cringed at the deception I was playing upon this kind old lady, but hoped she would forgive me if I managed to free her niece.

I opened Felicity's testimony with eagerness. This is what she had written.

> My family and I had been invited to take tea with our neighbours, the Hebrons. The day being very pleasant, we had tea on the lawn at Kessell Court. At

length, the conversation turned to the subject of artists who painted landscapes and how they decided upon which particular view to paint. This led Rachel to comment that she believed Kessell Court to have the most beautiful views in all the world. This remark was laughed at by both my parents and Mrs Hebron and Mr Hawke, who declared that while the gardens of Kessell Court were very fine, they could hardly provide inspiration for a painter. Rachel, a little put out, for she has a great love for her family home, stated that she did not mean the garden in which we sat but the view beyond which could only be seen from the rooftop. I knew, as we all knew, that Rachel enjoyed walking on the leads of Kessell Court and was therefore qualified to make this assertion. Our families grew tired of this subject of conversation and fell to talking of other matters. But I was intrigued and asked Rachel to show me the view she thought so very beautiful.

Agreeing, we left our families in the garden and made our way into the house. Rachel led me up a narrow staircase that took us to the roof and there we looked out. It was indeed a very beautiful prospect, and I told Rachel I wholeheartedly agreed with her assessment. So taken was I with the view that I may have strayed closer to the edge of the roof than was sensible. I cannot truly say. All I can say is that I suddenly heard my mother screaming at me from below in the garden and that the whole party had been roused. My mother's screaming, my father's shouting, and the others alarmed cries confused me greatly, and I looked back at Rachel to see if she could comprehend what had so exercised them. She stepped forward and grabbed my arm to stop me from putting myself in yet greater danger, and it was this action that was so horribly misunderstood by the spectators in the garden. They saw her grab me and somehow came to the conclusion that she was trying to push me off the roof when the opposite was true.

What happened next is something of a blur to me. Mr Ralph Hawke burst out of the door behind us and took hold of me, dragging me away from the edge of the roof. He shouted at Rachel, but I could not tell you what he said. I was struggling furiously with him, for he was holding me most brutally. He dragged me down the stairs and out into the garden, where my mother shook me and screamed in my face. I was bewildered by their manner. I had, as far as I was concerned, done nothing wrong. Rachel had followed Mr Hawke and I, and my mother suddenly released me and struck Rachel across the face, accusing her of trying to kill me!

I do not wish to recall what happened over the course of the next hour or so, but suffice to say, my parents levelled extremely unfair accusations against my dear friend Rachel. She was given no chance to explain what we had been doing. Dr Cowdrey, she was not listened to. She had no friend on that day but myself and her aunt, Miss Beatrice, who did her best, I believe, to calm Mrs Hebron. It pains me greatly that it was my foolish, unconsidered action that led to my parents wanting to prosecute Rachel for attempting to kill me (the very idea is ludicrous!) and settling instead for her being committed to a lunatic asylum on the basis that Mrs Hebron and Mr Hawke could not bear to have their family name dragged through the criminal court. What abuses are allowed to be practised so families can avoid a scandal, Dr Cowdrey?

My parents would not listen to my impassioned assurances that Rachel had not meant me any harm. I could do nothing to free my dear friend. If you are helping Rachel, in whatever way that may be, then you have my eternal gratitude, Dr Cowdrey. She has not deserved the treatment she has been forced to endure. Please, do all you can for her.

Yours, most gratefully,

Felicity Polke (Miss)

This was exactly what I needed. I rushed to show Rachel, and watched as she read her friend's testimony, her lips curling up in a smile. When she had finished, she handed the pages back to me.

'I told you I wasn't guilty of trying to kill her, didn't I? Is it enough to free me?' she asked as I refolded Felicity's letter and put it inside my leather folder.

'It's enough for me to write to the Lunacy Commission and demand a review of your case. And then…' I shrugged, 'we can but hope, Rachel.'

'Then please go and write that letter to the Lunacy

Commission,' she cried, waving me away. 'I don't want to stay here a day longer than I have to.'

I took hold of her hand and squeezed it, then rushed off to my office to do as she bid me. Miss Frayn had returned from helping her sister during her illness, and when I had finished, I put the letter in her hand, telling her to post it with all haste and to tell no one.

27

A VIOLENT CONFRONTATION

A week later, I was summoned to Dr Wakefield's office. I knocked and entered to find him standing at his window, staring out at the garden. Mrs Wakefield was by his side, glaring at me.

'He's here,' she said quietly as I closed the door behind me.

Dr Wakefield turned to me. 'You've written to the Lunacy Commission,' he said.

For all of the last week I had been walking on eggshells, waiting for a reply and worrying that something would go wrong. That the Wakefields would hear of my letter before I did had not occurred to me. But I would not falter now. I raised my chin.

'Yes, I have,' I said defiantly.

His balled fist hit the back of his desk chair, making Mrs Wakefield jump. 'Explain to me, Cowdrey, how you have the gall to write to them without consulting me first? Explain to me how you have the sheer audacity to think you have the right to do such a thing?'

His voice had risen with each word. I had never seen him so angry. I knew there was no way back from this – my employment at Flete House was over. I had nothing to lose now.

'Because if I had told you what I was doing, you would have taken steps to make sure I wasn't able to send my letter,' I said, hoping they would not hear the tremble in my voice.

'You bastard,' he breathed savagely, and I saw Mrs Wakefield reach up to squeeze his arm. A check on his profanity or his anger? I couldn't tell which. 'I gave you a position, I've taken you in, you've eaten at our table, and this is how you treat us?'

'I didn't write to the Lunacy Commission lightly,' I said. 'I made the decision after discovering very unsettling matters that led me to question the validity of Rachel Hebron's incarceration here.'

'What matters?' he scoffed.

I had my answers ready. I held up my hand and checked them off on my fingers.

'Firstly, my own opinion that Rachel Hebron is no lunatic.'

'She is, she is,' Mrs Wakefield screeched, leaning over the desk towards me. Her husband pulled her back and whispered something in her ear. Her chest was heaving and veins were standing out on her neck.

'Secondly,' I continued, 'the fact that the incident which led to her being examined as a potential lunatic was woefully misunderstood, confirmed by written testimony of Miss Felicity Polke.

'Thirdly, that you were one of the two doctors to confirm her lunacy when the second signatory should have been someone who would not gain financially by saying she was mad.

'Fourthly, the suspicion that there was collusion between you and Mr Ralph Hawke to ensure Miss Hebron was confirmed mad and her incarceration here.

'Fifthly, the fact that Dr Dennison was dismissed from his position when he challenged the validity of Miss Hebron's alleged insanity and the subsequent vicious attack on his person that means he will probably be an invalid for the remainder of his life.

'And sixthly and lastly, the fact that on numerous occasions, you have highlighted the importance of not trying to cure the patients because that would mean they would return to their homes and you would lose their fees. All of this led me to conclude that at the very least, Rachel Hebron's lunacy should be examined to make sure it is the correct diagnosis, or what I suspect will happen, the Lunacy Commission will reach the same conclusion that Dr Dennison, Felicity Polke and I have reached, that Rachel Hebron is not mad.'

I stopped to catch my breath. Neither of the Wakefields said anything. Dr Wakefield stared at me in disbelief. Mrs Wakefield was desperately trying to control her anger.

'Cowdrey,' Dr Wakefield said at last, 'I knew

nothing of Dennison's attack. I had nothing to do with it, if that's what you're implying.'

'I'm not saying you attacked him, Dr Wakefield. But I am saying you warned Mr Hawke that Dr Dennison was planning to take the same action that I have taken and Mr Hawke made sure he was never able to do so.'

'Oh, for God's sake, now you're accusing Ralph Hawke of attacking him?' Dr Wakefield threw up his hands. 'What else, Felix? Are you going to say Nora did it next?'

'No, of course not. But if anyone takes the trouble to investigate, they will find a clear line between Dr Dennison wanting to free Rachel Hebron and the attack that nearly killed him.'

'Why? Why would Ralph Hawke want his stepsister in here if she wasn't mad?'

'Because he stands to gain substantially by keeping her locked up. He is her guardian and has control of her estate and fortune. If she were free, she might marry, and he would lose everything.'

'Oh, you're making this up,' Dr Wakefield cried.

'I've seen Lawrence Hebron's will,' I said calmly. 'I know how little Ralph Hawke and his mother were left.'

Dr Wakefield opened his mouth to speak, but could find nothing to say. He looked to his wife for help. She was trembling, her hands balled at her side. She didn't look at me when she spoke.

'That Jezebel has fooled you just as she fooled Cedric Dennison,' she said in a voice that chilled my blood. She turned her face towards me and I saw such hatred in her eyes. 'But you are the biggest fool of all. She has spun you a pack of lies and you have believed every one of them. She manipulates men, Dr Cowdrey. She flutters her eyelashes and she gains their sympathy and they fall for her. I've seen it. '

I was not going to put up with such an insulting accusation. Rachel had not beguiled me, nor made any attempt to do so. I had refrained from mentioning Dr Wakefield's impropriety out of respect for his wife's feelings, but if she was going to call me a fool, then I was not going to spare her.

'I know you've seen it,' I said, 'and I also know how you dealt with it.' I slid my hand inside my jacket and retrieved the letters I had found on top of the wardrobe. 'You missed these when you stole the others from Rachel.'

'What do you have there?' Dr Wakefield demanded, eyeing them warily.

'Your love letters, sir,' I said, holding up the bundle, 'to Rachel.'

'Oh God,' he cried, and drew his hand over his face. He turned back to the window. I saw his shoulders slump, a man defeated.

Before I knew it, Mrs Wakefield was screaming and running towards me, her arms outstretched, her fingers crooked like claws. She threw herself at me, trying to tear the bundle of letters from my hand. She was like a mad thing. I felt her nails rake down my cheek. I knew I had to retain possession of the letters at all costs – they were evidence I might need – and stuffed them back inside my jacket, allowing her to strike me again and again.

Then the blows stopped and I heard Dr Wakefield shouting, 'Nora, stop, stop,' and I opened my eyes to see his arms around her waist, dragging her away from me. She was still screaming. I heard footsteps in the hall outside and the door burst open. Two male attendants rushed in, drawn by the tumult. They stared at the writhing figure of Mrs Wakefield in astonishment.

'It's all right,' I said, waving at them to leave the room. 'It's under control.'

'You're bleeding, sir,' one of them said.

I put my fingers to my cheek and they came away red. 'I'll see to it. Thank you, but you can go.'

They hesitated, but then they backed out of the room and closed the door. I turned to Dr Wakefield. He was managing to calm his wife down, making soothing noises in her ear but still holding her tight, her arms pinned to her sides.

'What can I do?' I said.

'Get some brandy,' he said. 'In my desk drawer.'

I pulled open the drawer and took out the bottle of brandy. I poured a large measure. Dr Wakefield pushed his wife down onto a chair and held out his hand for the glass. I put it into his hand and he bent over her, putting the rim to her lips and telling her to drink. She obeyed him, her face screwing up at the taste. I'd never seen her drink alcohol before.

'I didn't know she would react like this,' I said.

'Didn't care, did you?' he said, turning to me but

keeping one hand on her shoulder as if worried she would jump up again. 'What did you think she would do when you waved those letters around?'

'Not this,' I said angrily, gesturing at my wounded cheek.

He sighed and told his wife to finish all of the brandy. He watched her as she did so, then she handed him the glass and leaned back in the seat, resting her head on the back. She seemed to have exhausted herself with her attack on me and had no energy left.

'Cowdrey,' Dr Wakefield said, moving towards me and speaking quietly, 'I know I acted like a fool with Rachel. It was a madness, a flirtation.' He came even closer and spoke close to my ear. 'You know what my marriage is like. You've seen it. Can you really blame me for forgetting myself?'

'Yes, I can,' I said. 'You were a married man and she was in your care. Two very good reasons why you should have restrained yourself.'

He sighed. 'Yes, all right. You're a better man than me. But Nora's right too. Rachel *has* fooled you. She is as mad as any of the women in here. She just hides it well, that's all.'

I shook my head. 'All the evidence I have gathered points to the contrary.'

I had said all I needed to and wanted to tend to my wounds. I headed for the door.

'You're going to ruin me if you do this, Cowdrey,' Dr Wakefield called after me. 'But not only that, you're going to ruin yourself. No one's going to give you a job when what you've done here gets out. And it will get out, make no mistake. The only doctoring position you'll get is tending the poor in the darkest corner of east London, dealing with whores and criminals, contracting filthy diseases and never getting a penny for your trouble. Is that what you want?'

I didn't answer him. I went out and closed the door behind me, wondering gloomily if Dr Wakefield had just prophesied my future.

28

LEAVING FLETE HOUSE

I returned to my office and tended to the scratches on my face. Mrs Wakefield had cut deep, and the wounds stung as I cleaned them. I wondered if they would leave a scar, then wondered how I was going to explain their presence to Clara when I arrived home with a scratched face.

I glanced at my desk and saw that there was a pile of letters on it. I quickly sorted through them and found the one I was most interested in, the one that seemed likely to be from the Lunacy Commission. I ripped open the envelope and pulled out the letter, reading it quickly. The Commission had agreed to conduct a review of Rachel Hebron and had set a date two weeks hence, the review to be held in the parish hall of Reverend Bute's church. I was instructed to appear to give testimony, as was Dr Wakefield, they having written to him separately, and I assumed this was how he had discovered what I had done. In the meantime, the Lunacy Commission would despatch an independent doctor to conduct an examination of Rachel.

I had achieved my goal. Rachel was to be re-examined, and I had no doubt the independent doctor would find her to be sane.

I left my office and went upstairs to my bedroom. There, I packed my two bags and went down to the hall, placing them by the door. I couldn't leave without telling Rachel what had happened. I found her in the music room.

'Dr Cowdrey,' she said, 'what is going on? What was all that shouting? The attendants are gossipping that you've had a quarrel with the Wakefields. Dear God, what has happened to your face?'

I waved her questions aside. 'I have good news, Rachel. The Lunacy Commission is going to review your case. I've had the letter confirming it.'

Her hands went to her mouth. 'Oh, but that's wonderful, Dr Cowdrey. I will be free.'

'We must hope so. Now, Rachel, I wanted to see you before I left.'

Her face fell. 'You're leaving?'

'It is not possible for me to stay.'

Although Dr Wakefield had not officially dismissed me, I could not believe he would allow me to remain. I wanted to be spared the ignominy of being thrown out of Flete House by leaving now of my own volition.

'I see,' she said, and I saw worry enter her expression.

'Rachel—' I began.

'They will punish me when you're gone,' she said, her eyes wide and frightened.

'No, they won't,' I assured her, hoping I spoke the truth. 'Not if they have any sense. They realise it's over. They won't do anything to you that will make matters worse for them.'

'Do you promise?'

'I promise,' I said.

She nodded, satisfied. 'What of Ralph and Lucinda?' she asked.

'They can do nothing to stop you being re-examined. I expect Dr Wakefield will inform them of what I have done, as will the Lunacy Commission. It is likely they will refute all the evidence I have gathered.'

'You mean they will insist I am mad.'

'Most likely,' I admitted. 'You must be prepared for that.'

She sighed heavily. 'Thank you for helping me, Dr Cowdrey. I don't know how I will ever be able to repay you.'

It occurred to me that I might very well need her help when all this was over if Dr Wakefield's words were to come true, but now was not the time to say so.

'I must go now. But I will see you soon,' I promised, and left her playing Bach in the music room.

I walked out of the Flete House gates, ignoring Danby's querying eyes at my bags, and made my way into the village.

I didn't want to leave Flete without telling the Butes I was going. I knocked on the vicarage door and asked if the Butes were at home. At this hour of the day, I thought it unlikely, and I was proved right. Both the Butes were paying calls in the village. The maid asked if I would like to wait as she knew they would be home for lunch, and I said I would. I settled down into an armchair in the sitting room and took out one of the reverend's books to pass the time.

I think almost an hour passed before I heard the Butes' voices in the hall. I closed the book which I hadn't really been reading, and rose to greet them.

The door opened. 'Felix, my dear fellow, what are you doing here?' Reverend Bute asked, his eyes moving to my wounded cheek. 'Dear me—'

Mrs Bute peered over her husband's shoulder. 'What's happened to your face?' she cried, cutting him off. 'Felix, what's wrong?'

'I've left Flete House,' I said.

Mrs Bute took my hand and guided me back into the armchair. She took a seat opposite, and Reverend Bute took the seat by her. They stared at me intently.

'This is very sudden, Felix,' Mrs Bute said. 'Has there been some upset?'

I swallowed. 'You remember I told you I had found Cedric Dennison. Well, I didn't tell you everything he told me because, well, it was confidential, I suppose.'

'You mustn't tell us anything that could compromise you, Felix,' Reverend Bute said sternly.

'Oh, I'm beyond that,' I said, laughing hollowly. 'Dr Dennison had concerns about a patient at Flete House, the same concerns, it turned out, that I have had. I believe a woman at Flete House has been committed there as part of a conspiracy to rob her of her inheritance.' I looked at them searchingly. 'Well, is it as ridiculous as it sounds?'

The Butes looked at each other. 'Cedric thought the same?' Reverend Bute asked carefully.

'He did,' I confirmed, 'and he acted on it, and he was beaten to within an inch of his life as a consequence. He told the parties involved what he thought, you see, and they didn't like that.'

Reverend Bute blew out a puff of air. 'I've heard about such cases of wrongful incarceration but I never thought to have such a case on my own doorstep.'

'Mrs Wakefield and her piety,' Mrs Bute scoffed. 'I always knew there was something unpleasant about that woman.'

'You liked Dr Wakefield, though, my dear,' Reverend Bute reminded her. He looked at me and smiled. 'But then, it seems many women do like that fellow. He's very handsome and very charming.'

I thought of how Dr Wakefield had charmed me that day at Sadlers, and could only agree.

'Handsome is as handsome does,' Mrs Bute said knowingly. 'But tell us, Felix, what happened this morning and why your face is scratched.'

I told them everything, my writing to the Lunacy Commission, being called in by the Wakefields to explain myself, the attack by Mrs Wakefield and my deciding to leave before they could throw me out. I gave them the unvarnished truth, exaggerating nothing so they would have a clear picture of the whole affair. When I finished, I waited for their verdict.

'You have acted very nobly, Felix,' Reverend Bute said. 'I cannot fault a step you have taken.'

'Quite right,' Mrs Bute nodded decisively.

'But I've had to leave Miss Hebron there. I promised her she would be safe, but I cannot guarantee it, can I?'

'They would be foolish to do anything to harm her or make her stay at Flete House intolerable,' Reverend Bute assured me. 'But I will look in on her and see her to ensure she is well. Will that satisfy you, Felix?'

I grabbed his hand and wrung it. 'Thank you. That will be a weight off my mind.'

'Are you going back to London?'

'Yes. I'm going home,' I said, and a warmth spread through my chest as I said those words.

'Excellent, but after lunch,' Reverend Bute declared. 'You cannot travel on an empty stomach.'

The dear Butes. They always thought a good meal was the remedy for every distress.

Clara was overjoyed to see me when I arrived at my parents' house a little after four o'clock that afternoon. We had an hour alone before Mother returned from her afternoon calls and discovered me, and another hour before my father arrived.

I told them what had happened as I had told the

Butes, and that I had instigated a review of a patient's incarceration with the relevant authority. My father asked if I had been dismissed and I replied honestly that I had decided to leave, but I could tell from his expression he knew I had only left before I could be thrown out. I studied his face, looking for any sign of disappointment in me, but I didn't think I saw any.

'So, what will happen now?' he asked.

'The Lunacy Commission has set a date for the review and I will have to return to Flete to give testimony. If we are successful, Miss Hebron will be released and can go home.'

'But what of you?' Mother asked. 'What will you do? Go back to St Eustace's?'

I glanced at my father and he answered for me. 'No, Felix doesn't want to go back there.'

'A private practice, then?' Clara suggested.

I opened my mouth to speak, my first instinct to reject that suggestion, but no words came out. Father saw my hesitation.

'Why don't we just wait and see, eh?' he said. 'Let Felix get this Lunacy Commission matter dealt with and then he can decide what he wants to do.'

'Yes, there's no rush,' Mother said encouragingly. 'I expect Felix will want to have a good, hard think about what he wants to do next. After all, he's got all this experience now.'

My parents decided it was too late to open up our house across the square, that it should be left till the next day, and we settled down to dinner and an early night. As we lay in bed, Clara pressed herself against me.

'I'm so glad you've come home, Felix. I have missed you.'

'And I've missed you,' I said, kissing her temple.

'You're not going to go away again, are you?'

'No, my love. I'm not going to leave you again. Whatever I do next, I shall do here in London.'

'Would you like to know what I think?' she asked, turning her face up to me. 'You're not going to like it.'

I smiled indulgently. 'What do you think?'

'I think that you've had a position at a hospital and didn't care for it. You've now had a position in a private institution and didn't care for that. You've never wanted a private practice.' She paused and took a deep breath. 'I wonder if you're really suited to a medical life, Felix. You don't seem to enjoy it, and I do so want you to be happy. We all do.'

It struck me as Clara settled back down into the crook of my arm that had she spoken so a year earlier, her words would have angered me a very great deal. But after all I had been through in the last few months, I couldn't be angry with Clara for voicing her doubts, for the truth was I had reached the same conclusion. I wasn't at all sure medicine was the career for me, either.

29

BACK AT FLETE

The next two weeks passed swiftly.

I enjoyed being at home, Clara and I having reopened our house and hired new servants. Unemployed as I now was, I had little to do, and so, to pass the time and to stop myself from thinking about Flete House and Rachel Hebron, I joined my father and Theo at the office, helping out with paperwork, running the occasional errand, and on one occasion, finding myself back in Doctors' Commons handing over a shilling to view a will.

But on the day before the Lunacy Commission review, I kissed Clara goodbye and boarded the train that would take me back to the village of Flete.

My stomach was full of butterflies during that train journey, not knowing what to expect during the review, but going over and over my notes to ensure that whatever the Board might ask me, I had an answer for them.

I had arranged to stay with the Butes for the night, and they greeted me warmly, and as usual, fed me very well.

The bed they gave me was soft and comfortable, but despite this, I did not sleep well. I suppose it was the importance of the next day that kept my mind awake, but I do not know what it was that caused me to dream, when I did manage to fall asleep, of the gypsy fortune teller once again. I hadn't thought about her since before my arrival at Flete House.

This time, the gypsy woman didn't speak to me or, indeed, even approach me. She was a dark figure loitering in the back of the room in which I was standing, a room that was dark and echoing, a room I did not recognise. There was another woman in the room with me, one I kept beseeching to turn and face me. I couldn't move in my dream. My feet felt stuck to the floor, and my voice was muffled, muted, so that by the time the woman did turn to me, I was trying to get her attention by shouting at her. I had thought it was Rachel Hebron standing before, but when she turned around, I was taken aback to see instead Harriet Frayn.

I awoke with a start, my skin slightly damp from perspiration, and though the morning had barely broken, I decided I didn't want to try to sleep again. I rose quietly, not wishing to disturb the Butes, and once dressed, descended the stairs to wait for the breakfast hour in the grey light of the dawn.

Unlike the coroner's inquest, the Lunacy Commission review was heard in relative private. It was not open to the public, though a significant number of villagers loitered in the grounds, knowing something important was happening and keen to find out what.

The review was set for ten o'clock, and I was not eager to meet the Wakefields while waiting for it to begin. So, I lingered as long as I could at the vicarage, leaving it until five minutes to ten before readying to leave for the church hall. At the vicarage door, I paused and looked back at the Butes, who were standing anxiously by.

'I don't suppose you would come in with me?' I asked, a little shyly.

I think Mrs Bute had been hoping I would ask. She readily agreed and nudged her husband to say yes too. He was a little reluctant, saying he didn't want to give the impression he was attending out of mere curiosity, but I made the excuse that the Butes might be asked to provide a character reference for Cedric Dennison should his testimony be questioned, and the reverend agreed, though I suspect he knew what I was really about.

Feeling stronger having the Butes at my side, we entered the parish hall. The Wakefields were already there and they gave me the meanest of looks before turning away.

I sat down, the Butes sitting on either side of me as if they thought I needed protecting, and looked around the hall. At the front were Ralph Hawke and Lucinda

Hebron. Mrs Hebron was dressed in a similar fashion to how I had seen her that day at Kessell Court, all in black, though here she had a veil covering her face. Mr Hawke was sitting with his arm around the back of her chair, his hand every now and then pressing her arm as if to reassure her. Next to him was an older man with whom he had some little conversation and who I thought might be his doctor, Mr Blamey.

My heart began to beat even faster as Mr Hawke looked around and caught sight of me. The look on his face was unforgettable, full of hatred. Mrs Bute squeezed my hand and whispered, 'Stout heart, Felix.'

I drew out my notebook and ran over the list of questions I had written down that I expected the Commission to ask me, refreshing my memory. I had written to Dr Dennsion and asked him to set down in writing his own medical opinion about Rachel, and in a separate document, his belief in the conspiracy that surrounded her. Dr Dennison had supplied me with both, dictated by him and written by his sister. I was sure my argument was good; I hadn't missed anything.

'Try not to be so nervous, Felix,' Reverend Bute said in my ear. 'I can feel your anxiety coming off you in waves.'

I rubbed my sweaty palms on my knees. 'I can't help it. This is so very important. I can't afford to get this wrong.'

'You have presented your argument. You have solid evidence. These good people,' he gestured at the men from the Lunacy Commission sitting at the long table, 'will weigh the evidence you give them and they will make their decision. The worst they can decide is that Miss Hebron is mad and should stay where she is.'

'That's not the worst,' I cried, a little too loudly, for I saw Mrs Wakefield turn towards me, her expression grim. 'If they disagree with me,' I said, lowering my voice, 'Ralph Hawke, even the Wakefields, could take me to court for slander, couldn't they?'

I must confess, this thought had been heavy on my mind, for that week Theo had taken on a slander case and had been talking a great deal about it in excruciating detail to my increasing discomfort. That it might happen to me filled me with horror.

'I doubt it will come to that,' Reverend Bute said soothingly, though I noted he didn't refute the idea altogether. 'Look, they're beginning.'

They were indeed. The chairman of the Board banged a gavel and the room fell silent. He spoke.

'This review has been called to re-examine Miss Rachel Hebron and her suitability for committal to a private lunatic asylum. This re-examination has been requested by Dr Felix Cowdrey following his belief that Miss Hebron is in fact sane and therefore should not be detained at Flete House. He bases this belief on interviews conducted with Miss Hebron and the medical opinion of his predecessor at Flete House, Dr Cedric Dennison. Dr Cowdrey has also called into question the professional conduct of Flete House's proprietor and chief medical doctor, Dr Miles Wakefield, in his relations with Miss Hebron and with her relatives.'

'An outrage!' Mrs Wakefield cried.

'Quiet, please,' the chairman said. 'We shall commence the enquiry with testimony from Dr Cowdrey.'

He called me to take a chair by the table. My legs felt unsteady as I walked towards it.

'Dr Cowdrey,' he began, 'you wrote to us to raise a concern you had that Miss Hebron has been wrongfully incarcerated in Flete House Private Lunatic Asylum and requested that her alleged lunacy be re-examined. Kindly tell this enquiry on what evidence you based your conclusion.'

I cleared my throat. 'I thought to make a study of Miss Hebron, that is to try and understand the mental affliction under which she was supposed to be suffering. To that end, I began a series of interviews with Miss Hebron during which we talked about her childhood and various incidents that had been documented in her case file. During these interviews, I failed to note any signs of madness.'

'You conferred with your employer about this?'

'I tried to, but he was reluctant to discuss Miss Hebron at all. He was always most eager to retain the status quo at Flete House. In my opinion, Dr Wakefield has always been overly concerned with the fees paid by the patients' relatives to care for them at Flete House. He was very insistent that I should not try to cure any of the patients in case they would be able to leave, and so lose their fees.'

'You claim Dr Wakefield put profit before his duty as a medical doctor?'

I nodded. 'It certainly seemed so to me. It is my belief that the foremost duty of a doctor is to treat and, where possible, cure any malady, whether that be physical or mental.' I glanced at Dr Wakefield. His lip curled up contemptuously at my words.

'You persisted in your belief regarding Miss Hebron's apparent sanity and took what steps to prove it?' the chairman asked.

'I sought out her previous doctor, Dr Cedric Dennison, whom I had replaced at Flete House. He too was of the opinion that Miss Hebron was sane and that she shouldn't have been put in Flete House. I have written testimony from Dr Dennison.'

The chairman held out his hand and I put Dr Dennison's testimony in it. As he read, I continued.

'He was on the verge of approaching Miss Hebron's legal guardian, Mr Ralph Hawke, when he was viciously attacked and forced to abandon his position at Flete House.' I took care not to mention what we truly suspected, that Ralph Hawke had paid a thug to attack Dennison and so shut him up. I could not prove it, after all. 'I also discovered evidence of Dr Wakefield's improper behaviour towards Miss Hebron when she was first committed.'

'No!' Mrs Wakefield called out, but quietly this time, as if the exclamation had been involuntary.

I had no real wish to pain her, despite my dislike, and despite the injury she had done me and which was only just beginning to fade from my cheek, but the truth had to be known if Rachel was going to be freed.

'Continue, Dr Cowdrey,' the chairman said.

'Dr Wakefield, despite being a married man and having a duty of care towards Miss Hebron, began an improper relationship with her. Miss Hebron had only recently been committed to Flete House and was in a very vulnerable state. He took advantage of her vulnerability until his impropriety was discovered by his wife. Dr Wakefield engaged first Dr Dennison, then myself, to have charge of the female patients at Flete House, I presume so he would be able to avoid them altogether.'

'You have evidence of this improper relationship?'

'I have love letters written by Dr Wakefield to Miss Hebron.'

The chairman asked me to produce them. I took them out from my jacket pocket and handed them to him. He read them, eyebrows raised, then passed them along to his colleagues. He looked back to me.

'Do you have anything else to tell us, Dr Cowdrey?'

I considered. Dare I say I thought that the reason Rachel had been put in Flete House was because her stepbrother wanted the use of her house and fortune? I had no evidence to prove it true, so I decided to keep that to myself. I was doing all I could for Rachel. I had to consider my own interests too. 'No, sir. That is all.'

'Then you may step down, Dr Cowdrey.'

He called Dr Wakefield next.

'Dr Wakefield, you were one of the signatories who

confirmed Miss Hebron to be a lunatic. What led you to conclude Miss Hebron was insane?'

Dr Wakefield cleared his throat. 'I had been told of incidents in her past that had worried her family and, on occasion, had endangered relatives and friends. When I interviewed her, she exhibited extreme anger, almost uncontrollable, and raged against her stepmother and stepbrother in a manner that was impossible to pass off as normal behaviour. She claimed the whole world was against her, exhibiting a paranoia that was extreme. I firmly believed she was a danger to others, and that she was insane. I had no hesitation in signing the Lunacy Order.'

'Moving on to the allegation of impropriety levelled by Dr Cowdrey. Did you write these letters?' The chairman gestured to his colleague sitting at the end of the table to hand Dr Wakefield the letters I had produced.

Dr Wakefield snatched them out of his hand and glanced at them briefly before handing them back. 'I did write them. They were a mistake.'

'A mistake?' the chairman asked, his left eyebrow arching. 'Do you think it excusable that a man in your position should write love letters to a patient in his care?'

Dr Wakefield sighed, and his pale cheeks grew a little red. 'In the cold light of day, no, of course not. But in my defence, I was under a great deal of stress at the time of writing those letters. Flete House had only opened a short while before, and my wife and I had invested a great deal of our savings in the venture. Financial pressures led me to act inappropriately in relation to Miss Hebron, I acknowledge that. But,' he said loudly and held up a finger, 'my inappropriate behaviour never once went beyond the writing of those letters.'

'You mean you never had physical relations with Miss Hebron?' the chairman asked, a little pruriently, I thought.

'Never,' Dr Wakefield declared emphatically, 'and I would never have so forgot myself in that way. Common sense and my duty of care would have prevailed.'

The chairman seemed satisfied with this answer, but I myself had no doubt that Dr Wakefield would have seduced Rachel had he not been discovered by his wife. I wondered what Ralph Hawke thought of this admission. Had he known of Dr Wakefield's flirtation with Rachel? Had he even encouraged it as a means of ruining her?

'Two of your doctors expressed concerns that Miss Hebron was not mad and should therefore not be in a lunatic asylum,' the chairman continued. 'Did this not lead you to perhaps re-evaluate your original diagnosis of Miss Hebron's condition?'

'No, it did not. Dr Dennison was a very ambitious and argumentative man. He frequently offended my wife with derogatory comments about her religious beliefs and often sought to belittle me in public. I believed his insistence that Miss Hebron was sane was simply another attempt to undermine my authority. If he had not become ill and unable to return to Flete House, I would have dismissed him.'

'But Dr Cowdrey came to you with the same concern regarding Miss Hebron,' the chairman pointed out.

'He did,' Dr Wakefield nodded, 'and I did not dismiss it as lightly as he makes out. I considered it, but I considered too his inexperience in the study of lunacy and his ill-considered attempts at treatment and cure. His efforts had already resulted in the suicide of a female patient of whom he had decided to make a particular study and I was anxious that a similar incident not occur again.'

My insides shrivelled. I had not even considered that my conduct with Mrs Blake would be called into question in this inquiry. That it had no bearing on Rachel was immaterial. Dr Wakefield was making it seem like I was a troublemaker, and worse, an incompetent doctor. Mrs Bute patted my hand comfortingly while the Board members conferred in whispers.

The chairman called Dr Blamey, whom I had correctly identified as the man sitting next to Ralph Hawke, and he reiterated what Dr Wakefield had said about Rachel. He too had had no doubt Rachel was mad.

Then the Board called Ralph Hawke.

He kissed his mother's cheek before striding across the floor and taking the chair by the Board's table. He cut an impressive figure, I could not deny, and I felt that the chairman cowered a little before him. My hopes were fading as I felt that, despite all the evidence provided, the Board would be impressed and intimidated by Ralph Hawke, the gentleman who had done his best for all his family and consigned Rachel to Flete House.

'Mr Hawke,' the chairman began, 'thank you for attending this inquiry today. We understand that it is an inconvenience for a man of your station.'

Of his station indeed. What station did he have? My family had more wealth and position than Ralph Hawke! Just because he could legally call Kessell Court his home and not need to work for a living while he lived off Rachel's fortune, these fools were treating him like an aristocrat.

'You initiated the examination of your stepsister, is that right?' the chairman asked.

'Yes, that is correct,' Mr Hawke said.

'What led you to do that?'

'Primarily, knowledge and observation of her behaviour over the years since my mother married her father. There had been perhaps a dozen incidents of greater or lesser severity that had made me and my mother wonder whether Rachel had some affliction of the brain that made her act so strangely. She exhibited extremes of mood, ranging from undue gaiety one moment to deep despondency the next. She acted in ways that were unaccountable for any normal person, and on several occasions, acted in such a way that presented her to be a danger to others. She also threatened to harm herself on at least one occasion if we didn't comply with her demands. It was one such incident when she seemed to be endangering the life of her friend that led me to seek help for her and put my family beyond her dangerous reach.'

It was a succinct and convincing account of his motives, but it was not all, as I very well knew. He was concealing the most damning motive of all – his desire to get his hands on Rachel's inheritance.

'Were you aware of the improper behaviour of Dr Wakefield?' the chairman asked.

'No,' Mr Hawke said, glaring at Dr Wakefield. 'I had no knowledge of that. Had I known of it, I would have removed my stepsister and put her in the care of another asylum. If you reach the correct decision, that my stepsister is indeed insane, then that is what I intend to do.'

I looked down the line of chairs to Dr Wakefield. He crossed and recrossed his legs, a sign of his agitation, but I doubted Ralph Hawke meant what he said, that it was all said for show. After all, another alienist with his own private asylum might not be so amenable to imprisoning a sane woman.

The chairman had no further questions for Ralph Hawke. He dismissed him, then addressed his audience. 'We shall have a short adjournment while our doctor, who has examined Miss Hebron, delivers his report to us. We shall recommence at two o'clock.'

He banged his gavel and the Board rose.

We all did the same. Dr Wakefield immediately went to Ralph Hawke, his face earnest, and tried to talk to him. But Ralph Hawke shook his head and gave his arm to his mother. Lucinda Hebron glared at me from behind her black veil as they passed.

'They've taken a private room at The Black Dog,' Reverend Bute said to me. 'I suggest we go back to the vicarage until it's time for the Board to reconvene.'

I didn't argue. I didn't want to be where either the Wakefields or the Hawkes could get at me.

The Butes deliberately avoided discussing the morning's inquiry over lunch and for that, I was grateful. I barely touched my food and kept looking over to the clock on the mantel, wanting yet dreading the hands to point to two o'clock. I wished for it all to be over, for Rachel to be freed. Until that moment, I could not relax, despite Mrs Bute doing her best to comfort me.

We returned to the church hall at ten minutes to two. We were the first to arrive, the Wakefields arriving a few minutes later, then Ralph Hawke, his mother and Dr Blamey. We all looked anxious, I noted.

The Board got straight down to business.

'The doctors have delivered their report on Miss Hebron's state of mind and we have considered the evidence put before us. The doctors can find no incontrovertible evidence that Miss Hebron is of insane mind and we therefore decree that the Lunacy Order be revoked with immediate effect.'

I could have cried out with joy and relief. I had done it. I had got Rachel freed from Flete House.

The chairman was continuing. 'Dr Wakefield, will you please stand up?'

Nervously, holding onto his wife's grasping hand, Dr Wakefield rose. He faced the Board.

'Dr Wakefield, we were greatly distressed by the evidence put before us and your own admission of impropriety with Miss Hebron. We do not feel such behaviour to be acceptable for a man in your position and will be writing to the General Medical Council to recommend that they conduct their own investigation into your fitness to practise medicine. You may sit down.'

Dr Wakefield practically fell into his chair. He sat staring blankly ahead. Mrs Wakefield buried her face in her hands and sobbed quietly.

'This inquiry is at an end.' The Board rose and the members dispersed.

'Congratulations, Felix,' Reverend Bute said, grabbing my hand and covering it with his own.

'Oh, well done, Felix,' Mrs Bute said, dragging me down towards her so she could kiss my cheek. 'You did it.'

'Thank you,' I said, a little dazed. 'I don't really know what to say.'

'Then don't say anything,' Reverend Bute said with a laugh. 'Just go and see Miss Hebron. I expect she will want to thank you.'

‘Yes,’ I said, ‘I must go and see her.’ I hesitated. ‘But the Wakefields will not let me into Flete House.’

‘They can’t stop you waiting outside,’ Mrs Bute said. ‘Go.’

I did as she told me and hurried out of the church hall.

‘Pleased with yourself, are you?’ a voice called out to me as I ran along the path.

I skidded to a halt and turned. Ralph Hawke was standing to the side of the hall entrance. I hadn’t seen him or his party leave the hall.

‘I’m pleased an innocent woman has been freed,’ I said.

He came towards me and I wondered with what intent. He had proved himself to not be afraid of violence but would he commit it himself and in plain view? I thought not and stood my ground.

‘Rachel’s not innocent,’ he said, keeping his gloved hands in his overcoat pocket. ‘I know what she is. I’ve known her for years. I probably know her better than she knows herself. And you? You’ve known her for what, a few months?’ He shook his head. ‘A man can live with a woman for a lifetime and yet not know what goes on in her head. What makes you so sure you understand Rachel after so short an acquaintance?’

I had no answer to this. ‘I’m not the only man to believe Rachel sane,’ I said instead.

‘Oh yes, Dr Dennison,’ he nodded. ‘He was another of my stepsister’s dupes.’

‘One who you had silenced.’

His brow creased. 'What are you talking about?'

'I know what you did, what you had someone do to him. He's probably going to suffer with his health for the rest of his life, however long that may be, because of you.'

He looked me up and down contemptuously. 'You should be a patient at Flete House as well as Rachel, Cowdrey. You're as mad as she is.'

'There's nothing wrong with my mind,' I assured him.

'And nothing about this pricks your conscience?' he asked. 'Do you have any idea the distress you've caused my mother?'

'What about the distress you've caused Rachel?' I countered. 'And I know why. I couldn't say in there, I couldn't go on the record, but I know you did it so you could get your hands on her fortune and Kessell Court.'

'Is that what you think of me? That I would commit a woman to a lunatic asylum for such mercenary reasons?'

'Don't bother to protest your innocence,' I said. 'It's wasted on me. Now, if you'll excuse me, I have to go and see your stepsister safely out of Flete House.'

I continued on my way. As I walked, it occurred to me that Rachel would need transport to Kessell Court, and I thought it unlikely Ralph Hawke would arrange this for her. Should I do so? Would she expect me to be waiting at the gates in a carriage to take her home?

I didn't want to see Danby skulking in his little hut by the gates, so I waited fifty yards or so down the lane.

While I waited, a carriage passed me, the blinds at the windows pulled down so I could not see inside, but I thought it likely it contained Mr Hawke and Mrs Hebron on their way home. I could see the gates from where I was, and I watched in surprise as the carriage came to a stop outside. No one got out. I waited a few minutes, then hurried over to it.

'Are you waiting for someone?' I called up to the driver.

'Yes, sir,' he said. 'Name of Frayn. I was to wait here, so the order went.'

I had no opportunity to question him further, for at that moment, I heard the gates open and the murmur of voices. I saw Danby with his hands on the gate, and Rachel and Harriet Frayn passing through them.

'Rachel,' I called.

She looked at me in surprise. 'Why, Dr Cowdrey, there you are. How nice of you to come and meet me.'

'You were quick to hear the news,' I said.

'Yes, the doctors who examined me told me they found no fault with my brain's workings. I started to pack as soon as they left.'

'I am very happy for you, Rachel.'

'Thank you,' she said, handing the bag she carried to Miss Frayn, who handed it up to the driver to place beside him.

Was I expecting a more enthusiastic thank you? I confess I was. I had just moved heaven and earth to secure her freedom.

‘Are you going to Kessell Court?’ I asked, gesturing at the carriage.

‘Yes, of course. Where else would I go? And Harriet is coming with me. She’s been a great friend to me, haven’t you, Harriet?’

Miss Frayn grinned. ‘A great friend.’

‘I’m glad you will have company on the journey,’ I said. ‘I’m not sure what kind of reception you will have from your stepfamily.’

‘It hardly matters,’ she said, and I wondered with not a little dread how their reunion would play out.

Miss Frayn said they should get going and Rachel climbed into the carriage. Miss Frayn climbed in after her and shut the door with a bang.

Rachel pulled up the blind and leant out. ‘You’ve been so very good to me, Dr Cowdrey. I thank you with all my heart.’

‘You’re welcome,’ I cried as the carriage pulled away, covering me with dust thrown up by the wheels, but I had no idea if she heard me.

30

LONDON, AGAIN

I returned to London.

My family asked how the inquiry went and I told them everything that had happened. They congratulated me, and I accepted their congratulations with pleasure, but I could not rid myself of a sense of guilt that I had almost certainly ruined Dr Wakefield's medical career. Whatever his faults, I did not feel he deserved to have his livelihood taken away from him.

Almost a month later, Clara asked if I would invite the Butes to come and stay with us for a few days. I had told her a great deal about the Butes, and she wanted to meet the people who had been so kind to me while I had been away from her. I thought it an excellent idea and wrote to them that morning.

They accepted my invitation and arrived the following week, meaning to stay for two nights. The first evening Clara wanted to give a dinner, just us and the Butes. The following evening was to be a family affair, with all of us gathering at my parents.

It was very pleasant to see the Butes again, and Clara took to them both at once. She and Mrs Bute chatted for hours, while Reverend Bute and I talked in my study.

Our maid, a girl called Susan (who was not a patch on Millie), set down coffee and cake on the small octagonal table between us. Reverend Bute took a bite of the cake.

'Mmm, delicious,' he said, wiping away crumbs. 'Now, do you want to know what's happened in Flete since you left?'

This was the first mention of the village since the Butes had arrived. I had been keeping our conversation away from Flete House and the Wakefields, having a disinclination to discuss them, but I knew we would get round to the subject eventually.

'You can tell me if you wish,' I said, hoping my reluctance was not too evident.

'I think you ought to know,' he said, a little too seriously for my comfort. He set his plate down. 'Flete House has closed. The patients have been packed off, back to their relatives or to another asylum, I suppose, and the Wakefields have gone. The house is up for sale.'

'I see,' I said uneasily. 'That's my doing, you're going to say. I'm to blame.'

'It is because of you,' Reverend Bute agreed. 'To say otherwise would be to lie, but you know that, Felix. But the Wakefields are also to blame. If they had behaved correctly, your suspicions wouldn't have been aroused.'

I nodded. 'I suppose so. Still, I didn't mean for them to lose everything.'

'What did you mean, then, Felix?'

'Just for justice to have been done,' I said, a little hurt by his tone. 'I wanted justice for Rachel. Are you saying I was wrong?'

'Not at all,' he said, holding his hands up to me. 'I supported you in the action you took, but I must confess, it has led me to consider things I had not considered before.'

'What do you mean?'

'It has led me to consider the consequences of our actions, Felix,' he said, taking a sip of his coffee. 'For example, if we do this or that thing, no matter how right it is, what will follow? Do the ends justify the means?'

'If one is in the right, then the consequences must also be right, mustn't they?'

'I wonder,' he said. He asked if he could smoke his pipe and I bid him light it. He occupied himself for a while, scraping out the bowl into the grate and refilling it with tobacco from a leather pouch. Then he sat back in the armchair and looked at me.

'Mrs Wakefield became quite ill. Something to do with her nerves. Oh, you will know the medical term for it, I'm sure, but by all accounts, she is a shadow of the woman she was.'

'By whose account?' I asked testily.

'By Dr Wakefield himself,' he said. 'You're

surprised, I can tell. But he came into the church the day he and his wife left. He looked a little lost, quite changed from his old self. I think he wanted someone to talk to.'

'And he found you.'

'That's what I'm for,' Reverend Bute smiled, reminding me that I had sought him out in much the same way. 'And I was very ready to listen, because, well, I was curious, I confess it. We settled down in one of the pews and he told me they were leaving. He had been investigated by the General Medical Council and received a rebuke, but that he hadn't been struck off, which had been his worst fear. He knew he had acted reprehensibly in regard to Miss Hebron, but he had been a fool and beguiled by her. He implied that his marriage is not as happy as he would wish it. Well, that won't be a surprise to you, I'm sure. We all saw for ourself the kind of woman Leonora Wakefield is. Controlling, oppressive, jealous.'

'You condone the way he behaved with Rachel?' I asked, aghast.

'I don't condone it, Felix, I'm saying I understand. I think the world could do with a little more understanding, don't you?'

'I suppose so,' I replied, a little sulkily.

'He also spoke of Cedric, how he regretted the way he and his wife had treated him. When I spoke of Cedric's attack, do you know what he said? He said he had never meant for that to happen.'

I sat up in my chair. '*He* never meant for that to

happen? Do you mean to say it was Dr Wakefield who hired a thug to attack Dr Dennison, not Ralph Hawke?'

'Well, that is what I thought he meant,' Reverend Bute, his eyes twinkling. 'So I asked him to explain. And he said that he never knew about the quarrel his wife had had with Cedric in the church, you know, the one Emma told you of. He only found out about it later, after the attack. But that if he had known, he would have forbidden—'

'Danby!' I cried, sinking back in my chair with sudden realisation.

Reverend Bute's cheeks rounded in delight, and he nodded. 'Jim Danby. Got it in one.'

'Danby was waiting outside the church when Mrs Wakefield and Dr Dennison argued,' I said, remembering Mrs Bute's words. 'He must have heard everything.'

'And he is devoted to Mrs Wakefield,' Reverend Bute said. 'He must have been angry at Cedric speaking so rudely to Mrs Wakefield and decided to do something about it.'

'So, he followed Dr Dennison to London and attacked him.' I sighed. 'I was so certain Ralph Hawke had been responsible.'

'Dr Wakefield told me Jim Danby came back to Flete House that night and presented himself at the lodge. He told Mrs Wakefield that he had "taken care of Dennison", and Dr Wakefield, hearing Danby, had demanded to know what he meant. Danby was not at all ashamed of what he had done and told him bluntly that he had beaten Cedric and had the blood on his shirt to prove it.'

'Had Mrs Wakefield sent him to attack Dr Dennison?'

Reverend Bute shook his head. 'I think not. No, I suspect Danby took it upon himself to avenge Mrs Wakefield. So, that's one mystery solved, isn't it?'

'Ralph Hawke had nothing to do with it,' I said, staring into the fire.

'You told me he pretended not to know anything about it, except he wasn't pretending, was he, Felix? He really didn't know what you were talking about.'

'I got that wrong,' I said.

'Yes,' Reverend Bute said with a sigh. 'You did.'

31

KESSELL COURT REVISITED

Almost six weeks after I left Flete for good and returned to London, six weeks of trying to work out what I would do now, I received a letter from Rachel inviting me to take tea with her and her aunt at Kessell Court.

To tell the truth, I was a little disappointed it wasn't more. I had hoped Rachel would invite me and Clara to spend a week or more at Kessell Court in gratitude for her freedom, but perhaps she wasn't quite ready to have guests just yet. The tea invitation did not include Clara, and I realised that I had never spoken of my wife to Rachel. It was possible she had no notion I was married. As it turned out, had Clara been invited, she would have had to refuse, as she had promised to accompany my mother on one of her charitable excursions.

So I set off just after lunch on the Friday named to take the train to the village of Alderley and Kessell Court. A gig waited at the station to take me to the house, and I enjoyed the ride enormously, the sun shining on my face, the breeze just enough to keep the air fresh without being cool, and the anticipation of seeing Rachel back where she belonged.

How different was my journey from the first time I had visited Kessell Court. I was driven up the drive rather than having to walk all around and enter via the rear, and this time I was an invited guest, not an interloper.

The gig pulled up outside the front door and I climbed down to bang the twisted black circular knocker three times. Perhaps half a minute passed before the door opened and a maid bid me step inside. The interior smelt of lavender and beeswax and the dark oak panelling gleamed through centuries of polishing.

'The mistress is in the garden, sir,' the maid said, leading me through to the rear of the house. It was odd to hear Rachel referred to as 'the mistress'.

The sunlight burst upon me as I passed through a narrow door into the garden. I blinked, black spots before my eyes.

'There he is,' I heard someone say.

The maid led me to a metal garden table with four chairs around it. Three of the chairs were occupied, two by Rachel and Miss Beatrice.

'Good afternoon,' I paused, unsure how to address Rachel when we were in company, and settled on, 'Miss Hebron.'

'Dr Cowdrey, I'm so glad you were able to come,' Rachel said, holding her hand out to me.

I took it. 'Thank you for inviting me.'

It occured to me that I had not mentioned to Rachel that I had met her aunt nor that I had been to Kessell Court before. Had Miss Beatrice told Rachel we had met and that I had been shown her bedroom with all her private belongings? I said hello to Miss Beatrice, looking for some indication in her face as to what she had told Rachel, but she looked at me blankly, as if she didn't recognise me at all. She returned my greeting, then fell silent. I decided that I would not refer to our previous meeting, just in case it made things awkward for her with Rachel. I turned to Rachel's other companion, a young woman with thick blond hair and rather penetrating eyes. There was something oddly familiar in the tilt of her head, in the way she studied me, but I couldn't place her.

'Dr Cowdrey, this is my good friend, Miss Felicity Polke.'

I should have guessed. Who else would Rachel have at her side?

'I'm very pleased to meet you, Miss Polke,' I said. 'I've heard quite a bit about you.'

'And I about you,' she said. Again, there was something familiar in the sound of her voice.

I took a seat and Rachel ordered tea to be brought out. As the minutes ticked by, I found myself rather regretting accepting Rachel's invitation. Rachel and Miss Polke were merry enough, but their merriment was a little mean-spirited, as if they were sharing a private joke and having fun at my inability to understand it. As for Miss Beatrice, she didn't say a word, though Rachel piled more cake onto her plate that she had not yet touched, nor did she seem to have any intention of doing so. I wondered if perhaps she was ill and considered offering to examine her, but Rachel chose that moment to grow irritable with her aunt, telling her to stop sulking and to eat her cake. Miss Polke laughed at this, and I decided then that I did not like her.

When we had finished tea, Rachel told Miss Polke to show me around the garden. It had grown a great deal warmer and I would have preferred to stay where I was, but Miss Polke jumped up obediently so I could not then refuse.

It was an extremely large garden, perhaps four times larger than Flete House, and a dozen times larger than my garden in Milton Square. Miss Polke showed me the kitchen garden, which Clara would have envied, the rose garden with many beautiful specimens, the bee hives that had been Lawrence Hebron's passionate hobby, and lastly, she took me down to the very bottom where the trees grew thickly and through which I had walked on my first visit to Kessell Court.

'How was your holiday in Dorset, Miss Polke?' I asked, glad of the shade the trees provided.

'Dorset?' she frowned. 'Oh yes, Dorset. Dorset was fine.'

'Glad to be home?'

'I'm glad to be here,' she said, gesturing at Kessell Court. 'Rachel has asked me to stay here to keep her company, so that's what I'm doing. I couldn't bear to be at home with my parents while she's so close.'

She truly seemed devoted to Rachel, though I deplored her contempt for her parents. I was finding her a rather unpleasant young woman, and I wondered what Rachel saw in her.

'Have you been friends for long?' I asked.

'All our lives.'

'You must know each other very well, then.'

'We are as sisters, Dr Cowdrey,' Miss Polke said with sudden seriousness. 'I would do anything for her.'

'And she for you?'

She glared at me. 'Of course she would.' She suddenly looked over my shoulder with a great intensity and I turned towards the trees, wondering what she was looking at. 'Who's there?' she called. 'Why are you hiding?'

I heard the snapping of twigs, and suddenly, striding out of the dappled light was Ralph Hawke.

'I wasn't hiding, Felicity. Just walking. Rachel has company, I see,' he said, looking at me.

'Does Rachel know you're here?' Miss Polke asked.

'I've done my best to keep my whereabouts from Rachel, so no, she doesn't know I'm here.'

'She won't like it,' Miss Polke said with pleasure. 'I'm going to tell her you're here and she's going to see you off.' She turned and hurried off towards the house. I wondered if I should go with her but Mr Hawke spoke to me.

'Why are you here, Cowdrey?'

'Rachel invited me to tea.'

'I see. Well, she must thank you, I suppose.'

I cleared my throat uneasily. 'If Rachel doesn't know you're here, does that mean you're not living at Kessell Court?

'Of course we're not living here,' he growled, kicking at the root of a tree. 'Do you imagine Rachel would allow my mother to stay here after everything that has happened?'

'But then, where are you living?' I asked, feeling a little sick at this news.

'In town, for the moment,' he said. 'A friend of mine has been kind enough to put us up.'

'I'm sorry.'

'Are you?' he asked, looking sideways at me. 'You'll forgive me if I doubt you truly are.'

'I didn't mean for your mother to lose her home,' I protested. 'I just wanted your stepsister to be released from the asylum where she had no place being.'

Mr Hawke smacked the trunk of the tree beside him. He raised his hand, the index finger out straight and pointing at me. His jaw tightened. 'You have no idea, Cowdrey, no damned idea.'

He turned to leave, but I needed to know what he meant. 'No idea of what?' I called after him.

He stopped, but kept his back towards me. Then he turned and hurried back towards me, so fast that I had to take more than a few quick steps back to avoid him running into me.

'Do you know why I'm here?' he growled. 'I've brought my mother to see Emily's grave. Emily is buried just over there.' He pointed to the right where a church tower showed above the trees. 'And now, because of you, she may never be able to visit her daughter's grave again. You have no conception of the grief my mother still feels at the loss of Emily.'

'I pity her,' I said, 'I really do, Mr Hawke. But Rachel cannot forbid your mother from visiting the churchyard.'

'No, not even Rachel can do that, but she can cause my mother to have to live abroad. Her late husband left her a pitiful allowance, one that is not enough for her to live respectably here in England. I came to Kessell Court to speak with Rachel, to beg her not to treat my mother so, to give her a small allowance so that she might take a cottage in the village and so be close to Emily. And do you know what Rachel did, Cowdrey? She laughed in my face and said she enjoyed seeing me brought so low that I would actually resort to begging.'

'I don't believe you,' I said. 'Rachel would not be so cruel.'

'Because you know her so well?'

'I know her well enough.'

He shook his head. 'You don't know her at all.' He suddenly looked up and over my shoulder, his brow creasing.

I turned. There was nothing I could see that could have engaged his interest so. I could see Miss Polke. She was sitting at the garden table again, eating the cake that was left. She was alone. Both Rachel and Miss Beatrice were nowhere to be seen. Presumably, Miss Polke had decided to wait for Rachel to reappear to tell her about her stepbrother rather than go searching for her.

I looked back to Mr Hawke, and saw now that his narrowed gaze was not on Miss Polke, but on a point much higher. I turned back to the house and, shading my eyes, tried to see what he was looking at.

And then I saw it. I saw her. A figure that could only have been Rachel, standing on the roof.

'It's only Rachel looking at the view,' I said to Mr Hawke.

He shook his head. 'She never looks at views.'

I frowned. 'Of course she does. She was looking at the view when everyone claimed she tried to push Miss Polke off the roof.'

I turned back to the house. Rachel was spreading her arms wide, her face turned up to the sun, and in the silence between us, I heard her laughing.

Despite my earlier assurance to Mr Hawke, I did begin to grow a little concerned. She was very near the edge, and if she wasn't paying attention, could quite easily fall. I saw another figure emerge from behind Rachel and squinted. 'It's all right. Her aunt's there. Miss Beatrice will tell her to be careful.'

Miss Beatrice was moving towards Rachel, her arms outstretched, ready to pull her niece away from the edge and back to safety. I saw Miss Beatrice's hands go around Rachel's slender waist.

And I watched as the old woman shoved with all her might.

32

BEATRICE AND A BODY

The rest of that day is etched on my memory. I fear I shall never forget it.

I saw Rachel fall, head first, her arms and legs flailing, her scream loud and sharp while it lasted. That was all too short a time, and yet, an eternity too. I heard Miss Polke scream, and this spurred both Ralph and I into action. By the time we reached the verandah, Miss Polke was sitting on the ground cradling Rachel's bloodied head in her lap and sobbing wretchedly.

'Do something,' Mr Hawke said to me.

I moved to Rachel's broken body. I extended my hand towards her throat, hoping to feel a pulse beat there, but Miss Polke yelled when she saw my hand and slapped it away, bending low and blocking Rachel from my view.

The next moment, Mr Hawke had placed his hands beneath Miss Polke's armpits and hauled her away from Rachel. She kicked and screamed at him, but he was too strong for her and held her fast. I put my fingers to Rachel's throat and felt nothing beneath them.

'She's dead,' I said. I took off my jacket and covered Rachel's head.

'Where's Beatrice?' Mr Hawke cried and released Miss Polke, who crumpled to her knees and sobbed into her hands. He ran back onto the lawn and craned his neck to the roof. 'I can't see her. Stay with Felicity,' he ordered me, and darted into the house, disappearing into the darkness.

Nothing could be done for Rachel, and I was too stunned and shocked to offer comfort to Miss Polke. I moved back onto the lawn as Mr Hawke had done and squinted against the sun. I could see nothing, but a minute or so later, heard his voice. He had found Beatrice on the roof and was talking to her, but I couldn't make out what he was saying.

Another few minutes passed, and I heard footsteps coming from inside the house. I dashed inside. Mr Hawke was coming down the stairs, his arm around Miss Beatrice's shoulder, gently guiding her down the steps. She was crying and trembling. Mr Hawke led her into the drawing room and sat her down in one of the armchairs. He turned to me.

'We have to send for the police. I'll despatch one of the servants. What have you done with Felicity?'

'She's still outside.'

'You're a doctor. Tend to Beatrice. She hasn't spoken a word. I can't get anything out of her as to what happened up there on the roof.'

'She's probably in shock,' I said, kneeling before the old woman. There was a shawl hanging over the back of the armchair, and I placed it around her shoulders. 'Was it an accident? Did she mean to pull her back and Rachel lost her balance?'

He hesitated before answering me, causing me to look up. 'I don't know. Probably. Yes, I suppose it must have been. She intended to pull Rachel back, but Rachel moved away and lost her balance. That's what happened.'

He looked at me with meaning in his eyes. I nodded agreement and he left to send for the police. An officer arrived about an hour later. Mr Hawke told him what we had seen and how he believed it had been an accident. The policeman nodded and wrote in his notebook.

But then Miss Polke appeared in the doorway. I have no idea what she had been doing all that time. Both Mr Hawke and I had completely forgotten about her.

Miss Polke raised her arm and pointed her finger at Miss Beatrice. 'She murdered Rachel,' she declared.

Mr Hawke tried to quiet her, but she was having none of it.

'She pushed her off the roof,' she cried. 'I saw it, we all saw it.'

The policeman's attitude changed. His eyes narrowed as he contemplated Mr Hawke and myself, and he put his head on one side as he studied Miss Beatrice, as if trying to work out if there could be any truth in Miss Polke's accusation. Whether he thought it possible or not was, ultimately, immaterial. An accusation had been made, and he did his duty by placing Miss Beatrice under arrest. It was heartbreaking to see the poor old woman climb meekly into the police waggon and to hear the doors bang, locking her inside.

Rachel's body was taken away, and Miss Polke insisted on going with her. I was glad she left us. Mr Hawke had not spoken a great deal after the police left with Miss Beatrice. He slumped down on the sofa and just sat there, staring into space as if he couldn't quite believe what his own eyes had witnessed.

'I need to see my mother,' he said at last. 'She'll be wondering where I am.' He rose and brushed past me.

'You can bring her back here now, I suppose,' I said as he reached the front door.

I had meant it as a statement of fact, but as soon as I spoke those words, I realised how tactless I sounded. Mr Hawke thought so too because he paused at the door to give me a glare of utter contempt.

'You really are a piece of work, Cowdrey,' he said, and slammed the door behind him.

33

REVELATIONS

It was a few weeks after that dreadful day at Kessell Court, and Clara and I had been to see an exhibition at the Royal Academy. When we returned home, our maid informed me a Mr Ralph Hawke was waiting in the sitting room to see me and that he'd been there for an hour.

I exchanged a look of dread with Clara, for she knew of my last encounter with Mr Hawke and how crassly I had spoken to him. She kissed me and wished me luck, then mounted the stairs to our bedroom. I waited until I heard the bedroom door close, then gingerly opened the sitting-room door.

Mr Hawke got heavily to his feet. He seemed to have aged since I saw him last. There were dark circles beneath his eyes and a hollowness in his cheeks.

'Forgive me for keeping you waiting, Mr Hawke,' I said nervously. 'I wasn't expecting you.'

'I've come from the prison,' he said. 'I didn't expect

to be coming here any more than you expected to see me.'

I asked him to sit back down and I took the armchair opposite. 'How is Miss Beatrice?'

'She's very frail. That she should be in such a place is a… a…, I don't know.' He shook his head.

'She will need a barrister. My brother, Theo, is a solicitor. He could put you in touch with a very good one—'

He cut me off. 'There isn't going to be a trial. Beatrice has confessed to murder.'

'But it was an accident,' I said, recalling what Mr Hawke and I had agreed had happened on Kessell Court's roof. 'I know what Miss Polke said, but she was upset. The police surely cannot suspect Miss Beatrice of murdering her niece?'

'Beatrice told them she intended to kill Rachel. She told them she knew exactly what she was doing, and that she knew she would have to pay for it with her own life.' He let out a deep breath. 'She's going to be hanged, Cowdrey.'

His voice broke on my name and he turned away to hide his tears. I was confused by this man before me. Where was the villain I knew him to be? Villains didn't cry over old women.

'Anyway,' he said, savagely wiping his cheeks, 'I've come because Beatrice wanted me to deliver this to you.' He reached inside his coat and pulled out a thickly stuffed envelope. He held it out to me and I took it. 'She asked me to stay while you read it.'

I nodded and slid my finger beneath the flap and gently eased the paper apart. To treat it roughly, it seemed to me, would be the same as treating Miss Beatrice roughly. I drew out the sheets of paper with their beautiful copperplate writing, unfolded them, and began to read Miss Beatrice's letter to me. This is what she wrote.

Dear Dr Cowdrey,

Ralph has told me you two were together when I pushed Rachel off the roof, and I feel you deserve some explanation, especially since you were so instrumental in obtaining her release. Ralph has been very kind to me and is so upset at what must happen next that I feel I cannot add to his distress and my own by explaining my actions directly to him. I have asked him to remain while you read this letter in the hope that you will explain its contents to him. You are a gentleman and I trust you will do this.

You must have thought I was very rude to you that day at Kessell Court. You were polite to me and I barely acknowledged you. I apologise for my conduct, but I was greatly troubled by a conversation that had occurred before you arrived and I was trying to work out what I must do. My mind was only on that matter, not on being polite to guests, I fear.

It is time for the truth to be told. I am only sorry that I never acknowledged what was clear to those who loved Rachel less than I. I speak here of Lucinda and Ralph, of course. They saw her for what she was. Lawrence and I, alas, never heeded their fears. What a happier time we might have had had we done so.

As I've grown older, I find the distant past more vivid to me than yesterday. I can now recall a dozen incidents that should have alerted Lawrence or myself to Rachel's dangerous nature, but we loved her dearly and always made excuses for her more extreme acts while downplaying the lesser ones. I think perhaps we can be excused for not putting all those acts together and seeing a pattern. We were too close to her, I think. I discovered that dreadful day exactly how dangerous she was, and I was horrified. I have made so many mistakes in regard to Rachel, thought ill of people who were good. May God forgive me.

I honestly believed she should not have been put in Flete House. I did not think her mad. I believed her story about showing Felicity the view, and tried to defend her when the Polkes and Lucinda insisted she had been trying to kill her. I thought Lucinda, who has been weighed down with grief since little Emily's death, was speaking out of spite. She brought up all the incidents over the years which she believed showed Rachel at her worst. But I saw those incidents not as viciousness on Rachel's part, just the product of rage and frustration at being so obviously unloved by Lucinda. I do not blame Lucinda, but it is true that once she had Emily, she had no time for Rachel, although when you asked me this, I tried to make out that she had not neglected her. I didn't want to admit the truth.

The Polkes, too, had never liked Rachel. They thought she was a bad influence on Felicity, and in that, as in so many things, they were right, though I did not see it. They were all for prosecuting Rachel, but Ralph, in his goodness, didn't want the Hebron name dragged through the courts, and persuaded them she would be better put in an asylum. They took a great deal of persuading, I believe, and I never thanked Ralph for what he did to convince them. Another failing on my part.

It was such a lovely day, that day you came to Kessell Court, that we, Rachel, Felicity and I had spent most of it in the garden. Felicity had been drinking lemonade and made such a vile slurping that Rachel kicked her beneath the table and told her not to make such a damned disgusting noise and that she was a filthy bitch. It pains me to write those words. So I was shocked to hear her use such words and rebuked her, saying it was not ladylike. She laughed at me, and Felicity joined in. I was rather put out at this, and said Rachel would never get a husband if she behaved so rudely, that she must try to act like a lady.

Rachel grew annoyed and said she would rather not be a wife, for being a wife meant being powerless and she would never allow herself to become so. I asked her what she meant by this, for if I know one thing, Dr Cowdrey, it is that women, whether married or doomed to spinsterhood, have no power in this world. This is a world of and for men.

Rachel said a woman could have power over men, she just had to know how to wield it. I told her she didn't know what she was talking about, that she was acting like a child, and I refused to pay her any more attention.

It was the wrong thing to do. She grew even more angry and said she would prove it to me. I was angry and dared her to do so. She looked at Felicity with a proud look on her face, and I saw Felicity nod as if to encourage her to tell me. Felicity, I realised then, knew a great deal more about Rachel than any of us ever realised.

What follows, Dr Cowdrey, is what Rachel told me.

You will remember my telling you of the stable boy, Ned, and his dying from eating yew berries. That was Rachel's doing, I know now. She and Ned had been friends, and when Ned began following Ralph around and wanting to always be with him, Rachel felt betrayed. She told me she paid Ned back for abandoning her like that. She persuaded him to eat berries from the yew tree in the churchyard. We all thought his death to have been an accident, the boy having no notion the berries were poisonous. Now I know he was Rachel's second victim.

Her first was Emily. She killed her half-sister on her fifth birthday. Rachel had been particularly sulky that day because all the attention was, quite naturally, on Emily. It was a great relief to all of us, myself, Lawrence and Lucinda, when Rachel took herself off to her bedroom to sulk alone. With her gone, the mood lightened considerably, and we were all enjoying ourselves to see Emily so happy. Perhaps we should consider ourselves to blame, for it was our delight in Emily that caused Rachel, out of sheer jealousy, to take her life from her. I don't know if you have heard how it happened. The pony Emily was riding suddenly reared, and she fell, breaking her neck. Lawrence was too shocked to think or do anything. He just sat staring blankly ahead while Lucinda was beyond hysterical in her grief. I was busy trying to calm and comfort them, so several hours passed before my mind turned to Rachel. She had not come out of her room, even though she must have heard the commotion. I went up to see to her, thinking she must be crying alone. But when I went into her room I found her entirely dry-eyed and unconcerned. I thought it odd, but that perhaps she hadn't truly realised what had happened. I closed the bedroom window. A slight breeze was blowing the curtain about, and I cleared away the toys she had strewn on the windowsill. These toys included a couple of dolls, a pack of cards and a catapult. I put these away and thought nothing of it.

Looking back now, I realise what a fool I was not to have put two and two together: the open window, the catapult. In her boasting, Rachel told me she had gone up to her bedroom that day and opened the window to watch us. She grew so jealous of our happiness that she took her catapult and shot a bolt at the pony, hoping that a strike would cause it to bolt. She wanted something bad to happen to Emily. She laughed and said she couldn't have hoped for better when the pony reared and Emily fell to her death.

Then there was Ralph's fiancée. Charlotte Burnley was a charming young girl and so obviously in love with Ralph. I rather fancied Ralph was in love with her too, but he is a man who keeps his feelings to himself and I cannot say for sure. Yet I do know he was very upset when Charlotte broke off their engagement. We all wondered at that; they seemed so perfect for each other. But Ralph never said what happened, and we assumed they had quarrelled. But now I know Charlotte ended the engagement because of Rachel. I knew Rachel had been fond of Ralph and perhaps she had hoped that they might marry one day, there being no blood ties between them. I do remember when Ralph announced his engagement to Charlotte, Rachel was furious. Not in front of him or Lucinda, you understand, but she showed her jealousy to me. In my mind, I excused her feelings, understanding them as a disappointment of the heart. I have never married, Dr Cowdrey, and I understand too well loneliness. I thought Rachel believed she would never be married and thought she spoke out of fear of ending up alone. I had no idea then that her jealousy would lead her to put a knife to Charlotte's throat and threaten to kill her if she married Ralph. I remember now that on the day Charlotte left Kessell Court, she had tied a ribbon around her throat and I remarked upon it. She normally left her neck free of such encumbrances. She looked nervous, and gave no answer, but I suppose there must have been a cut or mark made by the knife. Charlotte must have believed that Rachel would carry out her threat enough to break off her engagement, though it must have broken her heart to do so. I understand she hasn't married anyone else.

There are a dozen other incidents I could recount now that I trouble myself to look back on our lives. But there is the one incident where Rachel overreached herself. She admitted this, that last day at Kessell Court. She told me that she should not have tried to persuade Felicity to jump off the roof in front of everybody. Then she looked at Felicity and asked if she agreed. You can imagine my astonishment at this. Felicity did agree! Felicity was devoted to Rachel. Rachel wanted to see just how much power she had over her friend. Could she get Felicity to kill herself just by asking? she wanted to know. And that is why they were both on the roof that day. The Polkes were right. Rachel had been trying to kill Felicity, not with her own hands, but with the power of persuasion. Felicity said she would have jumped had she not been prevented, and she said this with an ease which, quite frankly, Dr Cowdrey, made my blood run cold. I have never particularly liked Felicity – she has always seemed a very odd girl – and this remark confirmed to me that Felicity should be locked up in an asylum just as much as Rachel.

Now I come to the part of my tale that I fear will cause you much distress, but I must tell it. From the very start of her time at Flete House, Rachel was plotting how she could leave. She plied her charm on Dr Wakefield, encouraging him to deceive his wife and making him believe she loved him. She was winning him over to her side when his wife discovered their relationship and put an end to it. They couldn't afford, I understand, to put Rachel out of the asylum, the fee Ralph was paying to have her there was too great. Mrs Wakefield insisted her husband no longer treat the female patients in an effort to keep him away from Rachel, and he agreed.

So Rachel had to start all over again when Dr Dennison arrived at Flete House. She began by using the same trick as she had used with Dr Wakefield, but Dr Dennison was indifferent to her charms, and so she tried instead to convince him of her sanity. She was succeeding when Dr Dennison left and she became ill soon after. Ralph, only having Rachel's best interests at heart, insisted on taking her away to a sanatorium, and by the time she was well enough to return to Flete House, you had arrived. She was annoyed that she had been thwarted again but grew to realise that you might be the easiest of all to manage. Forgive me, Dr Cowdrey, but she said you were a sensitive man, one who cared too much, and that made you easy to manipulate.

Rachel grew annoyed when she discovered you were preoccupied with another patient, a Mrs Blake. This didn't suit her at all and she began to plot how she might get rid of the detestable old loony, as she called her. Felicity was still her devoted friend and the two of them cooked up a plan to trap you. Felicity obtained a position at Flete House disguised as an attendant. She and Rachel had often dressed up and performed plays for us at Kessell Court in their youth, and Felicity had demonstrated a very great talent for pretence. She enjoyed playing Harriet Frayn.

Rachel had the room next door to Mrs Blake, and the two were joined by a communicating door. As Harriet, Felicity could get hold of all the keys of the house, and she had the keys to the communicating door copied and gave them to Rachel. Rachel would creep into Mrs Blake's room during the night and talk to her, telling her that you were intending to send her back to her brother's house where she had been so badly treated. Rachel terrified her with this talk, so much so that given the opportunity, namely Felicity unlocking her bedroom door and she and Rachel leading her down to the stream, this poor Mrs Blake felt compelled to take her own life. Rachel boasted of how she and Felicity watched as Mrs Blake walked into the water. Oh, it is so horrible to write. Can you imagine how horrible it was to listen to coming from the mouth of someone you have loved as your own child?

With Mrs Blake gone, Rachel had you all to herself. And she began to tease you with snippets of information. She was very clever. She made no direct accusation but led you to make assumptions. This was the power she had over you and of which she boasted to me. She thought you weak, Dr Cowdrey. She gambled that, given enough clues, you would investigate and deduce wrongly that Ralph had conspired with the doctors to commit her to the asylum. She felt sure that once you knew you believed an injustice had occurred, you would do all you could to free her, and I'm afraid she was right. She has always managed to read people very well.

You mustn't blame yourself. You are a good man, Dr Cowdrey, and you did what you thought was right. It was not your fault an evil creature took advantage of you.

There was a time not so long ago when I would never have used those words to describe Rachel. Never having had one of my own, I loved her as if she had been my own daughter, and I was ready to forgive her anything. She played on this when she told me all she had done during that conversation before you arrived for tea. She thought I was so entirely in thrall to her that I would never speak of what she had told me or act upon it.

For once, she was wrong. It was clear to me that Rachel simply had to be stopped and I could see no way of stopping her other than the dreadful action I took. After you and Felicity had gone off, she said she wanted to go up to the roof and watch you as you walked about the garden.

I followed her and waited until she went near the edge. Even at that point, I didn't know if I had the courage to do it. I held back for several minutes. But then she spread her arms wide and laughed, and it was the sound of the devil that came from her lips. I knew then that I had no choice but to push her over the edge.

I am a murderess. I know that only God has the right to take another's life, and so I must be punished for Rachel's death. But I hope that those I love and who have showed me such affection find it in their hearts to forgive me. I hope I have made the world a safer place for them, and for the others who Rachel may have made her victims.

I am glad Ralph and Lucinda will now be able to call Kessell Court truly their home. Ralph has always loved Kessell Court, and he has worked so hard to maintain it and be a kind landlord to the tenants. And, of course, it means Lucinda will always be near poor little Emily.

I hope I have explained everything and left nothing out. I do not want there to be any loose ends or questions asked when I am gone.

I'm sorry to have distressed you, Dr Cowdrey, as I feel sure this letter will have done, but we must not hide from the truth. I have done that for too long. You can move on with your life a wiser man, I hope.

Farewell.

Pray for me.

Yours, in sorrow,

Beatrice Hebron.

I handed the letter to Ralph. He took it with a frown, but I nodded for him to read. I watched him as he read, imagining that the astonished, horrified expression on his face was not dissimilar to that I must have had on mine.

So much was now clear to me. Had I not thought Miss Polke familiar when I met her at Kessell Court? That was because we had met, many times, when she was in the guise of Harriet Frayn. Mrs Blake's death was explained. I recalled how Mary said she was unusually tired that night, that beer normally never left her so fatigued. Her beer had been drugged to make her fall asleep as she had claimed, and that drugging had enabled Rachel and Miss Polke to lead Mrs Blake to her death. A poor woman enticed to her death because Rachel had been jealous of the attention I had shown her.

My mind turned to Charlotte Burnley and the scar on her neck. That was caused by Rachel holding the knife to her neck. No wonder Charlotte feared Rachel would make good on her threat to kill her if she married

Ralph Hawke. And as for Mr Hawke, it seemed that he had done what he could to control Rachel and care for his mother and Beatrice, to keep Kessell Court running and providing homes for the tenants. Dr Wakefield had been weak and fallen for Rachel and Dr Dennison had been as foolish as I in believing her lies. She had fooled all of us.

It took Mr Hawke about fifteen minutes to read Beatrice's letter. When he had finished, he folded it up and placed it on the table beside him. He said nothing.

'Rachel used me,' I said to break the silence. 'You told me I knew nothing about her and you were right. How much of what Beatrice wrote did you already know?'

Mr Hawke put a hand to his forehead and sighed. 'I knew Rachel was dangerous, that she could make people do what she wanted and that what she wanted wasn't always good for them, but this…' he gestured at the letter. 'That she killed the stableboy and Emily, this Mrs Blake of yours! I can hardly believe it.'

'I must ask your forgiveness, Mr Hawke,' I said. 'I thought you a villain. I thought you were after Rachel's fortune.'

He looked at me with weary eyes. 'I shouldn't blame you. Beatrice didn't realise what Rachel was like, and she had known her all her life. But God, Cowdrey,' he slammed his fist against the arm of the chair, 'if only you'd left well alone. Rachel would be at Flete House, out of harm's way, and Beatrice would not be facing a hanging.'

He was right. If I hadn't gone to Flete House, two women wouldn't be dead and a third waiting to die.

'Is there nothing we can do for Miss Beatrice?' I asked quietly.

Mr Hawke shook his head. 'I've tried to persuade her to retract her confession. I've told her I will affirm Rachel's death was an accident, but she won't have it.' He rose and I did the same. 'Do you have any message for Beatrice?'

'Just that I admire her greatly for her bravery in doing what she did and regret that I was so taken in, and that she will be in my prayers.'

He nodded, satisfied. I extended my hand, but he stared at it. 'I cannot shake your hand, Cowdrey,' he said. 'Not after what you've done. You dragged us into an inquiry, accused me of mad conspiracies and villainy, and did your best to ruin my family and Dr Wakefield's career. I cannot shake your hand.'

He strode out of the sitting room. Susan, who had been waiting in the hall, hurried to open the front door. I waved her away to do it myself.

'I am truly sorry for all the trouble I have caused, Mr Hawke,' I said as he passed through the opening. 'I know it will be no consolation to you, but I swear to you that I have been taught a valuable lesson and am, as Miss Beatrice hopes, a much wiser man than I was before.'

He looked back at me. 'That's something, I suppose.'

And then he was gone, walking across the square

until he disappeared from my sight. I closed the door and returned to the sitting room.

When Clara came down a few minutes later, she found me with my head in my hands, unable to stop crying.

34

LESSON LEARNT

Fate was kind to Beatrice Hebron. She died in her sleep the night before her scheduled execution and so was mercifully spared the hangman's noose. I read her obituary in *The Times*, placed there by Ralph Hawke. He wrote of a kind, brave woman much missed by her family.

A few weeks after that, I read another notice in *The Times*, this time announcing the engagement of Miss Charlotte Burnley to Mr Ralph Hawke of Kessell Court, Essex. I was happy for them.

As for myself, I gave up medicine. I had made too many mistakes; people had died because of me. I no longer wanted to be a doctor. When I said as much to my father, he cried, 'Oh, thank God. Now, will you do what you should have done years ago and come into the family firm?'

I stared at him in frank astonishment, making him laugh.

‘Felix, your mother and I knew you were making a mistake when you decided to become a doctor. Oh, the sleepless nights you caused your mother when you told us. She was certain you were going to catch some dreadful disease or move to the East End to tend the poor and get hit over the head by a ruffian.’

‘So, why did you not try to stop me?’ I asked, now a little indignant, and perversely resentful that they had not.

‘Because you would have done what you always did when you were a boy. Dug your heels in and gone your own way out of sheer stubbornness. You had to find all this out for yourself. And now you have. Your mother will be very relieved.’

And so I did what he asked. I returned to the law, and I found that this time, I enjoyed it. The truth was to be found in legal documents, in clauses and codicils, and I rarely had to test my judgement, which had proved to be so very faulty, when meeting with a client.

I enjoy my work, so much so that it is now my greatest hope that in a few years’ time, the brass plate on the door at Tremlett Street will read ‘Cowdrey, Burkett, Cowdrey and Cowdrey.’

RESEARCH BIBLIOGRAPHY

Beeton, Isabella, *Mrs Beeton's Book of Household Management*, Chancellor Press, 1982

Flanders, Judith, *The Victorian City: Everyday Life in Dickens' London*, Atlantic Books, 2012

Goodman, Ruth, *How To Be A Victorian*, Penguin Books, 2013

Juxon, John, *Lewis & Lewis: The Life and Times of a Victorian Solicitor*, Collins, London, 1983

White, Jerry, *London in the 19th Century*, Vintage Books, London, 2008

Wise, Sarah, *Inconvenient People: Lunacy, Liberty and the Mad-Doctors in Victorian England*, Vintage Books, London, 2013

To find out about my other books and to get in touch,
visit my website:
www.lauradowers.com

or Follow Me on:

facebook.com/lauradowersauthor
goodreads.com/lauradowers
amazon.com/author/lauradowers

ACKNOWLEDGMENTS

A huge thank you to my brother, Malcolm, and sister-in-law, Siobhan, for reading the unfinished manuscript of *A Woman in Room Three* and providing feedback that has made it an immeasurably better book than it was then.

ALSO BY LAURA DOWERS

THE TUDOR COURT

The Queen's Favourite

The Queen's Rebel

The Queen's Spymaster

The Queen's Rival: A Short Story

The Queen's Poet: A Short Story (*Exclusive to subscribers*)

The Tudor Court: Books I-III (Omnibus Edition)

Master Wolsey

Power & Glory

THE RISE OF ROME

The Last King of Rome

The Eagle in the Dovecote

STANDALONE NOVELS

When the Siren Sings